The Dark Side of the Hill

Rodney Stone joined Government service after the RAF and Cambridge University. He has held senior posts in five Government departments, and was the recipient of a Nuffield Fellowship. He has travelled extensively on various official assignments but now writes full time. Rodney Stone is married and lives with his wife and their two children in London. His highly successful thriller *Cries in the Night* was published in 1990, and is soon to be filmed for television.

RODNEY STONE

THE DARK SIDE
OF THE HILL

HarperCollins*Publishers*

HarperCollins*Publishers*
77–85 Fulham Palace Road
Hammersmith, London W6 8JB

This paperback edition 1994
1 3 5 7 9 8 6 4 2

First published in Great Britain by
HarperCollins*Publishers* 1992

ISBN 0 586 21738 X

Set in Meridien

Printed in Great Britain by
HarperCollinsManufacturing Glasgow

The Dark Side of the Hill

1

The house nestled under boulders, close up against the mountain.

'Tan-y-graig,' Peter announced. 'It means "under the rock or cliff".' He produced a pocket Welsh dictionary with a series of place names.

It lay in a natural hollow between the surrounding hills at the end of the empty valley, and even in the late sunshine of the autumn evening it had a certain bleakness: a two-storeyed, slate-roofed farmhouse, stone-built and painted white, with a small front porch and outhouses across the yard.

They turned off the road and rattled up a rough track, pulling up in a kind of forecourt. She noticed a small round pond, a dew-pond or witches' bath, washing lines hanging limp, wire fences barbed on top surrounding the fields at the sides, the leaning barns closed off by the cliff at the rear, old milk-churns, a disused kennel, the clutter of an abandoned hill farm. A rainbow arched from black clouds and the ferns on the hillside were tossed like waves in the wind.

'Heavens, Dad. You do pick 'em.'

He climbed out and tried the front door. The key fitted but he stood back for a moment before they entered, surveying this bolt-hole in Snowdonia. It had been a long drive from London, picking Sandie up from school in Shrewsbury for the promised weekend, after which he planned to stay on alone for a few more days – his school had a longer half-term – and he hoped it would all be worth it. He wanted it to work, he willed it, smiling at his daughter now. He felt they needed each other.

1

The road over the mountains, after they had stopped for tea at Llanybindon, had been a switchback, curving through granite hills with naked scree on one side, brown and grey-green, and woodland and fields on the other, hills like the backcloth to one of those model railways in Christmas toyshops. High, bald hills folding into secret valleys with trees on the lower slopes, hawthorn and oak, mountain ash and birch. They had seen frothing waterfalls and confused sheep, fat-rumped and silly, running the wrong way. The water flowed fast in the ditches.

'It'll be all right,' he said. 'A chance for peace and quiet.'

'You can say that again.' There was a curious inertness, a stillness she found unnerving.

He unlocked the black door and carried their cases inside, her small one for a couple of nights, his larger one for the week, and then the boxes of supplies. A narrow passage opened into front rooms at either side, a parlour and a kitchen, with two more rooms at the back. They inspected each of them in turn and Sandie switched on electric fires.

'It smells a bit damp. And spooky.'

'Well. I don't suppose it's been used for a while.'

The kitchen had lattice-work windows, a chunky table and chairs, a stone-cold Aga which she inspected. She began to unwind, feeling some satisfaction in imagining a farmhouse kitchen that could be piled with produce, hams hanging from the rafters, strings of onions, a steady fire in the stove . . .

'Let's explore —'

The living room was at the rear: low beams and cream-papered walls, an inglenook stained with soot, high-backed chintz settee and a suite of well-worn chairs, even an old TV. With the simulated coals of the fire it became immediately cosy.

'Who owns this place?'

Peter Fellowes said, 'This chap in Birmingham. Steadman.' James, Sandie's elder brother, now studying engineering at Bristol, could be blamed for the idea. He had found the ad in one of the local rags, and suggested it to his father as a half-term retreat: 'Furnished farmhouse to let in remote valley, North Wales. Suit couple seeking to get away from it all. Rates on request.' Lanky and uncooperative James, anxious to get on with

2

his life, had suddenly had this vision of Eden and suggested that his father should go there with his sister, as if it was a necessary step in bringing them together again.

They wandered upstairs and inspected the bedrooms, which were neat enough, with solid beds. Sandie chose the room at the rear, looking up to the mountain, and Fellowes had the one at the front with a view over the bleak little forecourt. There was an adjacent bathroom and a third bedroom converted to storage.

'Furniture by Oxfam,' he said.

'Oh, come on, Daddy, don't be unfair. It's just that it's been shut up.' She warmed to her task of home-maker, sorting out the sheets they had brought, pulling blankets from the cupboards. Across the yard at the rear she saw more sheds and barns, dilapidated and locked.

Sandie opened the cupboards and ran her fingers inside for dust. Watching her Fellowes was reminded once again of Stella; she had her mother's figure and face and that similar frizziness of hair, though Stella's had been darker. But Sandie was seventeen and there was a distance between them that was still unbridged, that peculiar anxiety of father and teenage daughter relations, compounded by boarding-school after his wife had died. He remembered the times, before Sandie went away, when she had been sullen, argumentative, wearing. Society didn't pay you to bring up children. But now it would be different.

Sandie was bouncing on one of the mattresses.

'Well comfortable.'

'So glad you like it.'

She smiled at him uneasily, then ran downstairs again, eager to unload the provisions, and he followed. The sun had come back, a late golden flame which kindled the end of the valley and flooded the little house against the hillside. The rainbow had disappeared. They stood for a moment, aware of their isolation, and he began to wonder whether she was having second thoughts about their weekend commitment, a promise to rescue her from the school which she was beginning to find more constricting now that she was in the sixth form.

'Listen!' She paused.

'What?'

'That weird sound.'

'I can't hear anything.'

'Maybe it's at the back.'

They walked round to the sheds, outhouses crammed up against the rock of the hillside, overgrown with blackberries and hawthorn, nettles, old man's beard, sycamores. The presence of the animals that had once wintered there was almost tangible. Sandie shivered.

'Dad. This place gives me the willies. It's . . . as if there are ghosts.' She began to look round for them.

He smiled. 'Don't be ridiculous.'

She gave up the quest and returned. 'Oh well, all right. It must be something underground, like water coming out of the mountain.'

But Peter was already carrying inside the books that he had brought, his drinks and their boxes of food.

Sandie smiled to herself, picking up bottles of wine from the boot of the Ford. A brief vision of Monica Wilson and Miss Clarke, the Head of History, catching her in the corridor and asking where she thought that she was going for the weekend.

'Off to a cottage in Wales, with my father,' she had said, shovelling things into the suitcase and rushing off at midday. She saw their glances compounded of suspicion and envy; the tension of school was shattering, shut up together seven days of the week. Everyone needed a hide-out.

Inside, in the stone-flagged kitchen, her father was opening a bottle of sherry. They clinked glasses and sat at the table in the last of the sunshine, which seemed to lift their spirits. At eight o'clock the air was soft and swallows flew over the house. There was a distant murmur of aircraft but after that, nothing. Sandie put out a hand, then drew back as if surprised at herself.

'You hungry? How about some nosh?'

'I'll buy that.'

'Glad we came?' he asked.

'I hope so,' she whispered.

4

2

They ate together in the kitchen, secure in each other's company as the shadows lengthened. Fellowes had got the Aga working after a fashion and lit two candles on the table. A salmon light flooded the room from the west-facing window and sitting opposite her father, a little drunk from the wine after she had cooked steaks and sauce au poivre and tinned vegetables, Sandie felt her inhibitions about the weekend beginning to peel away.

She wanted to make him happy, yet an inner reserve – something she took from her mother – stopped her from being sentimental. She had an old head on young shoulders, and had come there not just to please him – after accusing him of never relaxing – but because being his daughter had become increasingly important to her. A serious-minded girl in fact, under the jeans and sweater. Well-built, open-faced, with freckles and her mother's hair, a golden-red frizziness that never quite responded to styling. Tomorrow she would go exploring.

Her father breathed on the glass and inspected the colour of the wine as if it was a sediment sample. A good face, she thought, fair-haired, cheerful and sensible, with that curious quality of being focused only on her, giving his features in the candlelight a flickering, eighteenth-century gravity.

'A dorm feast,' he said.

'I wouldn't know. We never have them. Only in *Girl's Own Annual* stories.'

He lifted his glass of Sainsbury's Medoc.

'To us.'

The farmhouse was like a ship becalmed. When they stopped

5

talking she was conscious with a slight shudder that there were no more noises. No sounds, no bird-song, nothing. It was beginning to rain.

'It's stopped. That rumbling. Like something hollow.'

He listened. 'You're right.'

'Why can't we hear it now?'

'I don't think I ever could.' Stella too used to have these 'feelings' about places and people. He classified them as something feminine, like intuition.

'Why can't we hear anything?' A note of alarm in her voice: not even a rustle of wind, and she felt the hairs prickle along the back of her neck. 'It's crazy,' she said. 'We could be the only two people left in Wales.'

Peter considered the statement carefully, head on one side, as if he was marking an essay.

'Oh, come on. This is the country. It's bound to be quiet.' Silence didn't upset him: school masters preferred it to noise. He remembered for a moment the shrieking jungle of the boys' school in Barnes where he taught English, and was glad to be where he was.

What was it about this place that still left her running scared? Sandie couldn't be sure, and she didn't want to disappoint her father – nice of him to collect her, and she knew how much he needed a rest, stuck there in London with all the aggro of teaching – but something about the silences was disturbing. Uncomprehending, he began to eat cheese and biscuits while she was tense as a watchdog. Outside there was absolute stillness. She heard the noises of his mouth, the scrape of a knife on the plate, enough to stretch her nerves like piano-wire.

He saw her hesitate.

'What's up?'

Sandie prevaricated. She told herself not to be emotional, but in spite of herself said, 'It's dead.'

His smile of reassurance seemed to say, 'Come on now, don't be stupid.' She looked for a moment through the window at his back, but in mid-October it was already dark.

'It's good to have a chance to talk to you,' he began, as if he wanted to say something important, or difficult, such as 'What's happened to the boyfriend, Sandie?'

She stared again at the window, her eyes wide, and her mouth opened in horror.

'Oh my God. Daddy!' she screamed. *'What was that? That thing?'*

'What?'

Fellowes swivelled round in his chair, alarmed by her shriek, and saw her jump from the table.

'Daddy. That face!' she screamed again. Her complexion had turned white as ashes and in the next moment she was half-way across the room, rushing at the kitchen window, a closed, leaded casement. 'That terrible face.'

'What face?' He looked round in astonishment.

Sandie was scarcely coherent: even from where he was seated he felt her tremble.

'An old woman . . . like a . . . a witch. At the window.'

He saw only an empty pane, beyond which the night was black. A hawthorn branch tapped on the glass like a blind man's stick.

'What are you talking about?' Her total panic unnerved him. 'Sandie, calm down, there's no-one there.'

But she would not be comforted. He heard his daughter catch her breath.

'There is. *There is.* She's there – outside.'

She was shuddering at an apparition, a face that had suddenly assembled itself, less a face than a framed hologram nodding on a scraggy neck like some ill-treated and washed-out puppet. Wrinkled, dry lips clamped over shrunken gums, the nose little more than a beak of gristle, the eyes deep-socketed. An exhumed grizzly skull plastered with wisps of white hair.

'That old woman! Daddy, didn't you see her?'

Peter Fellowes turned round again. 'Don't be ridiculous. It's all right. There's no-one out there.'

They stared at each other.

'Don't leave me alone.'

'Of course not.'

7

The face had disappeared. He lit the oil lamp which hung from a hook on the wall, and opened the door.

The night bowled in at them, but he saw nothing, only a curtain of rain.

Sandie came and stood behind him. She swore that what she had seen was a figure in a plastic raincoat, a head illuminated by a torch, a head that seemed cut and grooved by a hundred years of experience. An old woman in the rain, watching them through the window. Or else a ghost.

'Oh, come on,' he said, 'forget it.'

But she could not wash the face from her mind. She had retreated to the window and was peering out, but the figure had vanished as if it had been an illusion: there was only the empty night, the rustle of trees in the dark, the fear of the unknown. Her panic communicated between them and she was visibly shaken.

'Sandie, don't upset yourself. It must have been your imagination. There's no-one there.' He poured her a glass of wine, but when she tried to drink it she choked. The colour reminded her of blood, and somehow the drink tasted bitter.

'But Daddy, there was. There was. She seemed to be looking for something. Searching. What was she doing here?'

'I don't know.' Fellowes laughed. 'Perhaps you've seen a poltergeist. A visitation.'

'She wasn't a poltergeist. That's for sure.' He touched her arm but she flinched. 'What can she have wanted? Where on earth was she going?' Sandie asked, shuddering. 'Why didn't she come in?'

'Well, if there was someone there they've got a long walk.' He remembered the length of the valley with its jigsaw of stone-walled fields and the nearest settlement five or six miles below them.

He opened the window and leaned out into the night, but the figure had dematerialized as though she had never existed.

'I'd better go down the lane and make sure . . .' Make sure of what, he wondered: that Sandie had seen a ghost?

'Don't you dare abandon me here. Not after that.' Sandie's voice was strident, as if she could not bear to be left.

8

'Oh, come on, Sandie, forget it.'

'I can't . . . she frightened me. Why should she . . . come . . . here . . . to us?'

'I don't know. Imagination plays strange tricks.'

'Imagination. Oh, my God.'

'Don't let it spoil things,' Fellowes said. 'I'll draw the curtains. Then we can't see anything. No hallucinations.'

He pulled them quickly across, orangey and cheerful, blotting out the darkness, and Sandie's terrible vision.

3

'Do you believe in ghosts?' Sandie asked. 'Spooks? You know. The supernatural? Spirits back from the dead?' She stood in the kitchen with him, half-serious, half-joking, as they began to clear the table.

Fellowes assumed that she meant her vision, that vacant but querulous face which she described so graphically. It showed she had more maturing to do. 'Forget it. Of course not.' He walked through the passage to the rear door, which opened on to the main yard, as if to make sure it was locked. Sandie seemed to be tied to him.

'Don't worry, love,' he said. 'Let's try and enjoy ourselves. And hope the weather improves.'

But he could sense she was nervous. There was an electricity meter and he inserted another coin, to make sure the fires kept going.

'I know,' she said. 'But how can you be so sure there's no such thing as spirits? I've got this feeling we're being watched. As if there's someone out there . . .'

'Out where?'

'There!' She pointed through the rear door.

'That's only the yard.'

'Daddy, please check.'

He shrugged. 'OK.'

The lock turned easily, and they peered out across the darkness. A crescent moon hovered between piled clouds, illuminating the run-down farmyard with the barns on the far side built into the mountain. Higher up on the hillside they could see straggling trees, then the white shapes of boulders, huge rocks of granite which seemed to have been shaken loose by some primaeval force. There was a fine curtain of rain.

She shivered. How strange the moon was, appearing and disappearing like that. He put his arm protectively around her, worried that he'd made a mistake in choosing this lonely place, a spur-of-the-moment decision.

'Nobody there. Forget it, my dear.'

Fellowes shut the door, turned the key and put it on the table inside.

'Come on. It's late. And it's been a long day. Coffee, then bed.' He wanted her to relax, and have a good day tomorrow when they could enjoy the country, and talk about each other. In mid-October the trees in this part of Wales were slowly turning brown and gold and the land seemed colour-coded: olive, conifer-green, soil-brown, furze-yellow, shale-grey and the orangey-red of bilberries on the slopes. It would be good to walk there in the fresh air, the two of them together.

He yawned, and escorted her back to the kitchen to search for a coffee pot, passing the door to the scullery.

'What's in there?' she asked.

'I don't know. Junk and stuff.' He had looked in briefly when they had first arrived and seen it was piled with old furniture, stored from the rest of the house: tables, old chairs, tea-chests, cardboard boxes and cases, cabin trunks with yellowing labels. The relics of someone's life, presumably left there by Steadman. 'Leave it alone.'

But something impelled Sandie to look. Some childish inquisitiveness, or sense of intrigue, and he let her explore with a feeling of indulgence. This place was full of surprises, he ought not to be heavy-handed; treat it all as an adventure, an adventure between them, exploring mysterious Wales.

He found a coffee pot in the kitchen and busied himself setting things up. He could follow Sandie's movements next door, and heard her sneeze.

'Come on. Don't start getting dirty in there.'

'Just having a dekko,' she shouted. It was fun to investigate, clambering around the packing cases and across a stack of chairs.

11

With the coffee now bubbling Fellowes returned to the doorway to summon her, when she called out, 'Look –'

'What is it?' He went in to find her.

She was at the far end of the room, the storage coming up to her shoulders, and he could see her moving some packing cases from the outside wall.

'Some sort of stained-glass window. Come and see.'

He picked his way inside, and as she restacked the cases saw it more clearly: a simple blue glass window in half-a-dozen leaded panes, two of them with white clouds.

'It's like it's been a church or chapel,' Sandie breathed.

He shook his head.

'I shouldn't think so. There are no other signs.'

She peered more closely, hoping to find some further clue.

'What's this then?'

The light from a single bulb suspended from the ceiling was just enough to indicate that one of the stones in the wall, below the window itself, had been chiselled with a cross and an arrow.

Fellowes shrugged. 'I don't know. Builders' marks. You get them in old buildings. This place could go back hundreds of years. Come on, coffee's getting cold.'

But she traced the incisions with her fingers, as if trying to decipher them.

'It's not as old as all that, Daddy. I think they're sort of symbols.'

That intuition again. He smiled and tried to humour her.

'All right. Perhaps somebody put in the window as a memorial.'

'Yes. But what for and who?'

'Ask Steadman,' he said.

But she persisted.

'Blue glass and white clouds. And then a cross and an arrow?'

'Maybe it was a dairy. I once saw blue glass in a dairy. Something to do with calming the milk.'

'Rubbish, Daddy.'

'Look. We're getting filthy in here, and anyway, it's not our business. Do you want coffee or don't you?'

Reluctantly she gave up the enquiry, thinking there was further exploring that she could do in the morning. The house had its shades and messages. It was beginning to be exciting. She scrambled back across the store-room: re-entering the kitchen was like returning to a different world. The candles had long since burned down and Fellowes switched on the full lights, bringing it back again into the twentieth century.

She accepted the coffee gratefully, and found that her hands were throbbing. He wondered if she was still frightened by the spectre of the old woman.

'Forget her. Forget that funny window, and all that junk. Try and relax, now we're here.'

Her eyes dilated. Big and wide, they seemed to be staring through him.

'What is the matter, darling?' He felt both tired and concerned. 'Come on, let's get to bed. I'll sleep like a log.'

Sandie was not so sure that she would sleep at all. However much her father dismissed it, a sense of something dwelling and brooding there began to haunt her. It was a sense of presence, as if someone was watching them.

4

There had been times when Sandie had dreamed of this: coming back to her father again, away from the boarding-school she had so rashly volunteered for in the aftermath of her mother's death. Growing up and growing away from him was how she had put it then, but now she was not so sure, and had welcomed the chance to rethink. But anticipated events all too often turned out to be different from the idealized version, and she had not expected this particular place to be so . . . well . . . so frightening. It wasn't his fault, of course, and she ought not to blame him for it.

She lay in bed, a comfortable wooden bed, in the back room she'd chosen, with the view up to the mountain. The past could be shut down like a lid on a box, but she was still unable to sleep, her mind full of tension. Perhaps it was the strange bed, she told herself, perhaps the events of the day. Her eyes travelled round the room, from the chairs to the old-fashioned wardrobe and chest of drawers and the tightly pulled curtains. Why was she so on edge, so uncertain? It was not like her. She could hear her father taking off his shoes in the bedroom at the front of the house, followed by the cistern flushing along the passage.

Then silence, as she switched off the light and lay awake. What was it about fathers and daughters that made relations so fraught: at least this father, this daughter? As if he never expected that she would grow wings and have boyfriends, never thought that little Charlotte would stop holding his hand and blossom into Sandie. Growing up was like jumping a course of hurdles with your eyes shut. Oh well . . . try counting the sheep.

14

A tiny, tinny noise, like something falling, disturbed her. She sat up, puzzled. In the dark, in an unfamiliar place.

The explorations stopped, and she found herself calming down.

Then it was there again. A tiny noise. She shot up in bed, alert, and reached to switch on the light in the little bedside lamp.

It did not work.

Perhaps the bulb had gone. Nervously, she slipped from the bed and felt for the switch on the wall. It did not work either. For one terrible moment she thought she could feel hands, reaching and clutching at her, but her arms only beat the air.

Her heart was thumping like a pump out of control, but her father was sleeping opposite. If she dared open the door.

Of course she dared. She wasn't scared of the dark, it was only a matter of courage.

Her fingers gripped the door-knob and turned it gently, as if she didn't want them to hear. *Them?* The spirits of the place? Ridiculous ... but scary. She could feel herself shaking as she glided to her father in her new Laura Ashley nightdress. Ridiculous, too, to be sneaking into his room.

The whole thing was surreal, unnerving in the pitch dark. He was obviously fast asleep. When she opened the door she could hear his regular breathing.

She was inside the room. Perhaps she should go back now and not disturb him: but she could no longer face her own empty space in the dark.

Then another noise, downstairs, almost as if there were footsteps. But she could not be sure, not wanting to seem paranoid, shifting at every sound. And yet there was a noise, residual like a faint gasp, or a mouse perhaps, or the wind. A noise of something falling softly? Which room? She stood there frozen, unable to move, telling herself not to be crazy. The house could not really be haunted.

She seemed to stop breathing as she heard something again. The bedroom was pitch black, but there were candles downstairs. Someone else was in the house ... or else one of her father's poltergeists, she was certain of it. What if the place had been the scene of some terrible crime, some restless spirit

15

which was forced back to haunt there? Her hand felt for the bedhead.

'Daddy?' A whisper.

'Mmmm . . .' The figure in the bed moved, thought better of it, turned and lay still.

She shrank back, and then she touched him.

'Daddy?'

He grunted and roused. She felt reassured by his presence, as she made out the outline of his head and shoulders.

'Sandie? What's up?'

Peter Fellowes was stumbling awake. 'Are you all right?'

She hesitated again, listening for those faint sounds.

'Can't you hear?'

'No. What?'

'A weirdo noise. Something in the house. Downstairs.'

He must have been dog tired. For one awful moment she wondered what it would have been like if he had been a stranger, someone who had lured her there, only to wake and kill her and throw her body into one of those mysterious pools, dew-ponds or tiny lakes, dotted about on the mountains. Stupid, of course. Thank God her father was there, reassuring and steady. When she was a little girl he had comforted her in the dark.

He reached for the lamp.

'The lights have gone out,' she whispered.

'Out?' The meter was downstairs and he had put money in it. Surely it was enough? He began to grope for his shoes, then remembered he had some matches in the pocket of his jacket.

Another tiny sigh, somewhere. Inside or out?

'Daddy! Didn't you hear that?'

'No. What? Don't be a lunatic, Sandie. There's no-one else here. The doors are all locked. Nobody can come in.'

Her father sat on the edge of the bed, smiling at her, striking a match on the box. The flame fluttered and hovered, showing her clutching her arms in the white nightdress.

'I don't care. There was this peculiar noise. As if something was moving about . . .'

He began to feel more awake. 'I'll go down and fix the meter. And have a look.'

16

'Not yet. Just listen!'

But there was nothing more. That was an end of it, although she stood there petrified. Finally she said, 'It's stopped. It's gone.'

'What has?'

'I don't know. Like someone fidgeting, and murmuring.'

They listened to the silence.

'I swear there was somebody down there.' She was beginning to recover her nerve.

'I'll go down and check.'

'Daddy, be careful.'

'Don't be daft. You're imagining things. We shouldn't have had coffee last thing.' Wondering again if she was as mature as he had thought, Fellowes crossed to the window, intending to pull back the curtains.

'Don't,' she begged. 'In case that face is watching.'

'Who? Your disappearing visitor?'

But then he seemed to hear something too, like a hiss in the dark. It was stupid to be standing there hesitating.

'I'm going down.'

'Daddy . . . don't!'

'I can handle it.'

It was chilly. He pulled on his jacket over the pyjamas.

'I'm coming with you,' she whispered.

'No. You wait here.'

'I'd rather come with you.' Her hand felt chilled.

'For God's sake put something on. You'll catch cold.'

'I'm all right.'

'Here.' He took the jacket off again, and slipped it over her shoulders.

'I just . . . feel . . . something frightening . . . about this place,' she muttered.

'Don't be alarmist . . .' But he spoke cautiously, as if they were overheard. Sandie's nonsense was catching.

He struck another match, then opened the bedroom door and listened along the passage. Should he make noises and warn them, if there was anyone there, or try to surprise them? The farmhouse was stone and wood, with solid ceilings, but there

17

was no way they could move downstairs without being heard. Suddenly his own nerves were edgy.

'Let's go,' he said, and moved along the landing. The stairwell loomed; the match burnt out in the dark. They went down the stairs together, with Sandie holding his hand.

He banged into the lower passage and found the door to the kitchen. Like feeling the inside of a warm cave, smelling of their last meal. And reassuring. No-one was there, and yet they both had a sense of something strange. Something he could not pin down. Sandie fumbled in the jacket for coins.

'What is it?'

She shook her head. 'Nothing. It's just that I have this feeling . . .'

Out in the passage Fellowes found the meter, and put in two 50p pieces, all the change they could muster. The lights came on, comforting and dazzling.

'See . . . There's no-one here. Go back to bed and sleep.'

'I'm sorry,' she whispered.

'You had me worried,' he grinned. Imagination played strange tricks, but just to be sure he made a quick check: opening the doors to the kitchen, the front parlour, which was set out with a dining table they had not used, the back parlour with its high-backed settee and chintzy chairs, the scullery filled with old furniture where she had discovered the window, the bathroom and lavatory. There was no sign of life.

He began to doubt the wisdom of bringing her for the weekend.

'Look. We'd both better get some kip. Otherwise it will spoil tomorrow.'

'Are the outside doors locked?'

Fellowes checked again, front and back.

'Yup.'

She began to sway with tiredness, and he ushered her upstairs again. Opening the door to her room, he crossed over to the window and peered into the night. It was as dark as hell, he said, and still raining: not the sort of night to be at large in. The moon had disappeared. He sensed the brooding thumb of the mountain high above them and that was all.

He switched off the central light and helped Sandie into the bed, trying to be cheerful, but the atmosphere had unsettled him too.

'It's all as quiet as . . .' the words trailed off '. . . anything. Sleep tight,' he said.

As she kicked off her slippers, her toe touched something hard, just under the carpet. Something that ran away. She trod on it again, involuntarily, not knowing where it had gone, and this time it was inanimate, a small oblong of metal, lying under her foot.

She bent down to pick it up. It was a cheap little brooch, an oval inset with blue stones. Some sort of quartz. An old-fashioned, old woman's brooch. Somehow she had not noticed it when she unpacked, but it did not matter now. In the light it was harmless. She placed it on the bedside cabinet, and let her father turn out the light.

Peter Fellowes went back to his room and wondered why he felt so troubled. Life's rich pattern brought you to some odd places, and Tan-y-graig was one of them. But now that they had arrived, they had to make the best of it. An old woman's face that – in spite of what Sandie said – must have been hallucination, a few noises heard or imagined, inside or outside the old house under the hill, a surprising blue window: they did not amount to very much, he decided. The important thing was to see Sandie, and make her happy. Tomorrow if the weather improved they would take packs and go walking, up over Clawdd Mawr or Maen-Ilwyd or Tan-y-graig itself. But when he looked out of the window the night was still dark and wet.

5

In the unreality of first light someone was tugging at his sleeve.

'Tea, Daddy?' Sandie said, and as he groped awake he realized that it was his daughter, already up and sparkling, in her chunky white sweater and stone-washed jeans.

'Tea, Daddy. Careful, or you will spill it.'

Her mother's gestures again.

Peter Fellowes propped himself up on an elbow and muttered apologies.

'Are you all right?' She seemed to have forgotten the traumas of the night, with all the resilience of youth.

'Yes. Sure. Just coming out of a coma. How about you?'

'I'm fine. I woke up once thinking I still heard those noises, but you often do in old houses, don't you?' In fact she had lain there uneasily until she drifted to sleep. The bedroom had been pitch black, the door ajar, she would have heard if anyone had come up the stairs, but she was still sure 'it' was down there, that presence inside the house. Ridiculous. She had almost gone in to her father again, wanting his reassurance, but had finally slept. Even so she had woken early, gone down to the kitchen, made tea.

'Sorry if I woke you too soon.' What was there about this place, with its noises, its overhanging mountain, that gave her the frighteners? When she had first gone down the wooden staircase, standing there cold and sleepy, raking the ashes in the stove in the afterglow of the dawn as the sun rose behind the hills, she had at once felt that other presence.

'What time is it?' he asked.

'Just after seven.'

His eyes travelled round the room searching for his clothes, which had been knocked on the floor. He grinned like a schoolboy.

'Why are you up so early?'

'I dunno. Must be the air. The country.' She ran a hand through her brush of red-brown hair and asked what he planned to do.

'Explore. Go walking. Talk to you.' How did you get alongside teenagers today, he wondered: Sandie at seventeen was to him as distant as seventy. He knew that she had exams, three 'A' levels, to take, he knew that she had a boyfriend who hung around the school in Shrewsbury, he knew that she liked clothes and athletics and animals and might one day become a vet . . . and yet he really knew so little about what made her tick. What did she do with her time away from home, what did she really think? That was the purpose of coming there to spend a weekend together, he reminded himself.

'I'll get some breakfast,' she said. 'What would you like?' He realized they did not even know each other's preferences.

Downstairs she began to busy herself in what she called her traditional role, laying the table, putting rashers in the pan until the kitchen seemed full of the smell of frying bacon. The front parlour was opposite, with the table that made it a dining room, but somehow she did not want to go there, preferring to eat in the kitchen just as they had last night. The remains of that previous meal, the unpacked box of food and the empty bottle of wine were still perched on the old dresser.

By the time Peter appeared she was turning the contents of the pan onto plates and carrying them to the table.

'Hmm. Smells good. Did you know the Romans liked bacon? They used to boil it with dried figs.'

She looked at his straightforward face with the neat, short, fair hair just beginning to grey, and his blue eyes. He was a model of sanity, her father, so stuffed with facts, so logical; she could not imagine any circumstances in which he would lose control.

'Looking good,' Peter said, whether to her or in the abstract

21

she could not be sure as he sat across the table, between the teapot and the marmalade. 'What do you fancy? Day in the hills round here, climbing up to Carn-y-Geifre maybe, that's the peak down the valley? Or we could look round Maesteg, the nearest town.'

'It's your weekend,' she said. 'Let's stay around here. There's a mountain right behind us.' Looming over the farm like some testy giant. Tan-y-graig, the house under the cliff. She mustn't be nervous and start disliking places. It was quite pretty really, so long as the sun was out. From the back of the house her bedroom in daylight surveyed the old farmyard and the broken-down barns where the sparrows were chirruping, while the brown mountain above them disappeared in early mist. She mustn't imbue places with the spirits of people – that was outdated cobblers. Like all weekend rentals, however well-appointed, this place had a neglected air just because it hadn't been used. Don't hold that against it, she told herself. Get on your walking boots.

The car was standing outside, with their two pairs of boots in the back. Last night they hadn't troubled to unpack them, and she called out to ask for the keys.

'I must have left them in the other room,' her father said. 'Together with my maps.'

For some reason she again felt apprehensive as she walked across the passage and opened the door to the lounge or living room or whatever they called it, at the back of the house, opposite the scullery with the little blue window. The keys and the maps had been left by the TV and she had to cross the room to reach them and pull back the curtains.

She could not move.

When they had looked at the room last night the high back of the settee had blocked off the view of the fireplace, but now she saw something huddled there.

Words died in her throat, as she hoped against hope to be mistaken. Dreaming, or confused, or imagining. But she knew it was not so . . . she could see the outline of someone . . . lying crouched . . . lying immobile.

She screamed.

'Daddy! Oh God. My God!'

'What?'

Peter came running.

On the carpet at the foot of the floral settee, in front of the empty fire-grate, was a body in profile. Someone – a woman – resting on her side as if turned away in disgust. Without thinking, Sandie stumbled towards her and saw the half-open mouth in the mottled, grey head.

Sandie collapsed. She understood instantly what she had feared last night. They had been visited again by that old woman who had come up the lane. She had walked in . . . and died.

Peter Fellowes followed Sandie through and stood there. Shocked. Saying nothing, he slowly approached the body, touched a hand and then the face. The flesh was ashen and cold: the same face that Sandie had seen in the window that previous evening. He knew now that her visions had not been a flight of fancy.

The old woman lay there as if reproaching them, mouth gaping, slack-jawed, stiffening into rigor mortis. He had been stunned by the loss of Stella, but this was different, someone old and unknown who must have had some means of entering, and then expired in the night. She must have been coming to the house when they had frightened her off. Her clothes were still wet from the overnight rain. He felt filled with remorse and a kind of numbed pain.

Sandie knew her legs were unstable and leaned on him for support.

'Let's cover her up,' he said. 'Get a sheet from upstairs and cover her up. We've got to inform the police.' Wasn't that what you did first in situations like this?

He tried to be cool and rational now that the shock had passed, gently feeling for a pulse. There was no sign of life, and he confronted his daughter with the awful truth.

'Cold as iced wax,' he said.

23

6

Sandie had never seen anyone dead before. When her mother died in the accident she had been judged too young, and Peter had gone alone to identify the body. Now she touched the old woman's temple, lightly as a fly descending, before she stood back quietly, surprised to find she was not squeamish. She was no longer afraid: there was even curiosity. A smell was beginning.

'Daddy, I'm sure it's the same woman.' Dressed in a grey woollen top like a cardigan with white composite buttons, the skirt rucked up where she had collapsed on the carpet. The old woman's green plastic raincoat had been rolled into a pillow. She had then simply turned on her side, as if she had died quite peacefully, one limp arm revealing a clean white blouse. The end seemed to have come suddenly, without apparent pain.

'For God's sake, come away,' Peter said. 'We need help.'

He was more troubled now than his daughter. There was a double tragedy in the realization that the visitor had died, and that he had led Sandie here, to this abandoned place, in his illusory search for a peaceful weekend. The reality, the hurt, the uncertainty, pushed at the limits of his tolerance. The room seemed to loom over them, low-beamed and crushing, and he wanted someone else to take over. Take her away. Let's go. He almost wanted to run.

The elderly, lifeless figure reminded him of a discarded rag doll: brittle white hair, showing the scalp beneath, the cheeks already sunken where the mouth had collapsed. A line of dried spittle edged from the side of her lips. Locked up in that face he saw sadness, a haunting by memories. He started to search for a handbag, a notebook, some clue as to why she was there. But all he found was a key lying close to her hand. No name, no identification.

'I knew that there was something odd about this place as soon as we arrived. Then her face . . . and then those noises . . . but you thought I was imagining things,' Sandie reproached him. 'Daddy, why did she come? Is she someone who once lived here? How on earth did she get in?'

'Through the back door,' he said slowly. He had tried out the key and it fitted. 'That was when you heard noises.'

'But Daddy, why?'

He stood there, endeavouring to understand, fighting back a sense of panic. When he tried to move one of the dead woman's arms, he found that it was heavy. The sensation of handling a corpse made him feel sick.

But not so Sandie, who had got over the shock and was, if anything, excited. She began to touch the woman again, tentatively, gently, looking for marks of violence. He was uneasily aware that they did not know the cause of death: illness or suicide . . . or murder.

'Leave her in peace. The police may want fingerprints.' Prints? Why had he said that? There was no blood, no swellings. It looked like a natural death, sudden and complete. The only marks were signs of age, like rust stains in old linen: she must be near eighty, he guessed.

'I know.' Sandie had fully recovered and was interested in this anonymous visitor, looking at her stockings and footwear. Brown ribbed nylons, not fancy, held up by suspenders, and a pair of solid shoes. The soles were scarcely worn, a pair of hand-stitched brogues with sensible heels. Country shoes, and expensive.

'Please, Sandie. Come away,' Fellowes begged. 'There's nothing that you can do. We'll have to go down the valley and report what has happened. Don't let it distress you.'

The planned weekend had crashed in ruins, but he fought to get a grip on himself. Sandie stood back to admire that matter-of-fact side to his character, wanting to tell him to stop treating her like a schoolgirl, that this was an important adventure, a mystery as well as a tragedy. She almost wanted to enjoy it.

'Let's go in the kitchen,' she said. 'I'll make some more tea, and we can try and sort things out.'

Again he felt the need to cover the body, to seal up the sight, and ran upstairs to pull a sheet from the bed. The figure underneath made little hills and valleys in the shroud.

The reaction set in with Sandie as soon as she went back to the kitchen. She put her hands on the table, and then her elbows, feeling the firm wood. A table, real. But was this episode real, this extraordinary coincidence by which the dead woman had ended up there with them? She pushed her hands through her hair and rubbed her eyes till they were sore.

'Sandie, love. Don't cry. It's going to be all right . . . we'll find an explanation.'

She looked soberly at her father.

'We? Who are *we*?' As if she no longer wanted to be in partnership with him, and the fact of a death had opened up too many questions about her role in the world.

'You and me,' he said doggedly.

She ignored his answer. 'I just want to know why.' Almost as if she blamed him for this confusion. He began to feel cheated. 'And why it should happen to us.' Twenty-four hours ago he had been driving from London to pick her up and come on here, a chance booking through the small ads in the *Bristol Courier*. A teacher of English in a boys' school, boys like Rustler, wretched little Kevin Rustler who had asked where he was going for the half-term and told him not to do what he wouldn't do.

Sandie was staring at him.

'Peter,' she said slowly – it was the first time she ever had called him by his Christian name like that, signifying her adulthood – 'what I'm trying to work out is why it should have happened to us *here*.'

26

It brought him down to earth with a jolt. A stranger had appeared at the window, perhaps she had wanted to enter, and they had sent her, empty-handed, away. Had let her walk off down the lane. 'I don't know.'

'Weird. And those noises. What do you think she expected to find? Or perhaps she's a returning spirit?' She clutched her drinking mug tightly, in case it should suddenly disintegrate.

'Of course not,' he said firmly. 'There must be an explanation.' A rational reason. 'We'll find out more when we know who she is.' It reminded him he had to move. They had discovered the body over an hour ago and it was now nearly nine. There would be no escape from the official enquiries. 'Look. The first step is to get hold of a doctor to certify the death. And we shall need to inform the police.'

'What about the bloke who owns this place?'

'Yes. Him too, I suppose. As soon as I can get to a phone.'

'There was a phone next door,' she said, 'in the room with the stained-glass window.'

He was puzzled. Steadman had said nothing about the place being on the telephone, though, come to think of it, an isolated one-time farm was bound to be. He opened the door and went through into the cluttered scullery, an outhouse really, with the little blue window, and found the receiver, a modern handset, push-button, in a tasteful green. It had been disconnected. He showed it to Sandie.

'Did you see a line? I mean any phone wires, coming up the valley?'

She ran outside to look up at the slate roof. There was no sign of a telephone, only the thicker cable of the rural electricity. They were isolated and cut off at the back of beyond. But at least the sun had warmed up over the hills and the vaporous cloud on the mountain was breaking up.

Peter Fellowes found himself sweating.

'Let's get out of here,' he said. 'Look, I'm going straight in to Maesteg. There must be a doctor there. Got to inform the police. Get someone to certify death. Honey . . . I'm so sorry . . . but come on, for heaven sake, let's get rolling.'

He walked out to the car, expecting her to follow, as ready to get away from that house as he was. But when he turned round she was still standing in the doorway.

'You go,' she said. 'I'll stay with her.'

7

He stalled. He felt that Sandie was rejecting him, in spite of the bad vibes that she had had about the place, with its indefinable echoes of the past; that she preferred to stay there as an exercise in self-discovery. He fought against a sense of disturbance inside himself, an anxiety that was almost visible.

'Oh, come on, don't be awkward. I can't just leave you here.'

He stood helplessly in the morning mist, gesturing to the house behind her that he was beginning to hate. But Sandie had matured overnight, and was asserting her independence.

'Don't worry about me,' she said, and smiled. 'It's that poor thing in there all on her own.' A sense of pity, and intrigue, rooted her to the spot.

'Look, be reasonable, we've got to tell someone.'

'What about that big house we saw on the side of the valley, driving up?' A large white house which stood under the lee of the hill, isolated against a backcloth of grey and khaki conifers. In the trough of the valley, below the house, an overgrown railway cutting halted in a tangle of bushes, leaving only the road to Tan-y-graig.

Fellowes seemed doubtful.

'Hardly worth bothering them. May not even be lived in. We'll drive straight into Maesteg. It's only about twelve miles.'

Still Sandie hesitated, feeling very adult.

'But what about . . . the old lady . . . ? We can't just leave her here like that.'

He saw her mother's obstinacy lurking in the young face.

29

'She'll keep,' he said. 'No need to worry about her. We'll just lock the place up for a couple of hours, and come back with some help.'

She shook her head slowly, staring up at the mountain behind them. Inside herself, she felt they had turned the old woman away.

'I . . . I can't just do that. Somehow it doesn't seem right, simply to clear off like that. Supposing somebody comes while we've gone?'

'They won't. Who would?'

'But just supposing. And anyway I'd rather stay here. It doesn't bother me now, staying with her until you get back. I'd rather do that, somehow. It's the least I can do.'

'Don't be ridiculous.' But it rang a bell with him, and hurt again, remembering how he'd failed to believe her. He saw that petulant look that Stella had sometimes used when she was crossed.

'I'm not. It makes sense. You go, I'll stay. I feel I owe it . . . to her.'

'But Sandie, please . . .'

'Dad. Don't treat me like a kid. I'm old enough to know my own mind.'

He would have been inclined to argue, but saw the set of her mouth.

'Are you sure?'

'Quite sure.'

'I really don't like leaving you here . . .'

'Look – it would be very odd, wouldn't it, just locking up and sort of abandoning the poor old girl.'

He started to disagree, then threw in the towel, reluctantly.

'All right. If you insist.'

'I insist.'

Fellowes unlocked the door of the Ford Capri, anxious now to get away and put the sounds and sights of the house out of his thoughts.

'In any case I shouldn't be long. Just a question of informing the police. I'll come straight back as soon as I can and wait for the doc. Sandie, I'm sorry . . . but how could anyone know that this would happen?'

'Don't worry, Dad. Don't keep saying sorry. Just go.'

She stood by the front porch. Even then he prevaricated. It seemed an undesirable place to leave her with a dead woman, in the farmhouse at the end of the valley, with the mountain brooding behind it, and the mist shutting down again.

'Sandie, look, I can't simply leave you here on your own . . .'

'For Christ's sake, Dad. I've been on my own for years. An hour or two more won't matter.'

It wounded him.

'All right, darling. I know. It ought not to be like that.' He held out his arms and kissed her. She hugged him fiercely with tears in her eyes, but did not let them show. Turning away she said over her shoulder, 'Go on. Get moving.'

He slammed the car door and tried the ignition, winding down the window.

'Take it easy . . .'

'Don't *worry*, Dad.'

He edged the car round on the cracked concrete of the little forecourt and took one last look up at the mountain. It seemed to crouch over them, a raw, high hill of granite merging into the mist. How high was it, he wondered: twelve hundred feet? Two thousand? Must check it out on the map. Even its shape seemed unnatural, symmetrical as a coal-tip.

'Take care, honey.' He leaned from the open window. On impulse she kissed him again, knowing how much he wanted it.

'Bye, Dad. Don't be long.'

'I won't. You're a great girl,' he said. 'Love you.'

He jerked the car into life and bounced over the track, driving down to the road. Out of the rear view mirror he saw her smiling and waving.

31

8

Lake Maesteg was further from the farmhouse than he had thought, with Maesteg itself at the eastern end. He began to realize how remote the house was; had he known he would never have picked it. The evening before when they had driven along this same valley neither of them had dreamed that it would end in a nightmare.

Fellowes drove into a mist which wrapped round the sides of the valley, through which the tops of the hills poked out as bare as cardboard. The stone-built barns and scattered houses loomed up one by one like sudden rocks at sea. What did you have to do about a death like that? He wasn't even sure on procedure: Stella's had been so different, scooped up in an ambulance. Relatives would have to be traced. The police would be involved: Sandie and he would be witnesses, since they had found the body. There also had to be a certificate, a doctor would have to attend, and then the undertaker, before things could get back to normal.

Haunted by the shrouded valley, in his mind's eye he saw Sandie still waiting with the old woman inside that low-ceilinged room. Anyone's death diminished him as Donne said. Now it began to hit him with a sick self-pity as he sought to justify his weekend decision. 'All I did was to take up the chance of a farmhouse at £100 per week: reasonable enough when I was stuck in London. I wanted a break. I wanted to talk to my daughter, but then some wandering senior citizen turns up with a door-key, finds a warm room downstairs and pegs out in the night . . . Just my kind of luck.'

Shit. It wasn't what he expected from a half-term away. What would he say in the staff room? He could hear them laughing like drains, old Kingston and that crew, when he had to explain why the holiday in Wales had ended up with the police.

'The body in the barn, so to speak . . .' Old Kingston's jokes were primitive. And not even in the barn but the living room at the back of the house. Steadman's house. Mister con-man Steadman who had advertised peace and quiet. He'd have to tell Steadman too, or somebody would: perhaps the police could do that. Steadman was gradually assuming the proportions of an ogre. Fellowes felt like running away; Tan-y-graig could go to hell. Perhaps it would still be possible to rescue something from the wreckage, a couple of nights B and B at somewhere less jinxed.

Some two miles down the valley he came to the first house on the road, a not-very-hopeful cottage surrounded by broken fences and barbed wire. The Ford skidded to a halt and he opened the half-collapsed chicken-wire gate to a small farmyard. The retreating mist swirled in the air and pearls of water dripped from the eaves. Pen-y-banc, it said, whatever that meant. It might have been in Albania. The place was unoccupied but in his anxiety he hammered on the boarded-up door just to make sure, then peering in through the window saw that the curtains were rags concealing half-rotted floor boards.

Pen-y-banc was abandoned, left to decay. He wondered just for a moment if the old woman had squatted there and walked up the valley to see them. But the place was deserted: all the more reason not to have detoured off to the white house high on the hill. Wasn't there a Government policy of hill farm closures?

When he walked back to the car he saw his front tyre was flat.

Damn. Damn. Damn.

Some piece of farm debris picked up on these roads. He stood there in the damp morning and cursed his luck. Kicked at the useless rubber, swore, looked around for some minimal help, parked by the side of a wall, a crumbling tank-trap of stone. It must still be at least six miles down to the lake and the Maesteg road.

The spare tyre was in the boot, together with the jack and tools, and the walking boots they wouldn't now need. Nothing moved along this road – no, not quite true, for he glimpsed a car roof below him, through a break in the cloud, then heard the noise of the engine.

He stood by the Ford and waited but the newcomer only slowed briefly before accelerating. A red car, one of those German Audis. A woman, a blonde with a headscarf and shades, rendering her face expressionless, drove straight past. He could not say she had noticed the puncture but he was sure she had seen him as he made a half-hearted gesture.

It took him half an hour, by the time he had fixed up the jack and struggled with the wheel nuts. At least the mist was now clearing. At least it stopped him thinking about the ruined weekend, as he got the spare screwed on and eased his muscles back to normal. He began to crave for faces, human sympathy, but all around was empty country, full of hawthorn and rowan trees, red-berried, yellowing with late leaf.

Chilled and perturbed he manoeuvred back on the road and drove downhill, parallel with the old rail bed, towards the huddle of houses near the end of the valley. Now he could see their chimneys, roofs and TV aerials; and a flock of sheep in the road that blocked him off completely as he rounded the next bend. They pushed their rumps together, moving in front of the car like a sea of cream overcoats. A boy stood and waved at him, bringing up the rear, a kid with a round face and blank, almost Mongoloid, eyes. Beyond him, beyond the backs of the sheep, he saw a red telephone box, one of the old-fashioned kiosks.

The boy swivelled round to stare. Somewhere ahead of them both, over the backs of the sheep, he could see the man who was leading them, a shiny flat cap bobbing up and down as he walked. Thank Christ there was someone still living who might know the old woman. Fellowes leaned out of the car, half-minded to shout, urging him to turn round and listen, but somehow that vacant face grinning at the rear of the sheep froze him into inaction.

In the end he turned off the engine and waited in the middle of the road until the sheep had cleared the bend and disappeared. Then he restarted the car and drove as far as the call-box.

Sometimes you can't win, he thought grimly, as he saw the state it was in. Most of the glass was broken and what was left of the directory had been used to light a fire on the floor. When he tried to dial he realized that the handset had been vandalized. Deliberately smashed, as if someone hated telephones.

He reached the first houses at last, four cottages by the roadside, two of them empty, and a small working farm where a couple of angry collies had been roped to a post. He knocked at the first of the cottages, feeling suddenly shaky, not quite real to be standing there in his back-to-the-country cords and nylon jacket, clothes selected to match up with Sandie. Waited, staring at the ground-floor windows, half-expecting something else wrong, except that the man with the sheep flock must have a farm nearby. Waited, but all he could hear was the whine of a circular saw somewhere at the back of the houses. Then, after a while, footsteps. A woman stood in the doorway, dark-complexioned, early forties, in a cotton overall and carpet slippers.

The passive face was staring, as if he had come from the moon.

'Look. I'm sorry, but something's happened up the road,' he began. 'I've come from Tan-y-graig, at the head of the valley. Someone has died up there, during the night. I need to call the police.'

The shoe-polish eyes looked through him, dark and suspicious.

'Tan-y-graig? No-one there.' The inflexion told him she was more used to speaking Welsh.

'Yes there is. My daughter and I are staying there.'

She shook her head and turned away, as if he'd been selling brushes. Deeply distrustful.

He put his foot in the door.

'Look. I need to telephone. It's important.'

35

'No telephone,' she said, and pointed to the farm next door. As he withdrew his shoe the door slammed in his face.

He walked across to the farm and knocked at another closed door, set into a primitive porch, weather-boarded and then repaired with squares of hard-board. The down-at-heel dogs in the farmyard were beside themselves now. Lean-tos on either side were stacked with rusting equipment, boilers, a trailer, broken carts, implements he couldn't identify, and the compost pile steamed with old straw. James might have named the equipment, harrows and drills and spreaders, but Peter Fellowes felt as lost as someone in a foreign country.

He had to knock again. Sandie would already be wondering why he had taken so long. The buzz of the saw had stopped, and he had the uncanny sensation of people secretly monitoring him, as if he was calling on ghosts.

A man's voice shouted something he could not catch, probably in Welsh, and then the door was drawn back. Two people stood surveying him from the flagstoned hall, and beyond them he caught a glimpse of a hat stand, a long-case clock and a passageway into the kitchen. The woman was round-faced, high-cheeked like a Russian doll, and the man was the flat-capped figure whom he had seen with the sheep. He read in their defensiveness that the boy was their son and that they were stalked by sadness.

'Please, I need some help,' he began. Their eyes widened. 'We . . . I . . . have found an old woman dead in the house at the end of the valley . . . at Tan-y-graig . . .' – he hoped that was how to pronounce it – 'where I was staying last night. I don't know who she is . . . I don't understand how she got there, but I need to phone for the police.'

'Where . . . ?' A rusty monosyllable, as if he'd just learned the language. The cadaverous figure in run-down boots and trousers and a black waistcoat stood with his legs apart, puzzled.

'Tan-y-graig house. Right at the end of the valley. I've rented it for a week.' Fellowes's voice died away. The other man shook his head like a dog shaking off water, spoke quickly to his wife and started to shut the door.

'No farm there now.' The dogs began to howl again.

36

'I know that. We're just renting the house, from Mr Steadman.'

The wife laughed and disappeared along the corridor, leaving the two men to it. The sheep farmer's face was emotionless.

'Steadman is dead,' he said.

'What? Don't be ridiculous. I spoke to him on the phone in Birmingham. He advertised the house.'

That closed Welsh head was denying it, while he tried to find the English words.

'No. Steadman died over two years ago.'

'I don't understand.'

'He's gone, I tell you.'

'What do you mean? Steadman sent us a key. We stayed there last night.'

'Steadman is dead. I saw him buried. There were no children.' The man in the doorway shook his head again. In the kitchen the woman turned on a radio to listen to Jimmy Young. They understood English all right, but it suited them to be Celtic, conspiratorial.

'Look,' Fellowes said, beginning to understand the limits of this conversation, 'may I just use your telephone to call the police?'

The farmer eyed him suspiciously. 'What do you want with the police?'

'I need help. There's been a sudden death . . .' Fellowes found himself pleading.

'No . . . That can't be.'

'Please, just give me access to a telephone, for the police and an ambulance.'

The farmer shook his head. 'No need to call the emergency . . .' But he stood aside to let him pass, nodding to a black instrument on a side table.

'Do you have a police number?'

'No police for miles. Try the doctor first.'

'Right. Thanks. I need to telephone someone.'

The farmer pointed to a card, half-a-dozen ball-pen scribbles, pinned up on the wall.

'Which one?' How the hell was he supposed to know? Mind-reading?

A thick finger jabbed at the third set of numbers. Fellowes dialled and stood there unnerved while the number rang and rang. There was no reply.

'For God's sake,' he said, 'what happens in an emergency?'

'We don't have emergencies here.'

Fellowes was beginning to sweat. Time was not on his side, and his heart ached for Sandie, left alone in that house . . . Might as well give up with this pair and drive straight into the town. He began to feel locked in a puzzle where no-one was willing to help him.

He thanked them and turned tail, driving faster now, wanting to hurry to Maesteg. But on the road by the lake he came first to a small settlement, a handful of houses, a tiny shop and a pub, 'The Lakeside'. The water looked battleship grey.

The pub was shut.

He ran into the little store next door which sold paraffin and bread, matches and boiled sweets from tall jars, and racks of yesterday's papers. Somebody must come there. Somebody must know how to deal with emergencies, he shouted at the woman behind the counter.

'We always call Dr Bryn Jones, but he won't be there on a Saturday.' She was a woman in a housecoat, her hands caressing a jar of jelly babies which reminded him of tiny foetuses.

'Do you mind if I ring his number?'

'No. Go right ahead. If he's not available, you can always leave a message at the house.'

This was more hopeful. He was through at last to someone who understood, and rattled out his story to a wife at the other end.

'Of course. I'll let him know,' Mrs Bryn Jones said. 'And tell the police. Where did you say it happened?'

'Tan-y-graig, at the head of the valley.'

There was a pause, as if she was trying to remember.

'There's no-one there,' she said. 'The house is empty.'

'No it's not. I stayed there last night with my daughter. It's been let by a Mr Steadman.'

'No. You must be mistaken.'

'What do you mean, mistaken?' Perhaps after all there was a rational explanation, some confusion over names.

'Steadman is dead,' she said. 'My husband signed the certificate.'

9

The weekend had turned to ashes, and was close to disaster. At least if he called a doctor, between them they could sort out the formalities, hand over to the authorities, people who might know the deceased. He couldn't see Sandie wanting to stay on now, any more than he did himself. The half-term holiday had become a black dream. He saw the shop woman looking at him from the cover of the confectionery jars. The blood had drained from his face as he thought of the mess they were in.

'Are you all right?' she enquired, as he put down the telephone.

He nodded, feeling a little easier now that someone had decided to act. At least Mrs Bryn Jones had agreed to let the police know, and assured him that the doctor would be visiting, as soon as he returned for the message.

'I'm going straight back to the farm,' he said by way of explanation.

'Suit yourself,' the woman shrugged.

He tried to pace out his thoughts on the return drive, to explain to himself why no-one was interested, why no-one seemed to believe him. It was only ten o'clock but the day had lost its promise and the thick white clouds were reforming over the mountains as he headed back up the valley. Why should they refuse to believe him when he said that he rented Tan-y-graig? A stupid little local mystery.

Parochial, suspicious and bigoted. He threw words at them in his mind but doing so did not explain a night visitor and a sudden, unexpected death. Going past the sheep farm where he had first tried to telephone he noticed that the door was open and a red car had stopped: the same Audi that he had seen before, but there was no sign of the driver. Further on along the hillside the sheep had scattered across the lower slopes and Fellowes saw the son again, watching him from a stone wall. He must have been Sandie's age, but there was no life in the face.

It hardly seemed any distance going back, that eight or so miles, round the corners of the hills, past the deserted farm of Pen-y-banc that had been his first and last marker. Barely two miles beyond it the hard-top ceased and he turned up the gravel track, filled with rubble and crushed bricks, past the dew-ponds towards Tan-y-graig house. The mountain was looming behind it, shaded now, looking closer and more ominous. When they had arrived in the sunshine of the evening before only Sandie had thought in those terms.

The farmhouse was clearly in view at the end of the track, through the pair of open gates. He sounded the horn to alert her as the car bumped over the last hundred yards. Tan-y-graig, it said on the gateway; a shabby-looking white farmhouse crouching under the slope.

And silent as the grave.

'Sandie? Hi!' he shouted, slamming the car door.

The noise seemed to echo between the house and the mountain. He stood for a moment in silence and sensed again, uneasily, the immense and brooding age of the hills, while the farm itself was as quiet and secluded as when he had left it.

'Sandie!' But she did not respond. He had expected her to come running out, and hoped that she would want to embrace him after the traumas of the morning. He had been away far longer than he had anticipated; it had been less than two hours but seemed like a lifetime.

He ran to the door and opened it, into the now familiar passage with the kitchen and parlour in front and the living room with the old woman's body on the other side. Sandie was not in the kitchen so he called upstairs before he steeled himself to look at the lounge. The door was closed and he opened it softly, fearing to disturb the dead. What did he expect to see? Sandie? Or the old woman lying there under the sheet? Perhaps both. He could

41

not have said. The curtains were still drawn and for a moment he found it hard to adjust, looking for the white shroud.

But there was nothing. No sheet. No body. No Sandie. The room was hushed and empty, the blank fireplace like a vault.

'Sandie?' he roared. 'Sandie!'

The old woman's body had gone. It took a moment to sink in that she had risen like Lazarus. But that was ludicrous. She had been dead for hours when they had discovered her. He had felt her himself, and said she was cold as ice. His stomach began to heave, an indigestion of fear. The cover-sheet had gone, and the old woman's plastic raincoat. The room was empty. Even the seat cushions dislodged by her final convulsion had been neatly rearranged as if no-one had ever been there.

'Sandie! For Christ's sake. Sandie!'

He fled upstairs from the awful truth only to find a worse one. In the bedroom behind his where she had unpacked, her clothes and her case were missing. Vanished. In mounting panic he tried to trace her whereabouts, and then her movements. Only one used towel in the bathroom. Her toilet bag was also missing. Downstairs in the kitchen a single mug reproached him, the one he had used at breakfast, marked 'Captain' in red. Some lines from W.E. Henley, 'I am the master of my fate, I am the captain of my soul,' ached inside his head. And he was neither: he could not even find his own daughter.

Deciding that she had gone exploring, Fellowes ran outside to the yard, across the broken concrete to the barns. Perhaps she had fallen down somewhere, and lay concussed. But the barns were padlocked, and undisturbed. He looked around at the hills, the slopes behind Tan-y-graig, but nothing moved.

'Sandie!'

Outside in the warm air he screamed her name up at the mountain. The syllables screeched round, disturbing birds in the bracken which took off and circled warily. 'No! No! No!' He shouted in mounting panic. He had a fleeting vision that he was going mad, had even invented the story, the place, the illusion of the old woman, but he knew full well he was sane, and stone-cold sober. Persistent and not easy to fool. Yet someone was trying to fool him.

'Sandie!'

The ferns rippled on the slopes. The farmhouse stood empty behind him. He went back and searched it methodically, room by room. Every trace of the old woman, every sign of Sandie had gone.

He realized that he was alone.

10

Sandie couldn't have gone, not without leaving a note, some
kind of message. Perhaps she had been frightened, left there
alone with the dead, and started to walk down the road. But
if so, where was the body? So? Someone must have collected
it, some vehicle could have called: yet he hadn't left the road,
the narrow road down the valley, and he hadn't seen a single
truck. Only one car in fact, the little red Audi which had driven
past him and then, on his return, had been parked at the sheep
farm. Could she – the woman driver – have picked up Sandie
and driven her somewhere for help? But in that case why hadn't
Sandie left him some kind of note rather than abandoning the
place like the *Marie Celeste?* Even more chilling was the idea of
abduction. Yet the body had gone too, so that theory didn't make
sense. No way they could have crammed a corpse into the boot
of the Audi.

What if the old girl had somehow miraculously revived and
between them they had driven her to hospital? But that was
impossible. Fellowes had seen her and felt her. No pulse and
grey as a fish. Rigor mortis had set in, the skin was cold when
he touched her, and the arm had been stiff. They had found the
body at eight and delayed by the puncture and those obfuscating
locals – he glanced at his watch – it was now ten-forty-five A.M.
She must have been dead for some time when they discovered
her, probably five or six hours, for the body was chilled, and
purple-mouthed. He shuddered. No, she was dead all right, and
no way they could have transported her without a truck or an
ambulance.

He began to search even more thoroughly, going back over his tracks. There was no sign of disturbance: the place was the same as he'd left it except for those straightened cushions on the settee. Sandie's overnight case was missing from upstairs, her belongings had been removed from the bedroom, including her handbag, the little shoulder-satchel she used, containing her money and make-up. Again, he walked through room by room, methodically, telling himself to keep calm because there must be an explanation, rational and obvious once he could think of it. Four rooms downstairs, two front and two back, four more rooms upstairs including the bathroom. Odd cupboards, empty, a trap door into the rafters that clearly hadn't been used; he managed to force it open by standing on a chair and poked his head into dust. A small cellar. All of them dark and gloomy but also empty. The outbuildings in the yard were padlocked and boarded up and had been that way for years. Sandie had simply vanished as if she'd been plucked into air.

His heart began to race as the facts struck home. His daughter and a dead woman: both of them had disappeared, without so much as a chalk mark of explanation. All right. Sandie might be playing tricks, she was a high-spirited girl: but he knew inside himself that it wasn't in her true nature. She wouldn't upset him like that. She would not want to play tricks with the dead – after all she had elected to stay here. So someone else must have taken them, or disposed of the body somehow, and in two hours that scarcely seemed credible. Yet someone must have come – someone he hadn't noticed on the road – and taken them both. And now he had a doctor, the wretched Bryn Jones, coming all the way from Maesteg to see a non-existent corpse. The shock – the horror and fear – drove him back over events, and pushed his mind to its limits.

Tense and nervous, he jumped back into the car and turned it to face the gates. The anxieties for Sandie's safety were overtaken by anger, then a sense of frustration, followed by a feeling that she had betrayed him in some way he couldn't yet fathom by taking the old woman away and not bothering to let him know. Worried and confused, he waited there in the yard, hoping she would suddenly appear, or give a sign.

But no sign came. The day was beginning to cloud over, and he felt numb, fearful of an unknown danger.

Fellowes waited for half an hour, from time to time sounding the horn, which reverberated round the valley. Nothing moved and no-one came. He knew finally that she was missing. He began to fear that Mrs Bryn Jones had forgotten about informing the police. He hit the car into life, then sat there wondering about the next move.

He needed to contact the police. Leave the front door unlocked, just in case she came back when he had the only key. Leave things just as they were. Revving the car in the yard, his dislike of the place intensified. Its four-square appearance, the windows stuck in like eyes, seemed to be watching him. The sense of unease deepened and the new chill in the air only heightened his fears. He turned on the car heater. How could the old woman have risen up and walked? And why should Sandie abandon him just as their ties were strengthening?

It didn't bear thinking about. He had to talk to people. Shaken, he sped back down the track, out onto the road then down to the farm where he'd been blocked by the sheep. Less than three hours ago he'd seen the boy there and tried that telephone, but now there was no sign of life apart from the sheep themselves scattered far on the hillside. The farm and the cottages hadn't been much help earlier and now they assumed a closed and sinister significance. No sign of the red car either, and he decided to press on, to take his case straight to Maesteg. It would hardly be any slower than making another call from the settlement, three or so miles further down where he had stopped by the pub, so he joined the Saturday traffic into the little town. The main road here, he noticed, ran parallel with the narrow-gauge railway along the shore of the lake, one abortive branch of which had long ago climbed up the valley. Now there was only the road, which he followed into the main street before asking where the police station was.

The police house, and police office, Maesteg, was a double-fronted pebble-dash house with a slate roof, backing on to a field and situated at the far end of the town. End of the road, they said, right opposite the cinema. A law and order enclave with coal smoke hanging in the air.

Fellowes parked the car and walked up the path to the blue-painted door with the sign saying *Heddlu Gogledd Cymru*: North Wales Police. A lobby with wooden seats and a linoleum-topped counter fronted an empty office. There was a bell which he rang.

The duty officer was young and fresh-faced, looking scarcely older than eighteen.

'I'm reporting some disturbing events,' Fellowes said. 'Some-one – an old woman – has died at Tan-y-graig, at the end of the valley, but the body has been removed. My daughter, who was staying with it – her – has also disappeared, and I'm concerned for her safety. For both of them,' he added.

The constable looked at him cautiously. 'Oh, really?' he said quietly, as if this happened all the time, please pull the other leg.

Pressure built up in Fellowes now, and he found he was gabbling about a strange old woman with a waxen face, the reasons why he and Sandie had come there, and the way that he had tried to telephone the elusive Dr Bryn Jones.

'What house?' the constable asked slowly. His youthful face, the newest thing in the room, looked as if it had been oiled, as he stood behind the counter against posters on Colorado beetles and long-lost property. Dust motes swam in the air.

'Tan-y-graig, at the end of the valley.'

The constable pulled at his jacket and fingered a map on the wall. He traced the thin yellow ribbon of road that curled from the lakeside up into the valley, becoming more dotted and broken as it climbed higher.

'Where did you say?'

Fellowes told him again. For God's sake, there were so few buildings in this area they must know every sheep by name.

'I hope this is not a hoax,' the policeman said. 'We don't know of anyone living there.'

'What do you mean?' Fellowes said. 'There's a furnished farmhouse there. I've just come from it. That's where the old woman was found.'

'Old woman?'

'The body. This woman who appeared in the night but isn't there any more.'

'Oh yes. I see.'

'Look. I'll make a statement. I'm not joking.' A tingling sensation coupled with a dry mouth told him he was out of his depth. His story seemed horribly false when it was noted down.

The young policeman continued to stare.

'Tan-y-graig has been unoccupied for some years. It's more or less abandoned.'

'Look. For God's sake, it's a funny kind of abandoning, with blankets provided. And furniture and television.'

The policeman smiled thinly and shook his head, making a record in longhand.

'Abandoned,' he repeated.

'Please listen.' Fellowes found the certainties deserting him. 'All I know is that I rented the place, from this man Steadman in Birmingham, who sent me a key' – he took the mortice key from his pocket – 'and last night I drove there from London, after picking up my daughter.' Get the facts right, he told himself. Get them right from the start in case this thing, this chain of events which had festered with the first sight of the old woman, turns into something even more sinister. 'This morning I – we – found a body, and now my daughter's disappeared. I want somebody to come out there and investigate.' He was beginning to sound like a madman.

The constable shook his head again.

'I'm not certain what you're reporting.'

'A body.'

'Is it there?'

'No, of course it's not there. That's the problem.'

'Then how do we know? How do we establish that your daughter has been there with you?'

It had been bugging him too, all the way into Maesteg. Even her belongings had gone. He could see the copper trying to analyse his perspiring face. Fancy jacket, cost more than a suit, he would be thinking. No jeans, no scruffiness, but you mustn't judge by appearances, accents were a better guide, accents and use of language. This one was educated and articulate. The policeman was asking him what he thought he was doing there.

'This is my half-term holiday,' Fellowes explained. 'I wanted a few days away with my daughter Charlotte, who is at boarding-school.'

'I see, sir. The one who has disappeared?'

'Yes. For God's sake. Isn't that enough to report, let alone a disappearing body?'

The constable sucked the end of his ball-pen. Fellowes had a sinking feeling of events going out of control.

'How do I substantiate your story?'

'Oh, for Christ's sake. People don't make up this kind of thing. I've even called a doctor out. Dr Bryn Jones.' He repeated the story of his first attempt to get assistance, driving down to the farm and the shopkeeper and then going back to Tan-y-graig. The constable began to take fuller notes: name and address, name of the school in Shrewsbury, name of his school in London, and what he said had happened.

'When the sergeant comes back, I'll ask him to accompany you.'

Fellowes wanted to shout, but the words dried in his throat. Instead he stood there helpless, on the other side of the counter, which was stained and marbled with tea rings. He wanted to kick and bang at the partition, telling them this thing was for real, this story that he could detail, down to the brown-ribbed nylons and sensible shoes of the old woman and the clothes of his daughter. He explained that she had been christened Charlotte but taken to calling herself Sandie. Expanded on his job and credentials, including his son in Bristol who had first seen the advertisement. Requested an urgent visit to go back and search the vicinity. And finally admitted to an underlying, uncontrollable panic that his daughter might well be in serious danger. He was now so concerned that he was going straight back to Tan-y-graig, whether they liked it or not.

The policeman held up a hand, as if he was directing traffic.

'I think you'd be advised to wait, sir,' he said with a hint of compulsion. 'Sergeant Parry will only be a few minutes, and I'm sure he would like to accompany you. I'll telephone Dr Bryn Jones and arrange for him to stand down, until we . . . have a body.'

He did so in Welsh. Peter Fellowes, concerned and fuming, was forced to kick his heels until the clock reached midday, while suspicions were voiced and whispered over the telephone in a language he could not understand.

11

'A body?' A frown began on Parry's forehead, shifted to the
downturned mouth and transformed itself into a droop of
the shoulders. On Saturday afternoons Sergeant Emlyn Parry
watched rugby, so the sudden intrusion of a case of disappearance did not make him best pleased. The sergeant played with his
car keys, serious-faced and composed. Fellowes found himself a
suspect, simply by being there.

'So he says. And disappearance of a teenager. His daughter.'

The frown grew deeper, a body language of disquiet signalled
by a hand slowly brushed across the chin.

'What kind of body? Who?'

'Look,' Fellowes said. 'I don't know who. I'm not in a
position to identify her. An old woman inside the farmhouse
at Tan-y-graig.' Just his bad luck that she was there in the
morning, when they came down to breakfast, and now she had
disappeared.

'Why didn't you inform us earlier?'

He kept his temper and tried to explain. 'I left my daughter
with the body. I found a telephone and then went back there,
but she had gone. Vanished.'

'Who had gone?' Parry muttered obtusely.

'For God's sake, both of them. The old woman and my
daughter.'

'Then they must both be alive. It stands to reason.' Parry placed
thumbs in the flaps of his dark blue tunic.

But Fellowes knew his logic was faulty, and hammered home
his despair.

'Listen to me, for God's sake. I tell you there's something wrong.'

In his imagination he could almost smell that house, damp and dark under the hill. Again and again he had asked himself whether things could have happened there which were outside human experience.

Parry leaned on the counter flap, conscious of the young constable who would observe his example.

'Oh. You think so, do you? What time did the events occur?'

It was the signal for another briefing in Welsh. Fellowes heard his name mentioned as if he was a prisoner of war.

'Look. I've already made a full statement. What I want is some action. An immediate search of the farm, and the surrounding area.'

The duty copper stood back, leaving the running to Parry who snaked in with the bald statement that Tan-y-graig was empty. The last occupant was dead.

Fellowes tried to concentrate their minds on the likelihood of two disappearances, one of them his daughter, the other one a corpse. There was a possibility, he seemed to read in their eyes, that he might not be mad, but only as one of the options. And somebody was waiting behind him with ears as big as saucers to report the loss of a cat.

'Take Mrs Morgan's details,' Parry said huffily. He unlocked a door at the side of the office and led Fellowes into a corridor lined with old filing cabinets and an ancient Chubb safe. 'You're not playing games, are you?'

'No. I'm not playing games.' His face should have told them as much.

'Have you quarrelled with your daughter? Teenage girls, you know. Very headstrong.'

'No.'

Parry sighed. 'All right. Better sit down. I'll take a personal statement before we go.'

'Jesus —'

'If you please —'

Whether he liked it or not, he was directed to a small, square interview room with a table and a couple of chairs and another

52

map on the wall, while the sergeant went through the story. Was it possible, he wondered, as Parry elaborated the questions, was it conceivable he'd concocted a fantasy, a flimsy misinterpretation of some obvious confusion? But Sandie had been real enough, and so had the waxy pallor of the old woman's skin. No miracles had occurred.

Sergeant Parry was far from convinced. His dark eyes were unrelaxed, like those of a lay-preacher watching for sin. 'Do you ever have hallucinations? Or imagine things?'

Fellowes was slow to anger, but the fuse was shortening.

'Listen. The quickest way for you to find out is to come out there with me.'

Parry opened the drawers of the table as if looking for fresh inspiration or a forgotten book.

'If there is no body, and your daughter maybe has gone home, what are we looking for?'

God, these provincial police, Fellowes thought furiously, and wished he had never bothered. He tried to explain again, half rising, half unsure of himself in this odd corner of Wales.

Sergeant Parry closed the notebook and picked up his uniform cap.

'All right. You can follow my car.'

In convoy up the valley, the Capri shadowed the little blue and white police car back up the narrow road towards the mountain, past the landmarks that now seemed familiar: the pub and the shop by the lake, the farm and its neighbouring cottages at the unnamed settlement and then the deteriorating surface towards Pen-y-banc and Tan-y-graig house. High up on the hillside, beyond the abandoned railway, Fellowes saw the big house again and on the other side a scattering of isolated cottages which may or may not have been occupied: it was a puzzle how anyone could reach them. Silver streams chased each other down the sides of the hills. Parry turned off the road at last and bumped up the path to the gates of the farm, which he had to stop and unlatch. Closed gates. Fellowes wanted to shout that he had left them open, just as they had found them on the previous evening, and that someone must have pulled them across, but he forced himself to stay silent, his knuckles grasping the wheel. Perhaps Sandie had come back.

Parry seemed in slow motion, lifting the barbed-wire loop from its post in his stately, professional manner. He had taken off his patrol car cap with the blue and white checkered band and his black hair shone. But there was no sign of Sandie. The conviction grew in Fellowes that he had become the victim of some monstrous betrayal.

He drove through in Parry's wake, up the lightly rising ground to the front of the house. Tan-y-graig. The place under the rock. The name began to spell disaster. In his own mind he started to pray.

'Sandie?' he called.

At first he could not believe the evidence of his eyes as he pushed at the door. The farmhouse seemed nearly emptied, as if removal men had been at work. For a moment he tried to delude himself that he was mistaken, that this was a different house to which somehow they'd been misdirected, but Parry was standing there grinning. They were looking at a place that had been stripped.

12

'Well?'

Peter Fellowes leaned on the door frame. Tan-y-graig was no longer furnished. The chairs and tables, the television, the crockery, pans and cutlery that had been in the kitchen, even the curtains, had gone. He ran upstairs and shouted for Sandie, but saw only a couple of chairs and the bed frames with bare mattresses.

'Sandie!' His voice echoed emptily. He feared now for her safety, in a world of sudden violence, of rape and murder. Feared for Sandie left alone.

Sergeant Parry waited downstairs, and Fellowes was rushing past him, into the room where they had found the old woman. It was now an unfurnished space. Even the settee had gone, and the other big chairs, while in the kitchen only the deal table and the big old Aga, cold as enamel, remained.

In a mounting panic Fellowes howled at Parry, 'For God's sake, what is going on?' He stumbled through to the scullery at the other side of the kitchen, and saw it now for what it was, the store-room of an empty house. Those stacked boxes and cases, the jumble of tables and chairs piled on top of each other, had been left there to gather dust; and the strange little window that Sandie had noticed might have been put there to tease him.

'What the hell was this place?'

Parry smiled grimly. 'A farm. It was a working farm. But there's been no-one living here since old Steadman died.'

Fellowes swung round. 'When? When?'

'Oh. A good two years now.'

He found his sense of reality vanishing, leaving him confused and exhausted, fighting to retain his sanity.

'You've got to believe me. Listen. There was a fully furnished house here. Two of us slept here last night. I'm not imagining things. I'm not that kind of lunatic.' But in the space of a few hours, punctuated by one brief return after the call to the doctor, Sandie and the old woman had both disappeared, and now so had most of the furnishings. The policeman sensed his confusion.

'Are you all right . . . ?' Parry asked.

He did not know. 'Dear God, Sandie,' he whispered, half to himself.

The sergeant was walking slowly from room to room. Only the two store-rooms – one downstairs, one up – seemed to be as they were. The rest of the house had been gutted of indications that anyone had recently stayed there. His own case and spare clothes had gone. In the bathroom his sponge bag and towel, razor, toothbush and soap had all been carefully removed. The electricity had been shut off at the mains.

They were inspecting empty rooms with no indication that anyone had ever been there. Something was wrong. Very wrong.

'You say you slept here?' Parry asked incredulously. The main facts of Fellowes's story, the basic planks of his account, did not appear to stand up.

'I swear to you my daughter was here. Sandie. Charlotte. This place has been emptied within the last three or four hours.' He ran outside half-expecting to see someone explaining it was some kind of practical joke.

The sergeant was not amused.

'I suppose your daughter might have run off with the body.'

'Don't be absurd.'

'All right. What's your version then?'

'I don't understand anything.'

'Nor do I, sir,' Parry said heavily. 'But I do know there is a charge of wasting police time.'

Fellowes turned on him. Deep down he feared that some places could be evil.

56

'Listen to me, for God's sake. There was a body. My daughter stayed here with it. She wanted to. This place was inhabited yesterday. Heat, light, food.' He felt the Aga, hoping for some overnight warmth but it had already cooled. There must be a means of telling when they had used the electricity – or was it only how much? – and fingerprints could be checked, to show that Sandie had been there – unless they had all been wiped. It was ludicrous, crazy. He knew a crime had been committed but could not prove it . . . and far, far worse he feared that not merely the old woman but Sandie also could already be beyond help.

'Somebody is concealing a body. May have already buried it.'

The police sergeant looked at him closely. 'Now what makes you think that, sir? Who would have buried anyone?'

It did not fit the sergeant's experience, although Sandie's sudden flight – if flight it was – was the sort of thing young girls were sometimes known for. Sandie had packed her bags, or had them packed for her, right down to the last Kleenex. Fellowes's stomach tightened. Sandie had gone, or been abducted, because someone intended to fool him. Unless she had seen something that meant they had needed to silence her.

He swayed but came back to his senses, his mind still numbed by the shock of these discoveries. He began to see the marks in the floor, in the kitchen and the living-room carpet, where furniture had recently been moved. He saw the brighter wallpaper where curtains had been hanging. And, out in the yard, surveying the valley with the moulded hills all round and Tan-y-graig mountain looming behind the house, he could have sworn there was evidence of tyre-marks. Marks on the greenish concrete that did not come from his car.

Parry came and stood beside him as he pointed them out.

'There's nobody been here for a long time.'

Fellowes stared at him. They stood and doubted each other.

'Are you sure Steadman is dead?'

'Of course I'm sure. He's buried in the churchyard at Llangogarth.'

Fellowes walked back to the kitchen and sat on one of the two remaining chairs. He remembered Sandie's first premonitions of

57

the echoes and murmurings about this place, those 'feelings' that he had dismissed. No sounds now, no sounds of anything apart from Parry's heavy breathing. A curious, unnerving silence as if they had all been satisfied, those mysterious spirits. He took a grip on himself.

'There was everything here. Fully furnished. Television, bedcovers, china, cleaning materials, a vacuum cleaner. It was advertised as a holiday home.'

'Not in Maesteg,' Parry said. 'You ask in the tourist office. That's where you register.'

Fellowes felt he wanted a drink, but there was no sign of his bottles, or even the tea bags. He walked over to the sink and tried the taps; the water had been turned off and only a feeble trickle emerged.

Parry's eyes burned on his back.

'Not much more we can do here then . . . ?'

Fellowes swung round.

'For God's sake, Sergeant. I have reported the disappearance of my daughter. I'm now reporting loss of personal items. Doesn't that mean anything to you?'

'Oh. Well now. We only have your word for that.' Parry's Welsh monotone was full of doubt. 'Anyway, it's private property. We would have to inform the owner before we could pull it about.'

'The owner? Yes, you do that.' Fellowes extracted the crumpled letter which gave the address in Birmingham.

'All right. All right. We'll obviously pursue enquiries if your daughter doesn't turn up.'

'Turn up, for Christ's sake? She's got to go back to school. I'm responsible for her.'

'Yes. Quite. Well, that's your problem, isn't it?' Parry's stone face was unyielding.

'Listen to me. *Please*,' he begged, as Parry's eyes continued to track him, 'can't you see? Can't you feel it? Something is happening here. Something *unnatural*. Two of us slept here, in beds with sheets and blankets. Where is all that now?'

'You tell me?'

'I'm telling you. Somebody wants to pretend this place no

longer exists. So they've stolen our things. And abducted my daughter.'

But he had nothing to prove it. Whoever had planned the operation had carried it out methodically and quickly, removing every shred of evidence. The question was why, why, why; and it was compounded in his mind by the feeling that he'd screwed up his big deal with Sandie. Really screwed it up.

He straightened his back, wanting to tear the place apart with his bare hands. Then started to calm down, trying to make some sense of it. There must have been a truck or trailer, some kind of removal van on which they had loaded the stuff, and Sandie would have been there and witnessed it, or tried to stop them.

'Don't you see?' He thumped his fist on the Aga. 'Don't you see! Somebody came for the old woman as soon as I had gone. They wanted her out of the way, and because my daughter was here they had to take Sandie too. Then they came back for the rest.'

And Parry laughed.

'Quite so. But not in this part of Wales.'

That complacent unwillingness to listen made Fellowes dig in his heels.

'They must have come in here with a truck, round at the back, and taken everything moveable. Then shut the gates. I left them open.'

'Don't be stupid. Why would they want to do that?' Parry sat and scratched his head. Fellowes ignored him and went outside again in a vain attempt to see some pattern in the tyre-marks. Impossible. The marks were faint and beyond the yard the grass had simply sprung back.

The policeman followed and stood with him at the back of the house. Two faces lingered in Fellowes's mind: Sandie's and the elderly scarecrow's in a grey knitted costume who had wandered up the lane.

'You don't care, do you?' Fellowes asked bitterly. 'You don't bloody well care.'

The policeman looked over the valley and behind the house to the mountain as if he was measuring distances, and time, and money spent, and the loss of his free afternoon.

'We have a record of what you have said. If your daughter doesn't turn up in the next twenty-four hours let us know and we will begin enquiries. Enquiries that take time and resources.' He began to put on his cap, resuming the uniform. The white piping and silver buttons shone in the sunshine but already there seemed a rawness, an October nip in the air.

'You'd better follow me back,' he said.

Fellowes watched while he reversed the panda car, and in his mind swore at Tan-y-graig. He swore he would get even with it, and whoever was behind it, and Sandie's disappearance. Swore that he would find his daughter.

13

In the police office, Maesteg, a single loud, persistent voice singsonged from an inner room.

'What's the matter with you then, man? Bring him in.'

Fellowes found himself ushered to a room at the back where a Welshman in shirt sleeves, jacket over the chair, was standing before an electric fire. 'Owens,' the pale-faced man said. He paused, and his eyes darted at the visitor like someone inspecting a face ravaged by disfigurement then flickering away in embarrassment. 'Inspector Owens. What is all this?' He clicked his teeth like loose tappets. 'Someone missing at Tan-y-graig?'

A feeling of profound disquiet gripped Fellowes then, of one unknown following another, horror that might be piled on horror, as he faced the senior policeman, roused from his weekend, and told his story again. He reported the loss of his things, Sandie's case and his own, clothes, food, personal effects; he reported a gross deception carried out on them both by someone called Steadman and showed his letter from Birmingham confirming the booking; he feared his daughter's abduction in these mysterious hills; and something in Owens's eyes sowed the seeds of mistrust.

Inspector Owens said, 'Come, come, come,' and invited him to sit down, with bird calls along the corridor for tea and toast. He put his fingertips together and smiled behind a desk that somehow seemed too large for his limbs. There was a jumpiness about him, like a puppet not quite under control, and a neatly clipped moustache wriggled on his upper lip.

'What am I supposed to do next? Find a missing girl and a body?'

Fellowes wanted to scream. His daughter for God's sake, in that house which had been gutted as soon as he left her there in the secretive valley . . .

'If you paid your money – and that's your story – you takes your choice. Why don't you ring the man up?' Edginess sat in Owens's voice, as if he didn't want to know.

The policeman pushed across a black telephone – 'All calls are free' – and sat there watching with glass-bead eyes. In his white shirt and black tie he looked like some agitated pigeon which had flown by mistake through the window and perched on the edge of the desk. Suspicion shone out of his face, and Fellowes with a shock of recognition caught sight of his own strained features, reduced to a caricature, in a mirror on the wall.

He dialled the Birmingham number on Steadman's letterhead. It rang and rang for what seemed an interminable time with Owens and Parry listening, marking his card, before the receiver was lifted at the other end.

'Hullo, hullo?' The answering voice was not what he had imagined from Steadman's businesslike letter enclosing the key and brief, typewritten directions.

'I'd like to speak to Mr Steadman, please . . .' He was conscious of a fresh suspicion like a fall in temperature in the hot little room.

'No Mr Steadman here. This is JK Papers.'

He was speaking to a Pakistani newsagent somewhere along the Coventry road, who disclaimed all knowledge of Steadman. 'No, no, no. No Mr Steadman here, I say, and never has been. Please do not keep asking.'

'Well now . . . ?' Owens the inspector drummed his fingers. 'These things can happen of course. Confidence tricksters, you know. Not to be trusted. Not to be indulged.' He implied that only a fool would have been taken in and only a madman would have wasted police time.

'Don't you *believe* me?' There was a ragged edge to Fellowes now.

The senior policeman shrugged, as much as to say, 'You tell me.'

Fellowes was on his feet.

'Listen, Inspector, in God's name what has *happened* there? Two people disappear, and the contents of a house . . .'

'Possibly. So you say.'

'It was advertised in the *Bristol Courier*. You can check that out, for God's sake. I sent a cheque to pay for the place. Somebody will have drawn it from my account. You can establish that too.' Infuriated by Owens's off-hand manner, which managed to give the impression that none of this really mattered, he wanted to shout at them that Sandie mattered to him more than anything left in the world. 'Otherwise why send me the keys?'

'I don't know,' Owens smiled, his dark eyes turning away again.

By now Fellowes hardly cared whether they believed him or not. Sheer persistence should have drawn them out of their shells and made them listen but a smokescreen of disbelief, almost of indifference, hung in the room.

Someone brought in a plate of toast, but he was unable to eat.

'For God's sake, I'm telling the truth. Don't you understand?'

He might have been addressing the wall.

'Oh, yes. Of course. Naturally. But . . . you see . . . Mr Fellowes . . . we must have some evidence. You know . . . evidence of loss. Evidence of your possessions. Evidence of this here body.' A polite smirk spread across Owens's face while the pulpit head of Sergeant Parry nodded.

He realized these were local coppers, unable to credit a nightmare. 'All right.' He was sweating. 'And if my daughter doesn't turn up . . . what then?'

'Oh. Well. That would be another matter.' He saw the shifting focus of their eyes, away from him.

Both of them were switching off. Parry because duty – a reluctant and tiresome complaints duty – had already been carried out, the inspector because he either couldn't believe or didn't want to know. He wanted to jump the desk and bang their heads together.

'I can't go back to that house. Where do you expect me to stay tonight?'

Owens played with a pencil. 'Well, that will be up to you. You can make your own bed, so to speak, as long as we know where you are.'

The implication was obvious: he was a prime suspect, if he persisted with his account.

'Just you show us a body,' Owens added as Fellowes left the station, the words echoing round in his mind, 'and we will find you a criminal.'

He walked slowly back to his car, telling himself over and over that he must not lose his cool. Perhaps that was what they expected, to goad him into admission, but what had happened was not an hallucination, or some kind of bad dream. Sandie was his flesh and blood, and she had either walked out on him, or become a victim of some undisclosed and terrible event. The little town at the end of the lake now seemed sinister, as if these harmless shoppers coming in from the hills and jostling for parking space were all part of a conspiracy. If Sandie were alive, perhaps hidden somewhere among them, she would be living in fear. Anyone observing him would have seen his jaw stiffen.

14

Over that weekend he began to make telephone calls. He tried Birmingham again, but the Pakistani newsagent rang off on him, and later the line went dead. Inside the Angel Hotel he booked a room for the night, and explained why he had no luggage. They looked at him carefully, or so he felt, as if he was already marked out, but he nodded them down and swore that whatever it took, whatever the cost, he would hang on until he found her. Once before, when Stella died, he had faced a similar loss. Now, as he struggled with wild, alarming assumptions about what could have gone wrong, a bitterness slipped quietly but savagely over his features so that passers-by in the lounge, glancing at the figure in the corner, might have assumed he was ill.

James in Bristol had no news. Relations between father and son were easier than they had been with Sandie, but James had nothing to add.

'God, Dad, why ask me? I haven't seen her for weeks.'

'You sent me the ad.'

'Oh, come on. I just happened to see it, and thought it might suit you.'

Fellowes said, 'Help me. *Think*. Is there any reason why she would vanish?'

'How would I know? You sent her to that bloody school.'

It hurt him that they felt like that, both of them, about the educational arrangements that he'd made after Stella's death; he could see that it was unfortunate that he had sent them away, but he hadn't felt that he could cope with two children at home. And Sandie had wanted to board.

What did he know about her, really know, in the aftermath of that decision? He was aware that she had a boyfriend hanging around the school gates, one reason why James's plan had attracted him, out of sight being out of harm. But would she suddenly run out on him? Was she that kind of girl? He tried to think back to her attitude during their drive from Shrewsbury, and the way she had warmed to him as they started the weekend. Was it only forty-eight hours? Events could fade in the memory like water-colours in the sun, but Sandie's sense of premonition was scored in his mind. And so was the memory of that strange, shabby figure, the grey body by the settee. Ghosts? He couldn't believe in them but he felt his stomach contract.

This was no aberration of a wayward teenage girl: Sandie had had a conscience, she had volunteered to stay in the farmhouse out of a form of respect. He was haunted by the face of the dead woman under the spray of white hair, a face with a sense of tragedy in the sunken cheeks and wide-open mouth, as if she was not fully at rest. And yet she was dead as a door-nail without any mark of violence, a human being at the end of her road; or else – and the thought was appalling – the victim of some terrible crime. No wonder Owens was suspicious. Worse, if she should ever be found, he would now be in some way implicated.

It was no good counting the odds, he had to do something. From the bedroom of the hotel he put a call through to the school and asked them to make quite sure that Sandie hadn't come back. After another half-hour they replied that they had seen no sign of her, but again he felt a snare of suspicion on his own back. They were wondering why he should ask. His home in Barnes was a long shot, since there was no-one in residence, but he rang there as well to make sure. The telephone echoed in the empty hall; and Mrs Huxley next door assured him there'd been no callers.

On Sunday afternoon and evening the rain clouds closed over the hills in a steady Welsh downpour, but in his mind he felt calmer, better equipped, with a new raincoat, obstinate and determined.

He would undertake his own search, without waiting for the authorities.

In spite of the weather he made a new reconnaissance, back up the valley road, retracing his steps, running over the sequence again, and stopping to check at each point. The little store on the lakeside was closed but he rang on the bell and asked whether they had seen a young girl in jeans and a sweater, with uncooperative hair. He didn't even have a photograph; you never realized until too late how much you needed a record, a smile on a piece of paper.

'No. No-one like that,' they said, and shut the door.

It was the same at the pub, a small building tucked between a cottage and the shop, with two simple rooms inside, bar and saloon, opened into from the front door. The interior was cluttered and dark, with horse brasses and plastic chairs, a cord carpet on the floor and black and white photographs of what looked like mining disasters. The barmaid, brown-eyed, black-haired and gipsyish, with that circumspection of foreigners that he had come to believe was endemic, told him no-one had been there whom she did not know by sight. Over the bar was a sign of a hanging man, burnt into a piece of wood. 'Please don't hang around' it said, with an attempt at humour that struck him like a gallows laugh.

Higher up on the hill next to the sheep farm stood the four bleak cottages in a row, two of them already empty as if life was pulling out of the valley. He knocked in turn and got dumb shakes of the head, first from an elderly man carrying a scoop of coal, then from the overalled woman who had previously come to the door.

'I'm sorry,' he began. 'I wondered if you'd seen a girl. My daughter who was with me —'

She shook her head and tried to close the door but he pressed it back with his hand.

'We were staying at Tan-y-graig. I called yesterday morning, remember?'

A look froze her features, a sensitivity he would not have expected from the dumpy, middle-aged figure, as if he had posed a question someone had warned her about.

'No. I don't. Please go –'

'But listen – what do you know about the farm at Tan-y-graig? For God's sake, please help me.' He forced himself to hold on, foot in the door.

The woman's face seemed to grow darker.

'Tan-y-graig,' she said slowly, 'has been empty for two years.'

He did not try to argue further, aware that he was caught up in some much wider intrigue; next door was the farm where they had let him telephone and first told him that Steadman was dead.

The man who now appeared was a spruced-up and younger version of the flat-capped figure with the sheep flock, who stood there, lips turned down, when he recalled his visitor.

Fellowes repeated his question. Inside, he saw again the heavy old clock and the flagstones, a coldness and darkness that chilled him. He wondered where the boy was and pitied them confined there with the dogs barking in the yard. A breath of stale air seemed to creep along the passage.

'No. Of course I've not seen no-one.' The dark eyes glittered in the narrow face. 'All I know is you come here yesterday morning with that damned stupid story. No-one lives up in the valley, not any more. Only Davies in the big house.'

Fellowes found himself standing there, staring round at the farmyard and the yowling, chained dogs. There was a closeness about this area that he could not penetrate, something surviving from more primitive times, some mediaeval bleakness that was as real as the rusty machinery, the stagnant spillages, the damp grey stones of the house. He shrugged and turned away.

The road ran steeply uphill past the end of the abandoned railway, a cutting covered in saplings which had pushed their way through the track, and the broken-fenced farm called Pen-y-banc. Two more empty cottages – crofts they would have been in Scotland – were scattered up there on the slopes, too remote to be reached, and opposite, on the western side, he saw very clearly now the big house that he had omitted in his sweep down the valley because it stood high and secluded, way up behind the trees. The Davies house, they called it.

The driveway branched off to the right, a long elliptical curve through a screen of young conifers that gave it a faintly Scandinavian air, but the house itself was in the traditional style, white walls and and grey slates, dormer windows in the roof, and Bible-black paint. There were two large, imposing gate-posts, no gate, but a typewritten notice which he stopped to decipher. It was preserved in a plastic sleeve and pinned to one of the posts.

'Maesteg Railway Extension,' he read, in English with a parallel Welsh text. 'It is hoped a society will be formed to extend the Maesteg Light Railway on the old track to Tan-y-graig.'

They had a hope, he thought. The notice was yellow with age, and it would be a few years yet before that line was re-opened. What kind of steam buff, he wondered, could imagine it would ever be feasible to shunt parties of tourists up to these brooding hills?

There was no sign of life at the house but it looked well-enough preserved compared with the cottages below, as if money had been spent. Some weekend countryman or railway fanatic perhaps; but what would they know of Tan-y-graig?

He drove on, up to the door, and rang the bell, noticing another car parked there. A red car, the Audi two-seater coupé that he had seen before, on the morning Sandie had vanished: the woman who had passed by on the other side when he was changing the tyre. Passed by without stopping.

From the front step he looked back at the oval of grass that made up an unkempt lawn and beyond that to the gates and the surrounding box hedge. The kind of place, he decided, that would be lucky to find a buyer, certainly one who could keep it in the style of a country vicarage, with fresh curtains on the windows and paintwork in good repair. It began to rain more heavily.

He had ceased to blame himself for a sequence of events over which he had had little control, but there was still the problem of how he explained to others the fact of the empty house, the body that no-one believed in, and the loss of his daughter. The Davies house was two miles from Tan-y-graig; if anyone was aware of mysteries at the end of the valley it ought to be the nearest neighbour.

The door was opened by a young woman in a grey suit. She stood there policing the house, as if he was some kind of intruder, her hair cut short, streaked and lacquered: he could even smell the spray.

'I'm making enquiries about something that's happened at Tan-y-graig, just up the road.'

'I'm afraid I don't live here,' she said sharply. 'At least not really. I don't know about Tan-y-graig. I'm sorry.' The voice was English, straightforward, as if she was there on holiday.

'It's the nearest house to this one. Surely you must know something about it?'

She shook her head.

'I'm sorry. I've never been up there.'

'Look. Please. Is there anyone else who could help me?' He tried, and failed, to read the closed look on her face. 'Mr Davies for instance?'

She smiled. 'You'd better ask him when he comes down from London.'

'How often is that?'

She shrugged. 'From time to time.'

He began to wonder whether the absence was convenient: an absentee owner in London, a scheme for a defunct line, a house kept for occasional weekends by someone two hundred miles away, this girl, and the red car.

The girl was looking irritated, as if she wanted him to go.

'Is that all?' Her voice was brusque.

'No, wait a minute,' he said. 'That red car. Who does it belong to?'

A momentary annoyance, or was he mistaken?

'Just someone visiting on business.' She implied it was none of his. Yet the same car had been at the sheep farm when he drove back up the valley after his first telephone calls.

'Is that all?' the girl said again, increasingly on her guard. The rain trickled down his neck and she made no move to detain him. He felt that he was not welcome.

'OK. Thanks. That's all.'

Her eyes were on his back all the way down the drive.

15

In the car in the rain, Fellowes realized that none of them believed him, least of all Owens and Parry and the rest of the local police. Why should they indeed, if Tan-y-graig had been empty and he had been the victim of some con-trick? If he persisted with his ridiculous story he was either mad or guilty in the eyes of Inspector Owens, unless – and this was the difficult thing to someone who had played by the rules and implicitly trusted the police – unless Owens himself was involved, and knew more than he admitted. He switched on the wipers to try to clear his vision. Was he accusing the police of being part of a cover-up? The mere thought made him nervous.

He was comforted for a moment, as he turned again up the track to Tan-y-graig itself, by the sight of a uniformed constable. This one looked studious and cheerful, sitting at the wheel of an Escort. He waved as Fellowes arrived.

It was indistinguishable from any other farmhouse in that part of Wales, he thought, walking across. Four-square, hacked from the local granite and painted white, tucked up against the hillside. In spite of the disused air it looked far from derelict. Yet whoever had been there in the time between his leaving Sandie and returning with the police had stripped the essence away. Even the curtains had gone, and the windows were featureless sockets.

The young policeman emerged from his car, zipping up a white car-coat, the rain dripping from his cap.

'I'm sorry, sir. No entry. My instructions.'

'What do you mean?' He wound down the driver's window

and felt the cold wind blowing. 'I'm renting the place. I've got a key.'

'I know, sir. They warned me you might come back here' — words he pronounced in a soft local burr — 'but I wasn't to let anyone past. Including yourself.'

'Why not? I've got a right of entry. A legal right.' Perhaps he had, perhaps not, one thing he needed to check; but it didn't make any difference, the official face was obdurate.

'No. I'm sorry. Those are my orders, sir.'

'Supposing I said I just wanted to be sure that I've not left anything inside there?'

The constable leaned on the car. 'Police enquiries are proceeding, sir. The house is sealed pending investigations.'

'Sealed ?'

'Yes, sir.'

At least they were doing something. Dear God, he needed some help.

'All right. Any objection if I walk round the back?'

'Yes, sir. My orders are to prevent access, until the CID boys get here.'

He tried to tell himself that this was a good sign, the police had taken him seriously after all; yet his doubts about Owens remained, and every day that went by Sandie seemed further away.

'Are you a local officer?'

'Born in Llangollen.'

Fellowes got out and stood by the policeman, turning up his collar against the rain.

'One thing is very odd about this place. Everyone says it's not been occupied for the past couple of years. And yet when I came here on Friday – came here with my daughter – we found bedding and furniture, and there were all the signs that someone had lived here recently. What do you make of that?'

The copper stamped his feet and grinned, as if glad of someone to talk to.

'Oh, well. Of course the Steadmans have been living here on and off.'

The rain set in harder than ever, forming little gullies in the road.

'On and off? But I've been told Steadman died two years ago.'

'Oh, yes. But I think Mrs Steadman used to come here from time to time. I remember seeing lights in the house only a few months back.'

He felt a surge of excitement.

'Where does she live now then?'

The constable shrugged. 'I couldn't say that. Nursing home somewhere, I believe. But she gets out now and again . . .'

At last he was getting somewhere. If he could trace Mrs Steadman he could find if she was missing. Also he had a police witness who could swear to the place being occupied long after Parry alleged. It didn't bring Sandie back, but it might help to confirm his story about the old woman. As he drove off he was beginning to loathe the very name of Tan-y-graig.

The constable had seemed relieved that he was going. Fellowes wondered how long the police car would stay there, in some kind of lonely vigil — against what, against himself, against other unknown intruders? It looked a mere white dot against the brown of the hill, against the darker green of the trees, as if thrown there by some child who'd abandoned it in a game. But he knew it wasn't a game. Something deadly serious had happened there, something that Sandie had seen, and the cold, gripping sensation in his heart was a fear that when he found the answers he would already be too late.

16

'Are you saying she won't come back?'

Inspector Owens thrust his round and rather featureless face with its small disturbed eyes and push-button nose over the table in the police office on the following morning and continued in his high-pitched singsong. 'Why do you think that now?'

Accusations aimed directly at Fellowes, who appeared very alarmed. After a night in the local hotel he had woken at first light to find the long main street still grey with rain.

He tried to get Owens onside. 'Look, Inspector. The old woman may have been Mrs Steadman.' Even as he spoke he could see that Owens was scarcely listening. 'Somebody wanted her out of the way, and Sandie came in between.'

'Oh, I see.' Owens made one of his tappet noises by running a plastic ball-pen across his teeth. 'Well, I suppose we can check on that.'

For God's sake how did he *shake* them, really make them believe him? He could see them referring to his previous statement and penning more notes, mentally labelling him a lunatic, if not a criminal. His heartbeat jumped, and a sweat broke out on his brow, in spite of an attempt to stay calm.

It was a claustrophobic room overcrowded by four men, Fellowes himself and Owens, Parry and an elderly constable who was taking particulars. The only relief from the decor of cream and green filing cabinets and haircord carpet was a calendar from a Chinese take-away pinned up on one wall.

'Why don't you *do* something . . .' Above all about Sandie. The three faces stared back, confident in their authority.

'Well, we've already told the missing persons bureau in Cardiff, and from there it goes to Scotland Yard. It's all on computer,' Owens said. 'No stone will be left unturned, you can bet your life on that.' Tap, tap, tap went the teeth. 'I suggest you go back and wait.'

'Go back where?' Fellowes asked incredulously.

'Home. That's London isn't it, where you come from?'

The birdlike voice sang in his ears, and he seemed to be losing his balance.

'I'm not going back anywhere until I've found my daughter . . . or found out what's happened to her. There was a body, there was a furnished house . . . and now everything's vanished and you keep somebody there on guard. What are we playing – charades?'

The inspector's eyes glistened.

'You must remember, we only have your word for things. You say somebody in Birmingham . . .'

'Look!' He punched the letter from Steadman, dog-eared now, down on the table. 'Check back in the *Bristol Courier* over the last six weeks.'

'Oh. We shall be doing that, I assure you. I don't doubt your word, of course' – the inflection in Owens's voice conveyed the opposite effect – 'but it looks like you been taken for a ride, if I may say so.'

He leaned back in his chair, hands brushing over his hair as if he had scored a point. His cup of tea and one provided for Fellowes congealed to a mahogany rind.

'Why can't you believe me?' Did they really think he'd come there to dispose of his daughter, and invent a cock-and-bull story, he stormed at them, his face shining. Did they think he'd invented the idea of a house that had been emptied as soon as his back was turned? What was this, some practical joke for a television programme? Tan-y-graig had been occupied recently. 'Ask your young policeman,' he insisted. 'The one who was on duty there yesterday.'

Owens was looking at Parry, whose lips parted as if feeling better after an attack of migraine. Outside, the rain had stopped at last, and they could hear a bird singing.

76

'Send in PC Thomas.'

'Smoke?' Owens offered, holding out a packet of small cigars, then rolled one under his nose.

'Drink up your tea then.' The solidifying cup was pushed towards him, and they waited awkwardly while the young policeman was called. Smoke rings from Owens's cigar curled to the ceiling.

'Ah, Thomas,' Owens said, announcing him like a hymn tune. 'Our friend here would like a word.'

Fellowes leaned forward.

'You remember me? At Tan-y-graig yesterday?'

For one horrible moment he feared he would meet with a denial, but the young policeman nodded.

'Oh yes. Right.' But there was a nervousness about him, the look of a man in a wobbly lift shaft.

'Listen, please,' Fellowes said. 'Just tell us what you said then about the house being occupied, a few months ago.'

PC Thomas was looking from Owens to Parry: Fellowes could have sworn complicity.

'Oh no. That's not what I said.'

'What do you mean, not what you said? You said you'd seen lights in the house.'

'Oh no. I don't think so . . .'

'You don't *think* so? You told me someone had been living there only two or three months back.'

The policeman shook his head dumbly, implying that the recollection was vague and difficult.

'No. I don't think I ever said that.'

Silence, as they stared at each other. The constable's hands were rigid; he stood there on parade, parroting a message and waiting to be dismissed. And Fellowes then knew for certain that there was a conspiracy wrapping round that whole valley and blanketing the local police.

'Are you sure?'

Thomas nodded. 'Oh, yes.'

Fellowes let his anger subside in one long sigh. He heard but did not register Owens, with fingers together, saying, 'Well, I think that clears that one up.'

77

'All right. All right, I read you.' He turned on them. 'If you won't help I'll find out on my own.' Even though it was a cry in the dark.

Owens interjected sharply.

'I wouldn't advise you to take the law into your own hands . . .'

Was that advice or a threat? He had passed beyond caring, consumed by concern and mistrust.

'You wouldn't advise, Inspector? You wouldn't advise me? You want me to go home and wait? Wait to find out if my own daughter's still alive?' He banged his chair against the wall. 'Well, you've got the wrong man.'

17

Maesteg was one long street leading down from the police station to the heart of the town with the Angel Hotel on one side and the Raven on the other. The rain clouds had cleared, leaving the air refreshed, and a cool wind blew off the water as he drove back down the main thoroughfare.

The absurdity of his situation had begun to obsess him. They couldn't do this to him, he told himself over and over. Fate. It. They, whoever they were, the forces lined up against him. If he had unseen enemies equally he now needed friends. People who could help and advise. He could go to the Police Complaints Authority, or perhaps a local magistrate would listen, but who was really going to bother with a farrago of nonsense which seemed more garbled and unlikely with every day that passed?

And then he saw the car again, but this time she was standing beside it: the two-door red Audi that had been at the Davies house, and the blonde who was driving it. It was almost as if she was avoiding him; coming out of a clothes shop where she had been looking at something she had recognized his Ford Capri, and quickly turned on her heel in the opposite direction.

Fellowes pulled in.

'Excuse me?'

He stood there panting, slightly out of condition.

The face that looked up at him, perhaps it seemed to inspect him, was sensitive but – he thought – cautious. She was almost petite, smart without being beautiful in a conventional way, her nose a little too straight, her mouth perhaps not straight enough, fair-haired, with a regular fairness that had been carefully worked on. She had applied more make-up than Stella ever did, but Stella was dead, and this was a younger woman, both attractive and slightly evasive: evasive, that was the word, evasive in eye-to-eye contact, and even in her choice of dress, couture clothes, a sweater and skirt and matching jacket in discreet greens and golds, autumnal tints that showed a sense of style. She hesitated, smiled and stopped. Was it his imagination or did she also shiver?

For a moment she said nothing, standing in the small Welsh street, carrying a shopping bag in which he saw, incongruously, a packet of biscuits and a bottle of Bell's whisky.

'I hope you won't mind . . . but I would very much like to talk to you.' Fellowes was cautious but direct. 'I saw your car in the valley near Tan-y-graig.'

He thought to himself that she was backing off, that she was almost frightened, but then she slowly nodded.

'All right . . .' she said at last, softly and firmly, in an accent that was North American. East Coast, he decided. She paused again. 'Why don't we have a coffee? I'm Laurel Ericson, from New York.'

She led the way to a coffee shop and patisserie that she must have sampled before, for they nodded at her as she went in, under the tinkling bell; she was looking at him with the kind of reserved smile that encouraged him as she launched at once into one of those quick soul-searches between strangers. New York was one way of life, getting and spending, but she was digging up her roots, a grandfather two generations back, to discover how shallow they were. By the time she was thirty she had a job on *Harpers*, an apartment in Greenwich Village, and had suddenly realized she had seen all and found nothing. So she had taken a rain check on the magazine, not a great job but OK, and ended up on vacation in Wales.

The explanation disappointed him just as much as she intrigued him; it was as if there was a mutual suspicion that concealed the interest both felt. Yet she also seemed to be searching, rather than enjoying herself, judging from the places she had visited and the time she had spent there, at the Davies house and the farms up in the valley. On his side, he found himself trying to explain a mystery he could not solve, this lunatic situation that he said he was in, after renting Tan-y-graig. She listened with her hands on the table, bending her head towards him, blue eyes wide open as if she half-suspected that he was some kind of trickster. The details made him lower his voice. It was not the kind of story openly rehearsed in Maesteg: that someone had died and been spirited away, together with his only daughter.

Laurel breathed quietly, then turned her head away, gesturing out of the window of the coffee shop, across the street towards the lake. She stared round the tables of the little restaurant almost as if they were observed.

'Jesus. What can I say? It's like some kind of horror movie.' She stopped, then added, 'What in God's name are you going to do now?'

Did she know Tan-y-graig? She was shaking her head. The evasiveness began again: no, she had never been there, but Fellowes pressed her by saying he had seen her car, parked at the Davies house.

'Sure, I called in there yesterday.' The level tone gave nothing away, implying she had private business.

'I was told Mr Davies, whoever he is, wasn't there. Apparently he lives in London.'

'Right,' she said. 'There was a girl there: kind of housekeeper, I guess.'

The girl in grey who had also answered his enquiry. 'You must have been in the house when I was ringing the bell.'

Laurel shrugged; Fellowes had the impression she wanted to change the subject. 'More coffee?'

'No thanks. Are you interested in the railway scheme? That notice on the gate . . . ?'

Laurel laughed, relieved and throaty. 'No way. No sir. I had some personal business, checking on some relations who were over here way back.' But she was reluctant to say more: something about this countryside, these hills and the low, shut-in streets seemed to breed secrecies as surely as the coal smoke drifted over the terraces. Instead, she turned events back to him.

'What are you going to do?'

On the other side of the table, Peter Fellowes was determined.

'Find out about my daughter. And what the hell happened at that house,' he responded. 'They've made a serious mistake if they think they can fool me.'

They looked at each other again as if each had a separate secret, but neither would admit it. There was a steely resolve in the way that she would not be drawn.

'It must be tough for you,' she said slowly. 'I wish to God I could help you.'

He could have hugged her for that, as he paid their bill, and considered.

'Where are you staying?'

'Llangogarth, along the lake.'

He knew the name: a settlement a few miles on from where the road forked up the valley to Tan-y-graig. She was simply driving around to get the feel of the place, or so she said. It was somehow comforting to know that, to appreciate that he was not the only visitor to these sinister hills. She was walking with him to the door, and a feeling of mutual sympathy seemed to pull them together.

'This guy Steadman in Birmingham, who advertised the place,' he confided. 'I'm going to take him apart.'

She glanced up at him quickly, then nodded. 'I reckon that's right.'

He stumbled over his words. 'What . . . I mean where are you going now?'

Laurel shrugged. 'Oh, I'm sticking around.' Was that disingenuous, Fellowes wondered, or just casual, from this woman with no apparent ties, who had come over on holiday. He found himself wanting to know more, about her background, her job, her likes and dislikes . . . and why she would stick around. Such pleasure in a simple statement, as she held out her hand. 'Good luck . . .'

He took it with a feeling of regret, the sense that she was brushing him off, that she too only half-understood, and he was wishing it otherwise. But Llangogarth was very close to the valley that he had come to. He stored that fact in his mind as she drove away in the red Audi.

By now every day that he waited seemed only to confirm his fears, the sick, empty, hopeless dread of the unknown that came to haunt him, for he was starting to believe that some monstrous secret was locked up there in the valley. Yet all that he had in common with Laurel, after all, was the fellowship of strangers. There were sensations, emotions that he could not display in public, and he was close to despair.

He went back to the hotel to telephone.

The school in Shrewsbury was one of those red-brick, hospital-looking buildings behind formidable railings that architects seemed to think were required for the safe education of young ladies. Nevertheless it had a fine reputation and for some reason Sandie – Charlotte as she then was – had asked to go there when Stella died. St Cyprian's cost an arm and a leg but also took care of its own, and Fellowes knew they were deeply concerned that having taken her away for that brief and disturbed weekend he had now failed to return her. He had already warned them but he had to make sure.

He asked to be put through to the headmistress, feeling a common link in their professional anxiety.

'Has there been any word from Charlotte?' he enquired, imagining her in that study of light oak bookcases and bowls of flowers.

There was a significant pause.

'Well, not exactly . . .'

'What do you mean?'

'Didn't you give the instructions?'

'What instructions?'

He could feel the embarrassment now at the other end of the line, a tangible awkwardness as the headmistress's self-assurance drained away.

'To the police . . .'

'What police?'

Another embarrassed pause, and then the headmistress was rushing her fences.

'An inspector from the North Wales force came here yesterday evening. Said that he was making enquiries on your behalf. And that they wanted to collect some of her things.'

'What things?' Fellowes almost shouted.

'Clothes. A few personal papers. He said you would understand.'

'Understand! For God's sake, they're looking for a body . . .' His voice was a dry yelp.

'Oh, come now, Mr Fellowes. That's a little far-fetched.' But she was equally worried.

Fellowes calmed down. In an odd way it made it easier, this latest aberration. At least something was happening. And he guessed the name of the visitor.

'I presume it was a man called Owens . . . ?'

'Well, yes,' she said. 'How did you know?'

18

The next step was to trace Steadman. That meant a trip to the Midlands.

He arrived there in the late afternoon, after burning the miles in a way which limited the misery of what might be in store at the end if the police wanted examples of Sandie's clothes; although, by the same token, the fact that they'd taken so much gave him the persistent hope that they could find her alive.

Now he was hammering the car on the last leg of the switchback to Birmingham, where he invested in a street map and negotiated the suburban streets off the hub of the Coventry Road. One fear was that JK Papers, at number thirty-six Ramada Street, the address on Steadman's letter, would be closed when he arrived, but he need not have worried. JK Papers opened eight till late, selling a pot-pourri of papers and magazines, sweets, stationery and tobacco.

A sari'd woman behind the counter, dark-skinned and speaking poor English, called up to her husband in a room at the back and Fellowes recognized at once the voice that had answered his initial enquiry over the telephone from Owens's office. He opened the rental letter and pushed it across.

'Do you know who this is from?'

Mr Mukerjee shook his head, up and down meaning, No. 'No, no. Not here. I explain by telephone.' He was no fool. He smiled 'go away'.

But Fellowes was beginning to dig in.

'Somebody used this address. I wrote to it and they replied.'

'This is a holding address,' the newsagent countered.

'Ah. People pay you to have letters sent here, for collection?'

A flash of gold teeth told him he had hit the mark. The mysterious Steadman had come and gone. Too many people knew nothing. Fellowes's stomach tightened into hard little knots. He looked at the littered shelves and tight-packed trays of bon-bons, then left the shop.

He climbed back into the car and a couple of hours later was talking to his son in Bristol.

'James,' he said 'I need help.'

Half-way through his degree course and busy with his own life, this visit from James's father pointed to a mutual need. James, like Sandie, had broken away after his mother's death, set himself up as an adult while Peter had withdrawn into a shell, a carapace of school activities. Now something had happened which compelled both father and son to end their isolation: Sandie was a part of them both.

James had brought in a take-away meal – Kentucky fried – when his father arrived, and offered to share it with him, but Peter Fellowes shook his head. He looked drained as he recited the facts of Sandie's disappearance, sitting on a second-hand chair.

'Can you switch off that racket?' The room was a cage in which both men felt trapped.

James nodded, and they confronted each other in the sudden silence as the Stone Roses died. He found himself wondering at his father's vulnerability. Peter had once been a pain, pushing him to get his work done, and leaving home had been like coming up for air. Now his father was asking for help.

'Listen, Dad,' James said. 'Sandie doesn't play games. And she hasn't run away . . .'

'How do you know? How can I be sure?'

'God, man. Don't you think she'd tell me? Don't you think we communicate?'

'I don't know.'

'No. You never stopped to listen.'

'I'm sorry.'

'It's not a question of sorry.' He spoke with a new confidence.

The disappearance of his sister had bridged a gap with his father. 'Of course I believe you. The old girl dies, suddenly, unexpectedly. I don't think you're off your trolley. You rush off to get help and somebody else comes back who doesn't want her there. Don't ask me why –'

'– but?'

'No buts. Just listen. I don't know why, but Sandie was in the way. So Sandie had to be removed –'

'She could have been killed.'

'What, when the coppers want her clothes, and stop by to pick up papers? Have you asked why they collected her gear?'

Fellowes slowly understood. 'You mean if she's been taken somewhere they'll need that stuff . . .'

James nodded agreement. 'And then there's this bloke in Birmingham, the mysterious other Steadman who keeps himself under cover. If you ask me something is going on that those coppers must know about. That's why the young one had to contradict his story.'

'But why . . . ?' Fellowes asked. 'Murder or kidnap or some kind of terrorism?'

They stared at each other. 'That's what we're going to find out,' James said.

Peter Fellowes felt a flood of relief, sheer stark relief that the effort he had made, an appeal in its way, had sent a spark between them.

'Listen, Dad. We'll track down this Steadman guy between us. You go back to Maesteg, right? Have it out with the cops. I don't suppose it'll do much good but let 'em think that you trust 'em. I'll get a line on Steadman.' He owed his father that, having sent him the ad.

'He had a Brummie accent when we spoke on the phone –'

'OK. I don't reckon he'll be far away from Mr Mukerjee.'

Fellowes saw those small resemblances of himself, the tenacity that had driven him and James apart, now at last as some kind of virtue.

'How long are you planning to hang on, down there near Tan-y-graig?' the son asked.

'As long as it takes.' He had a week for half-term, but he would stay there until he found Sandie.

'Then I suggest you go through the estate agents, and any local shops that give credit, and the gas and electricity people, with a fine toothcomb. These days, you can't just shut up a house and go away into the night. What about the telephone rental, and the poll tax? They pin you down somehow, the bastards. . . . Somebody knows about the original Steadman, if it's only the people who buried him.'

That was another lead, Fellowes thought to himself, the other Steadman buried at Llangogarth, according to Parry. He nodded at James.

'Hey, Dad, where are you going?'

Fellowes hadn't really thought. Too late now to drive back to Wales; time seemed to have lost its meaning after Sandie had vanished, and the two days since – he had to count to be sure – seemed more like a lifetime.

'I don't know. I'll find a hotel . . .'

'Don't be stupid, man. You stay here and listen to me.' James could be obstinate too.

Peter Fellowes smiled at this clone of himself.

19

It was late on the following morning when Fellowes arrived back in Maesteg: the same small and sleepy main street in which he had met Laurel Ericson, but there was no sign of her now.

Facts. Stick to the facts, but the autumn had closed in like the end of his hopes and he had driven through a misty countryside over roads full of falling leaves. Even Laurel was a mystery, someone who moved softly on her undisclosed business.

Fellowes skirted the lake again, its water silvery-cold, and passed the narrow-gauge railway which had shut down for the winter. The lines were already rusty, indicating traffic was limited; it would be absurd to build an extension up to Tan-y-graig. He shuddered as he thought of the word, the farm and the biscuit-coloured mountain which seemed to threaten it. But this time he did not go there.

Instead he found the church at Llangogarth, half-way along the lake, and the adjacent graveyard. The village was a scattering of houses, slate-roofed, and stubborn cottages grouped round the small church with its witches' hat steeple.

He opened the gate and walked in. Leaning tombstones with half-forgotten messages, a path overgrown with rank grass, cow parsley and dock leaves. Memorials with withered flowers in dirty jam jars. Only a handful of headstones, local slabs of stone and slate, and a few marble crosses looked as if they were recent.

No-one was around to be asked.

It took him some time to find the one he wanted. The cold, grey day wrapped around him as he probed through the neglected churchyard. Three crows were picking over a rubbish tip in the far corner and flew away like disturbed souls, but in the end it was there, half-buried in nettles under a free-stone wall, that he found the tombstone he was looking for. He cleared the weeds away carefully.

It was an oblong marker, the same shape as a milestone, with a regimental badge and a simple inscription: 'Ivor Steadman, Major, Royal Engineers, d. 27 January 1990, aged seventy-nine'. Also chiselled in the stone were a cross and an arrow.

He brushed the dirt from the stone and stood there pondering. Steadman, or at least one of them. A good age, but not exceptional; a former military man. The headstone reminded him of something, and he recognized it was a war grave, one of those stone markers from the memorial cemeteries of two World Wars. It struck him as odd, the only official stone in the small Church of Wales churchyard, and it was of recent origin. As if Major Steadman, seventy-nine years old, had died on active service and been buried obscurely, without benefit of clergy or family.

But Sandie, dear God, Sandie: what did this mean for her? The stone was there telling him something if he could only understand it. That cross in the shape of a sword, where had he seen it before? And then he recollected, with increasing disquiet, the glass of the blue window at Tan-y-graig, with the cross and the arrow crudely incised beneath it. A military cross like this one and the arrowhead was a crow's foot.

Steadman of Tan-y-graig was buried in an official grave, that was for sure. And the duty policeman had said, before he contradicted his story, that he had seen lights in the house only a few months ago. What if the widow had returned in a secret act of pilgrimage? Well, she should be traceable . . . there must be people who knew her still living in the district. He raised his head and saw the church and the churchyard for what they were, ordinary grey stone artifacts of a small community at the foot of a secluded valley; but in the valley itself other forces were at work, forces that Sandie had tangled with. He looked from the grave to the trees with their leaves fluttering in a wind off the lake; the hills on the far side were changing slowly from green to a chill mustard-gas ochre.

He lingered for a while in Llangogarth, walking round the huddle of houses that constituted the settlement, hoping that he might run across Laurel, or catch a glimpse of her car, and found himself anxious to see her. But then, he had no address, only her throwaway mention that she was accommodated at one of the farms. She had not said how long she was staying and could well have gone away, but he felt a sense of disappointment.

Perhaps she would be in Maesteg, but Maesteg was scarcely awake; the three or four little streets might have been visited by plague, or perhaps he was a carrier by the way that they stared. Groups of people stood in doorways, chatting, mulling over fatstock prices, watching the world go by. It was not difficult to believe that he was at the heart of a mystery, as he listened to the Welsh voices murmuring of sheep and the weather. Something Sandie had said in those last minutes of parting reverberated through his conscience: 'I've been on my own for years. An hour or two more won't matter.' Now the hours stretched into days. *Think*. The old woman must have known Steadman. Perhaps she had been his wife, though he had not noticed a ring. And he did not believe in ghosts.

It hurt him to recount the facts to the bland, uncomprehending faces that greeted him when he tried to explain in the Post Office and the banks, the local Council offices, the shops and the library. None of them purported to know the Steadmans of Tan-y-graig and their puzzled faces shut like doors at the sound of his questions. It was as if they were concealing the past not merely from him but themselves, but whether from design or ignorance Fellowes could not be sure. The Welsh phrases flew across rooms while the polite faces murmured that they did not know. Even the tourist office had never heard of Tan-y-graig, until he pointed it out on the Landranger Series map pinned up on the wall among the holiday pamphlets and bed and breakfast cards.

He saw from the Yellow Pages that the nearest funeral directors were in Llangollen and Dolgellau, but there were small estate agents open in two of the streets, and he made these his next ports of call. One of them disclaimed all knowledge of property at Tan-y-graig, but the other one seemed less sure. A pleasant girl looked up with surprise as he entered the office at the end of the town and explained for the twentieth time that he was seeking information about the farm up in the valley last in the name of Steadman.

'Owned or rented?'

'I'm not sure.'

It was the mention of rental that appeared to ring a bell. Pert and pretty, she jumped up and rummaged through the card index in a four-drawer filing cabinet.

'Steadman? Steadman? We don't normally do rentals, we're sales you know, property sales and consultants,' she said proudly, 'but I do remember a young man came here, oh, three – four months back like, and asked if we could arrange something for him. Let me see now, let me see . . .' and she was busy enquiring, and consulting with a man next door.

Fellowes sat on a chair and looked at the photographs of small farms and cottages advertised for sale on the stands. Hill farms and coal-fired houses, even a converted school, all in the same vernacular of stone walls and grey slates. Some of them might well have been pictures of Tan-y-graig.

Might have been but weren't, the cheerful girl said, returning with a yellow card. 'Tan-y-graig farm? That right?'

He nodded, almost too weary to care.

'Well now.' She was reading a pencil scribble that someone else had made. 'Man came in three months back. Said he was a Mr Steadman, apparently had inherited the property. Asked us to rent it out.' She smiled, sensing Fellowes's growing interest. 'But we had to tell him no.'

'Why? Why?' He was on his feet, demanding.

'Oh. Well, when we asked for more details, it appeared that he didn't really own it – his uncle like had been in there but that was only a tenancy. It seems the farm was under lease, you understand?'

Fellowes felt his nerves tingling, a shiver of sensation working its way down his spine.

'Who from? Can you tell me that?' He held his breath while she tried to decipher the card.

'Oh, yes. Apparently some firm in London. Here it is. Secure Investments Limited.' She smiled again. 'That's all we've got, I'm afraid, we didn't take him on. Is there anything wrong then?' she added with sudden caution.

'I think so,' he said.

He dragged himself back to the hotel at the other end of the town to put another call through to James.

'If it's a registered firm, you can get the address from Companies House,' his son said.

'Where?' Fellowes sat on the bed and found himself close to tears at his son's loyalty. The acidity between them had vanished as the sense of loss brought them together.

'The Companies Registration Office of the DTI,' he heard James say patiently. 'In City Road, London. Shall I make some enquiries?'

It was one more step towards repairing the rocky road between them.

20

The secret valley haunted his thoughts, climbing up past the sheep farm and Pen-y-banc and the Davies house, up to the small, white farmhouse at Tan-y-graig. Suppose there was something unworldly about the forces up there, something beyond his imagining? But that was ridiculous. Beyond what, for God's sake? Try see over the mountains, to see inside them, inside the minds that had forced him into this hunt – the Steadmans, Parry and Owens, even Mukerjee the newsagent, and the closed faces at the farms – suspicious, guarding their secrets, all of them. He twisted in his bed, trying to make sense of what Sandie might be saying, somewhere out there on the mountains. Guilty because he had brought her, fearful for what he had done, the newsreel of that lost weekend running for ever in his mind. Even the weather had changed since he had come there with her, the thin October sun replaced by curtains of cloud that hung low over the town and seemed to dissolve in the lake.

What ate again into Fellowes's mind was the fear that it was all his fault: why hadn't he been more careful in answering that advertisement, in leaving Sandie with a body, in not getting other witnesses? He had fucked everything up just when father and daughter were coming to terms with each other.

Sandie at seventeen. No-one of course had up till now suggested that he had deliberately killed her ... and yet ... He woke up sweating, following the latest interview in that hot little police house where he had gone to find Owens and put his own accusations.

Owens had been in the interview room behind the deal table,

with another man instead of Parry, this one with an angular, planed, almost Asiatic face, and dark eyes which seemed to glitter under swept-back hair. A handsome, reserved coolness.

'Let me introduce Detective Chief Inspector Wishart of CID. He is here because some very serious allegations are now being made. And a lot of police time involved in searches.'

Fellowes had nodded, wanting to lay in to Owens, and ask what the hell he was doing picking up Sandie's clothes, but Owens cut him short. Wishart had a loose-leaf folder of notes lying on a black briefcase.

'Why didn't you tell us the truth about your daughter?'

Fellowes was angry, and launched into his own questions.

'Why don't you tell me first what you were doing at St Cyprian's?'

'I'll ask the questions, Mr Fellowes.' Owens's voice was less singsong now, more closed to argument. He stood up as if to gain height, his back to the map of Wales, his head blotting out Snowdonia.

They glared at each other. Wishart said, 'Tell him,' and Owens nodded.

'All right. We wanted to find material for fingerprint and DNA tests, and clothing in case we need police dogs.'

'Dogs?' The panic wrenched at him then, a blind and unfocused dread.

Owens's voice was a stick on a drum, rat-tat-tat. His face seemed to tighten. He frowned: 'We still have only your version of what has happened. So far as the police are concerned you are the last person to have seen her . . . alive.'

'Alive?' Fellowes's throat was dry. 'Alive?' he croaked. 'For God's sake what do you mean?'

Owens peered at him across the room with bloodshot eyes, as if he'd been working late.

'Don't give me any bullshit, Mr Fellowes, or we might level charges at you —'

'What charges?'

But Owens ignored him, his fist pounding the table.

'Listen to me, man. You didn't tell us the full truth about your daughter, did you? Little Miss Blue-eyed.'

'I don't know what the hell you're talking about.'

'You know, all right.' Owens half-turned, half-smiled at Wishart.

'Why didn't you say she had a boyfriend? A sexual relationship?'

Fellowes felt his heart miss a beat. Why should he? How could he be sure? Wasn't that one of the secrets that he had hoped might emerge from their aborted weekend, to know whether she was serious in talking about her guys? She broke bounds, so she had said, but never why or where, and in his ostrich-like way he had failed to enquire, failed even more to advise; then when he'd made his move, and suggested this weekend in Wales, fate had caught up.

He was forced onto the defensive. 'I don't know my daughter that well.' It was a terrible admission. 'That was one of the reasons for our little trip away last week.'

They had him on the run and Owens twisted the knife, openly doubting.

'Was it? Was it, indeed? Oh, I see. But you never really knew her, like?'

'I'm afraid we had drifted apart since my wife died,' Fellowes added miserably.

'Oh. So you suddenly take her to Tan-y-graig. Isn't that very odd, Mr Fellowes? Very peculiar . . . ?'

'It was advertised in the paper –'

'By someone who doesn't exist.'

'Someone who cashed my cheque.'

'We know that, Mr Fellowes.' Little beads of perspiration stood out on Fellowes's brow, but the policeman's stare was unbroken.

'I acted in good faith.'

But the inspector was attacking with fierce little jabs of speech. 'I hope you did, Mr Fellowes. I hope you did.' Owens paused, sat down again and said quickly, 'Put it another way, what's to stop you having a row with her, fit of temper most like, hitting her accidentally maybe . . . I don't know . . . and inventing this story to cover yourself?'

'That's nonsense, and you know it.' His heart was hammering.

The room was too small. He felt that he wanted to scream at them.

'Oh. Is it?' So you don't believe your daughter has been a naughty girl, like?'

The words were meant to be hurtful, and they went home. She had had a stable environment until Stella died; then she'd gone to the best of boarding schools. There'd been no hint of trouble. Why the hell should it go wrong . . .

'No,' he said firmly. 'I don't.'

And Owens sighed with satisfaction, looking sideways at Wishart.

'Well. We'd better produce the evidence.'

The man they brought in was young and self-possessed, twenty-three or four, good-looking, dressed in a sweater and jeans. He had short chow-coloured hair and a ruddy, out-of-doors complexion, the first things that Fellowes noticed. Almost by definition he would not have said he was Sandie's type . . . and yet inside himself were the old stirrings of unease. He tried to sound composed but knew that his worries were visible.

'Say who you are,' Owens said. 'Introduce yourself.'

'Terence Blackburn.'

'And what does Sandie Fellowes call you?'

'Well, she calls me Terry.' His tone was cheerful, almost cocky.

'Good.' The little arms unfolded and rested gently on the table. 'And what exactly do you do?'

'I work in avionics. The research branch of British Aerospace. They have a plant at Telford. Telford New Town.'

'And tell us how you met Sandie . . .'

'Climbing Wenlock Edge,' he said. 'One weekend in the summer.'

Owens was smiling and nodding.

'And then what happened?'

'We struck up a relationship.'

'A sexual relationship?'

Blackburn did not seem put out. 'If you like. Yes.'

'When?'

'That afternoon.'

'You're lying.' How could she have been there on her own? How could she deceive the school? 'I don't believe it,' Fellowes shouted.

Owens held up his hand. 'Please. I think you do.'

What were they expecting him to say: that he condoned it, that he was overjoyed? 'A pack of lies. A put-up job.' This was some scheme to discredit him as well as Sandie.

He saw Wishart's eyebrows rise.

'Come now, Mr Fellowes.' Owens reverted to singsong, a lullaby to smooth the tantrum. 'I think Mr Blackburn should tell us exactly how often it has happened.'

'She's in a boarding school,' Blackburn said slowly, 'so it wasn't so easy. But when she got Saturdays off, we used to go out. To a hotel in Shrewsbury – the White Hart.' He grinned. 'I had to pay in advance.'

Wishart intervened. 'Did she tell you she was going away for this weekend with her father?'

Blackburn nodded. 'She said she was coming here.'

'That's a lie. I didn't say where I was taking her until I picked her up. I didn't know myself until the last minute.'

Owens closed his fingers around his chubby little fist.

'I suggest you knew well in advance. I suggest you had a row with her about her conduct, and that something went wrong.' His voice was more menacing now. 'That's why we may need the dogs.'

Fellowes had come away chilled by their callousness, but unable to disprove the witness – as if any move that he made only confirmed their suspicion. The memory of that interview pursued him through the night as he imagined little button-nosed Owens and the Asiatic face of Wishart pow-wowing over the table long after they had let him go. He was the prime suspect and he was unable to fault them.

21

After all the fears, rumours and innuendoes, he was still holding on, and in touch with his solicitor Austen Collard, junior partner in the law firm he had employed at the time of Stella's death.

'Look,' Collard muttered over the line from London to Fellowes's bedroom in the Angel Hotel. 'I listen to some crazy story about a disappearing body, and Sandie taking off without warning leaving you legless. OK, so it's not delusions, I have to believe that – you're sleeping at nights I hope? – but don't give me the one about yet more local coppers bending the evidence.'

'You're my adviser,' Fellowes persisted. 'What the hell should I do – ?' His words trailed off in despair.

Finally, he had to admit that Collard wouldn't be much help; even his lawyer found it hard to believe him when the chips were down.

The one tip, however, that Collard did give him was to alert the media. 'Good way to draw attention and flush her out,' he had said. 'There must be some local rags. Ring up the press. You could also try BBC Wales.'

It took time, inevitably, time that seemed to him like Sandie's blood draining away, but he forced himself to carry on, using the hotel as his base, in case they needed him, as Sergeant Parry suggested, for continued help with enquiries. Time that he knew was not on Sandie's side, as he wandered round Maesteg or drove up to Tan-y-graig. But nothing changed: the farmhouse sat there closed up, with a police car in front and no means of access for him. From the gates, which had now been padlocked, he could just see the front of the house, its blank windows staring back, under the lee of the mountain.

In God's name why had he come there? Would there ever be an end? Sandie was seventeen, and she had gone.

He drove along Lake Maesteg, pinning up his own posters, using a blown-up photograph that James had given to him. A reward for any information. Owens would not be amused, but by now Fellowes was past caring.

He stormed into the local offices of newspapers covering Mid and North Wales: the *Clwyd News* and *Snowdonia Press*. They took the posters politely, saying they would give him a call. He could see their eyes reading 'nut-case'.

'For God's sake . . .' He thumped on the counter. 'I want to talk to one of your reporters.'

'I'm afraid they're all out, sir, today. A big event in Ffestiniog.'

'Listen to me, please. I believe that something terrible . . . something that my daughter stumbled on . . . has happened at Tan-y-graig.'

'Oh, yes. I'm sure that they will be interested, when they have a moment.'

But when he called back – nothing. Always evasive replies. He came away from their offices feeling that in their minds he was disrupting the tourist trade.

'It's really not appropriate,' one of the editors explained, 'for us to make too much of something that could, well, frighten people . . .'

'No human interest stories?'

'Human interest, of course. Bodies in bin-liners even, if one ever turns up . . .' He turned to the picture of Sandie on his desk. '. . . But this girl, you say your daughter, there's nothing to go on, is there?'

'What do you mean, nothing?' Fellowes stormed at him.

The editor smiled. 'Well, no evidence, really. I couldn't possibly run a story which suggests sinister forces, black magic if you like. Not in a National Park.'

Fellowes said very quietly, 'Listen. All I want is information. Someone must have seen something.'

'Rest assured we shall do our best.'

In the end he was relegated to small and innocuous paragraphs tucked away among the photographs of swimming galas, Young Farmers Club dances and sheepdog trials. 'Schoolmaster says daughter left him during walking weekend.' No mention of an old woman's body, or the transformation of Tan-y-graig. The Tourist Board doesn't like scandals, another one of them said, and Fellowes had the nightmare vision of that part of North Wales en route to some great theme park, a Disneyland where nothing went wrong.

Yet things had gone hideously wrong, so far as he was concerned; and he wasn't the man to run away. His persistence must have impressed them, because BBC Wales telephoned at last. They were sending a reporter from Cardiff, a girl with a tape recorder who came to the hotel and installed herself in the lounge.

'Right you are then.' She took off her bomber jacket and laid the black box on the coffee table between them. 'Tell us in your own words exactly what you say happened on this weekend.'

'Will this be a news item?'

'A magazine item,' she said.

'It's not some kind of fairy-tale. I'm seeking information on the whereabouts of my missing daughter . . .'

The girl waved cheerfully.

'No problem. Just give me the facts.'

And so he poured out his heart, the house, the body, the disappearance of Sandie, the contact address in Birmingham, the attitude of the police, watching her becoming agitated as she realized he was telling the truth. Appealing for anyone or anything to come forward.

When it was over the girl congratulated him.

'This will set them alight. Something big must be going on there, below the surface.' Her face was tight with excitement.

'When will it be broadcast?' He was in the open now, accusing them on the air, and felt a weight lift from his chest.

'I'll get it out tomorrow,' she promised as she switched off the tape and slung the machine on her shoulder like an all-purpose handbag. 'Jimmy Walker will jump at this one.' She smiled. 'That's my producer.'

He escorted her to the door and she thought he did not seem the sort to spin yarns out of the air: a typecast, solid professional, the kind of man who wore brown shoes.

'Thanks,' she said. 'That was great. Listen in tomorrow at six-fifteen, the news from Wales. I promise you it'll be number one.' She laughed. 'It'll rock 'em in the valleys.'

'I don't want to rock anyone. I just want Sandie back,' he told her stubbornly.

The next morning the police came for him, at the hotel, two young constables in a car, asking in that incriminating way if he would mind accompanying them.

For one brief moment he thought that they might have some news, some hopeful sign, but the now familiar chapel face of Sergeant Parry told him that nothing had changed. His waiting had to go on, and he assumed they were leading him to yet another of those interviews conducted by Owens and Wishart.

Owens was certainly there, sitting behind the deal table in front of the large-scale map that now had been marked with pins surrounding the Tan-y-graig mountain, but instead of Wishart there was a youngish man in horn-rimmed glasses.

Owens was angry, launching at once into a series of complaints.

'You're going round stirring up trouble.'

Fellowes flushed but kept his temper.

'I'm not.'

'Yes, you are. You've been talking to the press. And now you've given this ludicrous' – he hovered on the word and repeated it – 'ludicrous story to BBC Wales.' The inspector's podgy hand thumped the table. 'It's not on. It's bloody not on.'

In the school situation Fellowes had dealt with these types before, people who tried to bluster.

'It's a free country.'

'No it's bloody not when it comes to lying in public.'

'I'm not lying, Inspector.'

'Oh, don't give me that . . .' The cadences rolled out, and

Owens's face glowed. 'You know where your daughter is, don't you?'

'Are you accusing me, Inspector?'

Owens backed off.

'I'm telling you not to cause more trouble for yourself. You understand that, don't you?'

'No.' He wondered at the change of mood. Could it be that Owens was under instructions?

Owens jumped up. 'Listen. You weren't getting on with your daughter – you admit that, eh? – and you could well have a hand in her disappearance. That stuff about the house makes a nice story, doesn't it?' He turned to the other man. 'I think you understand that too?'

His companion had to introduce himself.

'My name's Walker,' he said. 'Producer of News from Wales. You did an interview for my programme. I have to say it's not going out.'

The cards were being reshuffled again, and Fellowes could do nothing about it. Walker told him that was final: there was some kind of embargo.

'Why not? Why not, for God's sake?' It was like hitting a brick wall.

'It would not be in the public interest,' Walker replied tersely.

Owens said, 'That's enough. There'll be no radio interviews because you're under suspicion and liable to face charges. Unless you're mad.'

But Fellowes knew he wasn't mad; nor had he misheard.

22

Mrs D.E. Jones was calling from the stairwell.

'Are you still there, Miss Ericson?'

Laurel opened the door and walked to the top of the stairs of the bed and breakfast farm at Llangogarth. Her case was packed. Mrs D.E. Jones wanted her money, or at least to be sure of it.

Laurel smiled at her. 'Time to be moving on.'

Mrs D.E. Jones finished wiping her hands.

'Oh, well. Time like an ever rolling stream . . .' They stood together awkwardly, gazing across the fields that Mrs D.E. Jones must have seen every day of her life.

Bears all its sons away, Laurel thought, her head full of the Englishman who had told her of his missing daughter. Ships in the night, maybe, but somehow she thought not. She turned to Mrs D.E. Jones.

'Mind if I use your telephone? Local call.'

The older woman put down her bowl of chicken feed, and Laurel saw the interest that at once came into her face.

'Oh no. Of course not.'

Laurel went through to the hall and phoned the Angel Hotel. She heard his surprise at the other end of the line.

'Hey. How d'you know where I was?'

'Easy. Everybody is talking about the guy who says his daughter disappeared. Goes round putting out posters. The cops keep an eye on him.'

'Nobody tells me anything. They just look the other way when I walk in.'

He heard her laugh.

'I guess that's what comes of being a homicide suspect.'

'Homicide?'

'Sure. Why don't we talk it over?'

It was a tongue-in-cheek invitation but the impression she gave him was that she meant it, as she found him in the hotel, and saw the pleasure in his face.

'I thought maybe you could do with some help.'

He wondered, and admired her, taking in the tailored jacket and thick blonde hair.

'How about helping with lunch?'

Strolling up the street with her was like turning a new page as he saw things through fresh eyes. He was conscious of people watching, a kind of suppressed gossip that seemed to permeate the town, and he no longer cared. When she slipped a hand through his arm he was mildly surprised but aware of how much he had wanted it.

'Peter, listen. People disappear round here. Others keep buttoned-up lips. What do you make of that?'

He countered, 'What do you mean?'

'I mean that something weird is going on, somewhere up round Tan-y-graig.' She leaned towards him confidentially. 'I get the feeling that your Sandie stumbled on a secret buried way back in the past. That's why the old lady returned. And that's why they both disappeared.'

It took his thinking one stage further, if he could find a theory to fit the facts, but he was still cautious.

'Sandie wasn't looking for secrets. She's just a lively kid.'

'Too right,' Laurel said. 'And curiosity can kill the cat.'

It was a chilling reminder as he stopped with her by the lake, watching her as she stood by the water, lost in thoughts of her own which she would not articulate. But bells rang in his mind too. 'Not in the public interest' was what the BBC man, Walker, had said, apparently going too far in front of Owens. Who exactly was Major Steadman, RE, who had lived at Tan-y-graig, and was buried close to the mountain, under an official but uninformative headstone? Yet none of it added up to a reason for Sandie's disappearance. He found that he was opening out to Laurel about all the things that disturbed him.

'I want to help you,' she said again.

He hesitated. 'Are you some kind of investigator, or reporter?'

'No kidding? I'm flattered.' She laughed. 'Put it down to personal interest. I want to find out what's happened there, and you want to find Sandie. We could make quite a team.'

Fellowes wished he could be that sure, but his hope was more negative: hoping to know something. If there had been a time when he would have cried off – and in his heart he doubted it – it would have been that morning, but now Laurel had given him a shot of adrenalin. Suddenly they were two conspirators, counter-intelligence agents making their plans together.

'I've got to crack this guy calling himself Steadman in Birmingham . . .'

'Peter, you will. You will. Another thing – you should check on the oldies, some of 'em must know something about what went on at Tan-y-graig . . .'

Strengthened in his resolve, he told her he was staying there as long as it took. Who had been paying the bills, who had delivered supplies or disconnected the telephone . . . he would comb all the possibilities.

Laurel picked up a pebble and skimmed it across the water, five, six hops like the jumps in his mind.

'You ought to do one more thing. You ought to hire a detective, a private eye.'

He joined her in throwing the pebbles, going back to the games of childhood. 'But I don't know any detectives.'

'Aw, come on. You pick one from the book. The business directory. Investigative agencies. Ask 'em to check out this firm "Secure Investments" that really owns Tan-y-graig, and do some background research.'

'Maesteg is not exactly the place where they lay on that facility . . .'

She threw her final pebble, expertly skipping the waves.

'Ask James,' she said. 'The more we have on our side, the better. Now how about that lunch?'

23

It took him the rest of the week to realize he was getting nowhere, apart from a heavier bill at the Angel Hotel. Whatever magic Laurel might have had to open doors of reminiscence seemed to desert him entirely when he approached the elderly in Maesteg to ask about Tan-y-graig. No information, nothing, almost as if they'd misheard him. He drove long stretches on remote roads beyond the valley, hoping perhaps that the mountains would tell him something, but all he saw were the hills, often clouded by rain, where the trees stopped and the granite began. When he cut the engine to look back over the landscape the lake in the distance glimmered softly. Autumn was shutting in, heavy with leaf-fall which seemed to have started in earnest as soon as the weather turned colder. The tops of the mountains were bare, the few plants struggled for life, and he gave little chance of survival to anyone abandoned there.

But Sandie couldn't be out there. He told himself it could not be: someone had taken her, and that someone must be keeping her. That had to be his hope. For if that hope was wrong . . . he looked at the empty hillsides and shuddered.

'It's no good coming back here,' Owens told him daily. 'We'll let you know as soon as there's any news.' His busy little eyes seemed full of suspicion, as he sat day in day out behind the wooden table in the interview room, a table like the ones in the staff room, but Fellowes's colleagues and cronies at school had no idea, as yet, of the grilling he was facing. Owens concentrated his efforts on the disappearance of Sandie as if he was conducting an enquiry in respect of an undiscovered murder.

'You wouldn't like to add to your story, Mr Fellowes? Perhaps there's something you've forgotten?'

'Yes. Why have you sealed off Tan-y-graig house?'

The little hands clapped together.

'Well done. You've been to see.'

'I'm always going up there.'

'Well, you shouldn't.'

'Shouldn't?'

Owens's face might have registered annoyance but Fellowes could not be sure.

'I think there's no point. Your daughter isn't there.'

'Then where the hell is she?'

Owens seemed to push the table as if he wanted to stand up, and then thought better of it.

'Ah. You tell us, eh?'

'Am I under investigation?'

'I wouldn't say that. Just let us know where you are.' He smiled ingratiatingly, and Fellowes waited for another barrage of questions about his relations with Sandie. Instead, Owens said, 'Tell me. After your wife died, did you . . . go about very much?'

'Go about much? I moved houses, if that's what you mean.'

'No, no. I mean, have you had . . . say, since then . . . an interest in other ladies?'

He found himself increasingly at odds with this policeman who offered no sympathy apart from a cup of tea, and seemed to think the worst.

'No.'

The inspector sat back.

'Oh. Right. Sorry. It's just that I wondered about the American woman. Whether you've known her long, like?'

Fellowes cut back an angry reaction.

'I only met her this week.' But in this small-town community such things were noticed at once, especially a woman like Laurel, attractive and asking questions.

'I understand.'

He was sure Owens winked, but it might have been the tic of an eyelid.

'Look. You find what's happened to Sandie, and then I'll tell you about my girlfriends.'

Owens was grinning again. 'That's what I intend to establish.'

When Fellowes had gone, Owens checked that Wishart had been listening over the intercom. The DCI walked along to his room.

Owens felt mentally weary. 'I don't know. I don't know how much he's telling the truth.'

'What about?'

'About his relations with the daughter. After all, he's got a blind spot. Didn't know about the boyfriend, or so he says.' Owens's lips parted as he ruffled his moustache. 'Doesn't want to think of her as less than perfect. I reckon we should pull in young Terry Blackburn and give him the works.'

'Listen.' The CID man's planed face, all hard angles, dark-chinned, stared at him, poker-headed. 'Blackburn may be a shit. The sort of man you hope your daughter won't find. I've put the squeeze on him, but he has a cast-iron alibi, working that weekend at Telford. Four people vouch for that. I don't want any bruises on him. All he proves is a may-be.'

'Maybe?'

'Maybe she could have scarpered.'

'On her own or with some other bloke?'

Wishart's face glared at him. 'That's up to you. But don't start fingering him: he's just the sort of bastard to go squealing to the media. A self-righteous lover-boy, who can prove he was nowhere near. Don't try and turn him over.'

Owens accepted the order.

'Better get on with your researches,' Wishart said.

When Peter Fellowes caught up with Blackburn, on the end of a telephone, the young man refused to answer his questions.

'Look: she may be your daughter, but what we did together is over. And whatever has happened now is nothing to do with me. Even the fuzz have had to admit that, so give it a rest, will you?'

Events drove him back towards Laurel as his one available confidante. She had told him where she was staying, and now he made a dinner engagement; Laurel at least made him laugh, attentive towards him with a flippancy which helped to dispel what otherwise would have been unbearable. But she learned more about him than she explained of herself.

'Peter,' she said. 'Don't give in. You've got to have faith in your kids.'

Well, he was in touch with James, he was in touch with Owens and the press, and none of them had found Sandie.

'Don't believe all they tell you, either.'

'It's not in my nature to do that.'

'No, sir. You just keep on looking. You got anywhere yet with that Secure Investments outfit?'

'James has found this man in Bristol who does commercial tracing and business investigations. We're putting him on to Steadman as well. Fellow by the name of Steve Hopkins.'

'That's great. I'd like to meet your James.'

Was she pressurizing, he wondered; was he at risk of being taken over? Christ, what a thing to say. Next thing he would be wondering what view Stella might take, as if he was starting a romance. A nonsense.

Maesteg that evening nevertheless seemed a more peaceful place, simply because Laurel was there. They wandered up the long main street towards the two hotels. The sky had a golden calm. A few cars nosed from the kerbs, a handful of youngsters wheeled mountain bikes on the pavement, looking for something to do, some sheep complained in a cattle truck. The hills grew above the town.

'It's all so damned quiet,' she said. 'You wouldn't think things could happen here big enough to screw you up.'

'No. That's right.'

They walked on in silence, then after a while he stopped. 'Laurel – ?'

She turned full face to inspect him.

'Yes, Peter?'

He wasn't sure what he had wanted, but the words would not come.

'Nothing,' he said. 'I suppose I'd better say goodnight . . .'

'You don't have to . . .'

He held her, but only to give one of those polite kisses on one cheek. He knew he had got it wrong.

'Goodnight, Peter,' she said.

24

The countryside depressed him now, as the falling leaves thickened like discarded wrapping. Stella had never liked autumn: she said it reminded her of compost. The bright weather of the previous weekend had been a misplaced promise, something that had not worked out. On the Friday when James telephoned and asked him to return to Bristol it was almost a relief to be leaving the quiet country town, the cold lake and the secret valley.

Fellowes told Laurel he was going, walking with her by the water, his hands in his raincoat pockets, her collar turned up against the wind.

'I wondered if you would still be here when I come back,' he said tentatively. 'Of course I've no right to expect . . .'

She slipped a gloved hand through his arm. He caught a faint drift of some perfume he did not recognize: not the one that Stella used, but no-one ever came back.

'If you want me to stay, I can.'

He swallowed, unsure of his emotions.

'I don't want to upset your plans . . .'

'Oh, Peter, don't be such a pain. Neither of us are children. I know what I'm doing. A few more days here won't matter . . . if you really want me that is . . .'

That difficult humour, careful yet sentimental, foxed him again.

'If you don't think I'm going bonkers.'

'Bonkers?' she grinned. 'No, honey, no way.'

After a while he had kissed her.

★   ★   ★

On the following morning Fellowes told the hotel he was leaving. He was standing with his bag on the steps, ready to take off to Bristol and whatever news James had, when he heard someone sounding a horn. His heart jumped to see the red Audi.

More: she was skidding to a halt, a slim figure in a white topcoat, her arms flailing.

'Peter! Peter!' He was startled by the new note of urgency.

He stood in the hotel doorway and Laurel almost ran into his arms like a train into buffers.

'Hold on!' He felt her weight pressed against him, and saw her flushed and breathless face.

'Peter, thank God I've caught you. I tried to phone . . . I was so scared you had left.'

'Why? I'm coming back after I've seen James.'

'I couldn't reach you . . .'

'I must have been downstairs. Having breakfast or something . . .' In fact he had left it late, and it was now after ten, but he could see things were wrong.

'What's going on, Laurel?'

'Tan-y-graig,' she said. 'Come and see. You tell me.'

In the early morning she'd looked out over the street, walked out to buy a newspaper and suddenly decided to drive. Automobiles were her form of therapy, get in, click-clunk and go, and she had warmed up in the car, pushing it along the lake then up the road in the valley where she was driving Fellowes now. He saw the familiar landscape, the narrow road climbing higher alongside the rusty railway, the scattered houses on the slopes, then the bleak little sheep farm beyond which were only the abandoned place at Pen-y-banc, the Davies house and Tan-y-graig. She refused to tell him what he would find.

'Wait and see.'

She took him to the head of the valley and turned off to the farmhouse that now held such bitter memories.

He saw the barbed wire across.

A barrier was in place, some fifty yards down the track, in front of the old gates. Closed. Beyond them was a uniformed man, whose head turned at the sound of the vehicle. No less than two cars, dark green official-looking Rovers, were parked in the roadway.

Fellowes and Laurel got out and walked to the gates. The road to Tan-y-graig was closed off by newly erected wire fences which were stretched on concrete posts. The silver mesh ran away as far as they could see, circling the neighbouring hills.

'Holy Moses,' Laurel breathed. 'What do you make of that?'

Fellowes found the pieces fitting together in his mind. 'It would not be in the public interest.' He shouted out to the guard, a blue-uniformed, officious-looking figure, who responded with jerks of his arm.

'Stay away. Stay clear.'

The guard was inclined to ignore them, but when he realized they were serious decided to come down. The new wire fencing had become a second line of defence at Tan-y-graig; the man in the dark blue serge was another kind of policeman, and the leather belt round his waist supported a walkie-talkie. He glared across. His shoulder markings read 'Secure Investments'.

'Sorry, people. No admittance,' he said, more apologetically as they came face to face.

'Since when?' Fellowes asked.

'Since now, that's when.'

'How far does this wire go?'

'Right round the other side. That should give you some idea.'

The voice now had that civilized menace adopted by someone on duty but not quite sure of his authority. Tough and cunning, it implied they should play by the rules.

'A bit sudden isn't it? Putting all this around an empty house? I was renting it only last week . . .'

The other man was struggling to register an improbable fact. 'Come again?'

'I said I was renting this place only last week.'

The guard laughed uneasily.

'Don't tell me you're the one who had that problem with his daughter . . . the girl who's gone missing?'

Fellowes stood firm, a stocky, obstinate figure looking over the other man's shoulder towards the house. That terrible house.

'That's right. My daughter and an old woman.'

114

'Yeah. I heard about that.' The eyes were suspicious. 'Well. Our orders are to seal the bloody place off.'

'Who from?' Fellowes was conscious of Laurel standing determinedly beside him, and the guard now shifted his attention to her.

'Who from, lady?' He indicated his shoulder tab.

'What kind of a firm is that?'

The guard was leaning over the fence to make his message clearer. He fumbled with the two-way radio as if deciding to call for support.

'You'd better ask the MoD,' he said. 'They sent us here.'

The fence was a no-go area, so far as they were concerned, and the once innocent house now seemed a trap. Laurel was tugging on his arm.

'Let's go,' she whispered. 'Please . . .'

'Let's go!'

It was a cry echoed by dozens of uniformed men who had started out with high hopes, as they combed through Welsh towns and villages, and set up watch in London and Shrewsbury. Owens sat tight, watching his men run up the overtime, while Wishart established a temporary office along the corridor and introduced a new computer. Since the CID had been called in, Cardiff had almost taken over.

'You see these bloody leaflets distributed by Fellowes,' Owens complained. 'It's as if he doesn't trust us.'

Wishart was unyielding. 'I don't suppose he does.'

'But he's monopolizing my policemen. Every time we get a sighting, somebody has to go there. And as for the house to house enquiries . . . do you realize the extra duties cost? Half the North Wales force is now looking for some woman who may never have been there at all.'

Wishart shrugged.

'Nevertheless it has to be done.'

25

He drove on alone to Bristol later than he had intended, full of uncertainty. It was almost as if he was acting in some surrealist drama, impressions one on top of the other – his attempt to talk to Sandie, and then her disappearance, the sight of the old woman, Owens's little dancing glances and the barriers now round Tan-y-graig, all superimposed on thoughts of Laurel as he hit the road out of Wales. He climbed through the high passes, skirting the road round Shrewsbury and joined the M5 at Worcester. In happier times he would have gone via Welshpool and down through the rich farmlands of Hereford and Monmouth, but he was fearful of delays, hold-ups over the Severn Bridge, and fast driving down the motorway was some relief from the pressure. He was in Bristol by five o'clock that afternoon, peeling off from the Avonmouth intersection.

James was shocked by his appearance.

'Christ, Dad, are you all right?' His son opened the door of the house off Whiteladies Road, a high Victorian house with stained cornices and sash windows looking over a neglected garden where the trees murmured of winter.

Fellowes saw there was another man present, sitting in the high-backed chair that James had acquired from the charity shop.

Father and son clasped hands, a touching formality James thought, as if neither could quite admit how close the relationship was.

'Dad, this is Mr Hopkins.'

'Call me Steve,' the man said, putting aside a mug of tea and standing up. 'Consultant from the Yellow Pages.' He grinned cheerfully. There was a quick-wittedness about him, a warm, mobile face and eyes. A sensitive, rather crafty face, matching the crumpled corduroys, someone who invited confidences.

'Ex-police Fraud Squad,' he said. 'And it sounds as if you've got a fraud.'

James said, 'We've found Steadman.'

Hopkins rubbed his hands together.

'No problem. I paid a little private visit to JK Papers. Mr Mukerjee was very helpful . . .'

Fellowes was beginning to realize just how much he needed to learn: Mukerjee had kept his lips buttoned when he had seen him. 'Not when I asked him,' he said.

'Tricks of the trade.'

Hopkins was pleased with his efforts, and cleaned his specs with a handkerchief. 'Had to lean on him a little, you follow. But he was no problem really.'

'Lean on him?'

'Well, tell him he might have trouble, know what I mean? He came clean as a whistle.' He whistled to prove it.

Fellowes said, 'What happened?'

'Sonny Mukerjee didn't make no objections to passing me Steadman's address. You with me? In fact I think he thought I was another copper.'

'From North Wales?'

'Right. They'd been round there earlier, checking out this Steadman, so no skin off Mukerjee's nose.' He sat with his legs outstretched as if they were cardboard tubes with brown shoes plugging the ends. 'Listen. I'll tell you something else. When he put that ad in the paper, Steadman was only interested in making a quick buck.'

Fellowes looked at James, reassured that his son was with him all the way. James was nodding at them both.

'Go on . . .'

'Well, I went straight round to see the bugger.' Hopkins was enjoying himself, sipping tea, stirring in a sugar mound. 'No problem again.'

'You traced him then?' Fellowes could hardly believe, after so much had gone wrong, or disappeared in the dark, that some things were being unscrambled, but the private detective had seen it all before, and nothing now surprised him in human nature.

'I specialize in jogging people's memories.'

James looked at his father, and thought how much he had changed.

'Sure you're all right, Dad?' He wanted to offer a pause, a drink perhaps and a meal when they could talk at leisure, but his father waved him away.

'This Steadman? We only spoke on the phone. Who is he?'

'Oh. A double-glazing salesman down on his luck. Lives in a flat in West Bromwich. I didn't even have to twist his arm. The police had been to see him too.'

Fellowes heard himself saying, as if the voice didn't belong, 'Sandie . . . Why us . . . why you?'

'Funny sort of place,' Hopkins recounted relentlessly. 'One of those maisonettes over a shopping parade with a big pub next door. Saturday nights the place must be bloody noisy. Two bedrooms, living room, kitchen full of bottles and bin liners, that sort of thing. Bit of a charlatan really. Things got difficult, apparently, when his last job folded. Only bit of luck in his life was when old Mrs Steadman over in Wales at this Tan-y-graig place told him he was going to inherit it –'

Old Mrs Steadman, he thought. 'Inherit it? The Steadmans were tenant farmers.'

Hopkins consulted a notepad pulled from his pocket.

'Well . . . I'm telling you what he told me.'

'What sort of man is he?' James intervened.

Hopkins's eyes danced. 'Physical characteristics – balding, nice line in sweaters, bit of a ladies' man I would say, but getting past the sell-by date. Average height, maybe five nine, starting to run to fat. Gift of the gab an' all.'

Fellowes said, 'I think I'll have that drink,' and Hopkins said he wouldn't say no. They sat round now with three whiskies, as the light began to fade.

'The fact is,' Hopkins declared, 'this aunt of his was going ga-ga, according to young Steadman, but when he went and visited her, after the old man died a couple of years ago, she gave him a spare key, said he could use the place to keep it aired. Apparently the old girl was going into a home but you know what it is, she couldn't bear to think that she wasn't coming back – been living there forty-odd years – and so she wouldn't sell the place, or so she said. Mind you' – he flicked through the pages again – 'this bloke Steadman could have been lying, but I doubt it somehow. When he's pinned down he don't wriggle.'

The excitement of discovery jumped into Hopkins's voice.

'So, anyway, it follows that the old lady left and didn't go back, and young Steadman used to visit. Kitted it out a bit for his own use as a kind of weekend place, last in residence he says about three months ago' – three months, thought Fellowes, would be when the young policeman saw lights, before he changed his story – 'but he'd rather lost heart, 'cos his missus had walked out on him, though they're back together again now. So we come to the interesting bit' – he smacked down the empty whisky glass – 'suddenly Steadman gets a letter from the real landlords telling him they was requisitioning the property, and he was not to go there no more.'

'Dad. You got that?'

'I'm not stupid,' Fellowes said.

'OK. You want to know who the landlords are?'

'I already know,' Fellowes said.

'Right.' Hopkins nodded. 'Secure Investments. And they tell our Mr Steadman not to push his nose in, for some reason. But Steadman is short of the readies and suddenly has this rental idea. After all he's got a key; and some of the stuff inside there is his. So why not make a fast buck by renting the place out, he thinks, and shoves an ad in the Bristol papers because that's where he happens to be. Unfortunately, your son picked it up.'

'But why use the cover address in Birmingham?' Fellowes persisted.

Hopkins became almost conspiratorial, lowering his voice. 'Because of the people who warned him off, that's why. Told him Tan-y-graig was none of his business.'

'You mean Secure Investments?'

'I mean the MoD.'

It was the second time that arm of government had been cited.

'Ministry of Defence?'

'Right.' Hopkins drew breath. 'Tan-y-graig is owned by the MoD, under cover of Secure Investments.'

Fellowes found himself bemused by the little ex-policeman's news. He might have anticipated it, even worked it out for himself, but that kind of security cover-up was far removed from his experience. Now he was shut out by fences, and somewhere inside had lost Sandie.

Hopkins was looking at his watch, and James switched on a gas fire against the chill of the evening.

'I don't know all what's going on,' the detective said, 'but I'll tell you one more thing for your money. I've been digging into the records, in London and Cardiff. This Secure Investments was registered in 1945 just after the War. It has other properties in England, old airfields, storage dumps and the like, but only one place in Wales.'

Fellowes felt his muscles contract.

'A secret store?'

Hopkins was on his feet, in his time-is-money pose. 'Something like that. And what's more there are some very interesting footnotes in the official histories about the cost of a tunnel used during the War for storage of stuff from the British Museum. You got that? Of course they don't say exactly where, but it was somewhere around in Snowdonia: they mention transporting treasures from London to Wales, great big statues and things, and building a rail link. Afterwards, the whole thing was taken over by Secure Investments.'

'With Major Steadman as tenant?'

'Probably, but I can't pin the man down,' Hopkins said.

Plausible enough in one sense, but it hardly explained what had happened to Sandie, or the disappearance of the old woman.

Hopkins was looking at him almost anxiously.

'That all any help?'

'Enough to be going on with.'

Hopkins said he had to be moving and they walked down the stairs together to the former policeman's car.

'Oh, I almost forgot. Your old biddy in the farmhouse. The stiff who disappeared.' He fumbled in his wallet, and produced a black and white photograph. Apologetically he added, 'I bought it off him. Thought it was worth a try, and that guy will sell his own aunt.'

There was no doubt in Fellowes's mind. The face stared up at him, solemn-featured, in half-profile, a head and shoulders portrait taken many years before when she was in her thirties. But she had the same pale, rather featureless face with mousy hair set in a wave, and a high-buttoned collared blouse, against a studio backcloth. The same heavy-lidded eyes, and down-curving lips that they had seen at Tan-y-graig. The woman with whom Sandie had stayed: the body that had gone missing.

The tips of his fingers ran cold.

Hopkins turned. 'Keep it if you want it,' he said.

Fellowes put it carefully inside his pocket.

'If there's anything more that I can do . . . ?'

Fellowes shook his head.

'You've already done a lot,' he said.

When he went back upstairs, James was making up the spare bed. 'No buts,' he admonished, 'you're staying. Let's get this straight. For some reason Sandie stumbled into some MoD can of worms. They must have realized it, and started sealing off the dump.' He looked long and earnestly at his father, his eyes alight. 'The question is, what for?'

Peter Fellowes bunched his fists.

'I'm staying there until I know.'

They looked again at the photograph and he told his son about the grave at Llangogarth. Major Steadman, RE.

'They can't do this to me,' he said slowly. Not ghosts, not ghosts, but humans.

26

'Girls disappear all the time.' One of the local reporters had at last
followed up Fellowes's hand-out about the affair and traced him
back to the hotel. 'No good unless it's juicy.' Perhaps they had
him labelled as some kind of manic-depressive, from the doubts
being expressed.

Fellowes bought him a drink in the bar.

'What about a body that disappears before the doctor comes?
Gets up and walks like Lazarus?'

That raised a flicker of interest. A cynic into the bargain, he
could see the man thinking. 'Oh, right. That's better, but we've
only got your word. The cops say it's all balls.'

Fellowes said, 'What about the place where it happened?
Tan-y-graig' – waiting while he wrote it down – 'why is it under
some kind of embargo? Why have they sealed it off?'

'What do you think is going on there, then?'

Fellowes drank another beer with him.

'I don't know, but there's a nasty smell of deceit. For instance
you'll find the landlord is a firm called Secure Investments, a
cover company for the MoD. It hasn't filed accounts for years.'

The other man digested this angle.

'Maybe I'll nose around. Talk to some of the coppers. There's
enough of 'em about.'

But Fellowes knew he couldn't leave it to them, these local
reporters, and the efforts of his MP. Why the hell should Tom
Kelvin care anyway, on the strength of one letter from Wales,
someone who said he was a constituent and talked about
vanishing women? People had noises in the head. No: he knew

he was on his own; like a match in a box, he was rattling around waiting to explode.

Waiting also for Laurel, who phoned him again that night.

'The answer must be up there somewhere,' she said. 'Behind all that barbed wire. Peter, I've decided to stay and help you . . . for as long as it takes.'

He was both pleased and concerned.

'Look, Laurel, I can't expect . . .' He was inclined to draw back, fearing an obligation, but she put on the pressure. She had found a small cottage to rent, and taken it for two weeks. Half-way along the lake between Maesteg and Llangogarth, it was going for a song in October. Also it had two bedrooms. 'England expects . . .' she argued.

His hand was sweaty on the telephone. My God, he thought, other people do this all the time. Maybe Sandie wouldn't hesitate, or James for that matter. Laurel meant something to him, perhaps more than he was prepared to admit.

'I'll think about it,' he said.

'Sure, honey, your funeral.' He could almost see her grin. 'One other thing, Peter. I've been up the valley again. They've strengthened the wire round Tan-y-graig, and put up new signs. It now says "MoD, keep out". And one of those official cars turned off to the Davies house.'

The Davies house.

The news was electrifying: he felt she had switched on a light. Hell was beginning to have geography.

The next afternoon he drove there himself, along the path through the trees, two miles from Tan-y-graig. When he had gone there before, he had only seen the girl in grey, and Laurel's red Audi outside. Come to that she had never explained what she was doing there, but now he saw Laurel was right. A new green Rover 820 was parked by the front door, almost certainly one of the cars that he had seen through the gates of Tan-y-graig.

This time the girl did not come. He was shown into the well-lit hall by a solid young man with a short haircut, who, when Fellowes asked to see Davies, disappeared upstairs to confer. Fellowes looked round while he waited. The place seemed substantial and large, fitted out with good carpeting, a series of Victorian portraits, a simulated coal fire switched on in the marble fireplace.

The man returned with the news that Mr Davies would see him. Would he mind going upstairs?

At the top of the carved staircase a corridor of cream walls was broken up by light brown doors. Davies, then, lived in some style, but the room into which Fellowes was shown had the soullessness of a waiting room in a small private hospital: a double-fronted bookcase, a couple of easy chairs, orange hessian curtains and a large desk in the window at which a man was sitting.

So Davies had appeared at last, coming forward to greet him, a thick-set fifty-year-old. He shook hands with a brisk friendliness but there was something intimidating about him, something that didn't fit in, in spite of the business suit and careful bonhomie. It was the eyes, Fellowes decided, eyes that were rather too bright in the over-florid face, like the glass eyes on children's dolls. Outside, close to the windows, trees bent in the wind and branches scraped on the panes, almost as if they were listening, darkening the room so much that Davies switched on the desk light.

'Do sit down, Mr Fellowes.' He smiled like a professional. 'Coffee?' A jug with two cups was in front of him.

Fellowes shook his head. He had been living on coffee and hastily snatched meals, and seemed to have forgotten hunger. His stomach was tight with tension as he geared himself to argue.

'Look. I would like some information about what exactly is happening at Tan-y-graig. I've seen the cars outside. I've seen the fences go up, and the security notices.' At the back of his mind he had read of these secret establishments tucked away at Porton Down and obscure places in Scotland, sealed by barbed wire and red flags. The ordinary citizen never really came up against them, just expected them to exist as some kind of last-ditch defence against unspecified dangers, but if he had breached the rules, if Sandie had stumbled on something, for God's sake he wanted to know . . .

Davies was smiling, a gentle decline of his head with the polite implication that Fellowes was being an idiot.

'It's really not like that at all.' He interlocked his hands, bringing the fingers together as if he was clasping at some private vision of his own. In the uncertain light he seemed a powerful figure, leaning back in his armchair. 'Excuse me.' He poured himself a coffee and held the cup lightly between both hands. For a moment he frowned at his visitor, then rose and stared from the window.

'Tan-y-graig,' he said slowly, 'is tricky territory. I'm sorry that you've been caught up in it.'

Fellowes sat up. 'What do you mean, caught up?'

Davies began to shake his head. 'I'm afraid it's not for me to say.'

Fellowes cried out in agony. 'For God's sake, I've lost my daughter.' And every day that went by meant time was running against him. 'Look. Tan-y-graig is owned by the MoD. Where the hell do you fit in?'

Davies put down the coffee cup. 'I'm afraid I'm only the area director for the PSA. Property Services Agency in North Wales. This is a regional office.' He gestured at the haircord carpet, the hessian curtains and chairs. 'Nothing to do with Tan-y-graig.'

Fellowes stared at him. 'Don't tell me you don't know why the barriers have suddenly gone up there. Secure Investments move in guards. For some reason we triggered a panic, and now the whole damned place is buzzing. As soon as I left that morning somebody stripped the house. That must have been locally organized. You just can't empty a place inside a couple of hours unless you've been waiting nearby. Whoever did that, took Sandie. And this is the nearest house . . .'

Davies's head moved in the shadows. 'Don't be ridiculous. Of course I don't know.'

'What? You mean it's not part of your estate? Not your barbed wire?'

The big figure laughed. 'Not my command, as they say. I don't put up barbed wire. That's another side of things. The military.'

'The military? Like Major Steadman, RE?'

Davies refilled his cup. 'Look, I really don't know what you mean. Fact is I don't very often come here. We've got property all round these parts, and this place is only convenient for seminars, that sort of thing.'

Fellowes knew he was lying. 'So Tan-y-graig is not your business?'

'Sorry. As for arranging to strip it from here, you can search the house if you like . . .'

Fellowes would have liked to do so, but had no means of enforcing it.

Davies looked out of the window. 'The fact is, I think you're wasting your time. What do you want me to do?'

Peter Fellowes seized on that. 'Give me some advice,' he said, and sat there daring him.

'I'm terribly sorry, but I'm afraid I can't advise you.' Davies had clearly decided that they had fenced enough, as he held out his hand. 'You really must excuse me. I've a good deal of work on hand . . .' He gestured to a file on the desk.

Fellowes disliked the tone. Now that they were on their feet he could smell the other man's washed, carbolicky cleanness.

'You don't fool me, and I don't believe in ghosts. I don't care what you're hiding, I'm here for one reason and one reason only, and that's to find out about Sandie.' He stared into that big, bland face. 'Help me to get her back . . . help me, that's all I want . . .'

Davies turned at the door, an overbearing physical presence. 'Don't be ridiculous. How can I? I also know what you've been saying, and trying to peddle to the media. The rumours in the press. But it won't wash. It won't work, d'you follow me?'

Fellowes stood his ground. 'Look, I don't want this horse-shit about area offices and seminars and not knowing what's going on.'

Davies closed the door softly, as if he wanted to shut him in, or no-one else to hear. The sensation of being abandoned in a dark wood, or in a house full of shadows, ran through the other man's mind.

Davies was smiling again. 'Listen to me, please. I fear that you're under strain, considerable strain. But you shouldn't be wasting my time or anyone else's dreaming up cock-and-bull stories about your daughter being abducted by some kind of government agency. It's not what the police think, is it? It's not what the press think, either, otherwise they'd follow up, wouldn't they?'

The voice was mellifluous, reasonable, but not prepared to be interrupted. 'For God's sake give it a rest, Mr Fellowes, or rather give yourself one. You may not realize it, I'm afraid people often don't, but you're obsessed with a theory and blind to other possibilities. I've been in the business long enough, connected with various estates, to meet quite a few like you, obsessed with some apparent malpractice or some personal fantasy. Psychotics, Mr Fellowes, or dreamers, like, if I may say so, yourself.' He laughed smoothly. 'I think you'd better be careful about making accusations . . .'

Fellowes waited for him to finish, and then said coldly and clearly, 'All right. But I've done some homework too . . . on the accounts of Secure Investments, from the days when they first started.' He watched Davies's eyes contract. 'It appears there is some kind of tunnel at Tan-y-graig, used for storage during the War, though why anyone should want it now, God only knows. That's not my problem, but for some reason Tan-y-graig house stands on the site. And when we happened to go there, the death of that old woman – listen to me for a change, I'm not mad and she did die – for some reason alarmed your security boys . . .'

'No –'

'Oh, yes. I'm going to check you out, Davies, all the way to the top. While I was reporting the death to the police, Sandie found out something, didn't she? Didn't she?' His voice rose. 'Have you got that? That's why she's missing. Or maybe killed. For God's sake, how much do you know about what is going on there?' Fellowes trembled for a daughter whom he'd loved since she was born, and disappointed, and sometimes seemed to ignore, and for whose loss he blamed himself.

'Wait a minute –'

'By Christ, I'll tell you this . . . if Sandie has come to any harm, harm in which you've been involved, I will never let you off the hook. You hear me: never. You or anyone else responsible.'

Davies was waiting for him to finish, and then spoke softly.

'I realize you're under strain, understandably so, after an argument with your daughter . . .'

'Are you suggesting I've done something to her?'

'No, I never said that. I think she simply went away.'

'Went away?'

'Of her own accord, with or without your knowledge.'

'Oh, for God's sake —'

'Hear me out, please. I want to help if I can. I realize this state of affairs happened on government property. I suggest you leave things to us.'

'Leave what to you? Searching for Sandie?'

'Nobody mentioned searching, Mr Fellowes. That's a matter for the police. Look —' he walked across to the largely empty desk and pressed a buzzer —' I'm afraid I'm going to have to ask for you to be escorted out. You're obviously under pressure, and I can appreciate that, but I don't think you can carry the world on your shoulders, running yourself into the ground. You look . . . ill, Mr Fellowes . . . ill.' His beady eyes were glittering, and the other man realized that the undermining was beginning. The next step would be to challenge his sanity.

'For God's sake, all I want is the truth.' But even that word had a hollow ring when set against Davies's blandness, that calculated bureaucratic stone-walling.

'Truth depends on what you want to see, Mr Fellowes.'

Fellowes could have hit him. 'What the hell does that mean?' His shout reverberated through the room and down the corridor, and he wondered if the younger man would come running.

Davies stood silently for a moment, hands in pockets. Then he said slowly, 'The Government interest has to be protected, you follow me? There are certain sensitive matters here which you have inadvertently touched on —'

'Don't try and shoot me that line —' But he remembered the similar warning from Walker the BBC man and threw the phrase back at Davies. 'What exactly does that mean?'

Davies's face was set rigid, almost ignoring him.

'I'm not in a position to say more than that, but I can assure you we'll do anything we can to help.'

He seized on the half-admission. 'Does that mean you know something about what might have happened to her?'

Davies was shaking his head. 'Not at all, I'm afraid. Merely that we shall double-check our properties.'

Fellowes said, 'For Christ's sake, don't you understand what I feel?'

He might have been addressing the wall, for Davies had switched back to his bland, uncompromising negatives.

'Don't try and bully me. I suggest you go back to London and stop agitating.'

'Is that some kind of warning?'

'You asked for advice. I'm giving it.'

Fellowes stood with his back to the door, as if refusing to budge, and tried one last appeal. 'Look. What is all this about? For God's sake stop this secrecy. If you know something, please tell me . . .'

Just for a moment Davies, he thought, seemed to hesitate, perhaps seeking some means of sending him away more satisfied, but ended with an empty gesture, almost wringing his hands.

'Sorry, but I've nothing to add. And if you value my advice, you won't hang around round here.'

Fellowes could hardly believe that he could come away so empty-handed, his questions dismissed by this public servant as if they were of no consequence, as Davies reopened the door and he saw the younger man standing there.

'You haven't heard the last of me,' he said grimly. 'I'm taking this to the top, all the way to Parliament.'

Davies smiled.

'You can try.'

27

Laurel was waiting for him when he returned to Maesteg. 'Let me show you this place I've found.'

The cottage that she had taken was one of a pair of ancient, stone-built farm houses looking out on the lake, modernized after a fashion. There was a tiny crossing over the rusting toy railway, a short lane and he was there.

She kissed him quickly, taking the initiative again. They stood outside and watched the water, anthracite silver.

'Getting colder,' Fellowes said, no good at the small talk. The lake was deserted, and the hills on the far side reminded him of those behind the Tan-y-graig valley. The greyness made her shiver.

'You're going to stay with me?' she asked anxiously. 'You haven't booked any place else? There are two bedrooms.'

He had packed up at the hotel, and took his cases from the car.

'If you'll have me.'

'Oh, Peter ... But we'll play it your way,' she whispered. 'Sandie comes first.'

He made no attempt to touch her; if anything he moved away, inspecting the cottage instead – the other one was empty. It was no more than a ground floor room with a sink in the corner, a fridge wedged in underneath, water heater and electric fires; a wooden staircase led upstairs, where the bedrooms adjoined each other, two rooms with double beds that almost filled them, and white quilted counterpanes. She made no mention of the sleeping arrangements but seeing she had occupied one room he carried his cases to the other.

'What news?' he asked, confident that his report on Davies would be the talking point.

Laurel was busy in the living space downstairs, beginning to prepare a meal.

'You should have had another look at Tan-y-graig itself,' she called out. 'The bulldozers have moved in.'

He switched on both bars of the fire: as the daylight shortened the cottage would be cold and dark.

'What?'

She offered him whisky.

'Drink this, it's good for shock. Bulldozers up at the old house. Two big yellow monsters. I saw them trundling up. Those SS guys in the uniforms unlocked the gates and let them in, then told me to piss off.' She grinned. 'How do you like that?'

He didn't like it, and the news filled him with foreboding. If they were taking earth movers up to the head of the valley something further was going on, and worse, he feared, something might be obliterated.

'They're going to dig some place,' she said. 'And that's for sure.'

'No armed guards? No soldiers?'

'Not as far as I could see. They just don't want to know you, those guys, that's all.'

He laughed uneasily as she talked about Macy's and the Big Apple and articles in the *New Yorker*, which they didn't even take in the staff room. And he wasn't there for romance.

'Tomorrow,' he said, 'I'll see for myself. Somehow or other, I'm going to have to go back inside that damned house.'

'Come on,' she said. 'Tomorrow is another day. These steaks need eating.'

Fellowes knew that Laurel was looking hard at him during the meal, her face serious. Stella had been dead three years, through a teenager out of control on a high-powered bike, and it was still too soon, much too soon, he told himself, to enter a seduction with honour. And that was what it was surely, a cheap little holiday affair on both sides, sharpened by misfortune. Her hair shone in the light, and her face seemed a good deal softer as she

131

pursued enquiries into his own past. He found himself a little drunk with the promise of her expectations.

'Tell me more about Sandie?' she kept insisting. 'I almost feel I've met her.'

'There's not a lot more I can say. Except she's a wonderful kid.' Is or was, he wondered; you realized your mistakes too late.

'You know something, Peter? This thing, this terrible thing is maybe some kind of fate for us.'

He felt the twists of desire. Also she was damned well right, but what did she see in him? Just a short-term affair, or even a believe-or-not story that she would some day write up? She flicked her head back as he pondered, almost as if she could read him, and he suddenly realized he wanted to know more about her own motives for being there. A whole lot more. Instead of which she ducked the issue, and talked about Sandie again.

'It doesn't make sense, that she would go off on her own.'

'There's a conspiracy . . .'

'Sandie fell into some pool, and we're going to pull her out. I mean that.'

He nodded. There was no mistrust of ideas as they touched glasses and began to plot. He had a lot to do – telephoning Collard, telephoning the school about another week's leave of absence, continuing his search and trying to find some people who had once known the Steadmans of Tan-y-graig. What would she do?

'Don't worry about me,' she said. 'I've got other records to check.'

He had almost forgotten the search for her family ties which had brought her there in the first place, but he saw that she was in earnest.

'Don't let me get in your way.'

'Honey, you're not.'

They smiled at each other. Oh God, he thought, if only I could find Sandie this might all come alive again, but the sense of her loss overruled him.

Laurel put out her hand. 'I know.'

At length she yawned. 'Give it up. It's been a long day . . .'

He nodded, putting off the moment of decision.

132

She laughed. 'Oh, come on, Peter. I don't mind if you sleep with me.'

'It's not that.'

She raised an eyebrow.

'Sure?' He wasn't clear what she implied.

'I'd rather not.'

'OK. Your choice.'

He heard her upstairs, singing in the bath, off-beat blues and rumbling water.

Concentrate, he told himself. Concentrate on finding Sandie. Get round the fences put up by Davies and Owens, come out on top. Maybe she isn't dead, maybe they're holding her somewhere. But why, why? And another voice said, don't be stupid, you're just making up excuses. Whatever the reason, however the old woman died there – Mrs Steadman on a last visit – Sandie will never come back, because something had gone wrong, and they were covering it up.

'I've finished, Peter,' Laurel called down the stairs, but he delayed, uncertain of his own reactions, almost as if he feared a trap. He switched off the lights downstairs and heard her go in to the bedroom.

Outside, through the small window, a curved moon hung over the water.

Then he was at the top of the stairs where the door to her room was ajar. Laurel was already in bed, lying back on the pillow, and as he came in she put her arms behind her head, then pulled him down to kiss her.

'Peter. Oh, Peter.'

He let himself be held there, then disengaged, as if he was dissuading a child who had rushed into his arms, James perhaps or Sandie, when they were young.

'Not tonight, Laurel. I'm sorry,' he whispered as he said goodnight.

28

In the small hours the noises began. Laurel could not be sure that she really heard them at first, but she was sleeping uneasily, with a weight on her conscience. If this thing was going to be serious she knew that she ought to confide in him, and yet her past experience had taught her not to trust anyone. She woke up, senses alert.

A sound like someone running. Outside, not inside. The house was dark and silent as she listened tensely.

Footsteps, definitely footsteps.

Clutching a wrap she sat up, thankful for Peter next door.

Again. Someone in the bushes outside, where the two cars were parked in front of the cottages.

She slipped out of bed, and gently edged back the curtain. It was a dark night, with the last quarter moon in cloud but just light enough to glimpse one if not two shadows merging into the bushes. Then one seemed to slip across in front of the building, below her line of vision.

Laurel was scared now. A break-in or something worse; her heart raced. She tiptoed across the bedroom and listened at Peter's door.

She could hear his regular breathing, and sensed rather than saw the outline of his head as she shook him.

'Peter!'

He roused, and thought for a moment that she was coming to him, but she put a hand on his mouth.

'Peter. Ssssh. Outside. I think someone's trying to break in.'

He was awake now, listening.

Together they went to the window, but saw only the shapes of the cars, the Audi and the Capri, and the brush strokes of the bushes, a wavering line in the background.

Fellowes switched on the lights and they blinked at each other in the brightness. He went downstairs.

The back and front doors were still locked. No signs of entry. None of the windows were broken. Whoever it was had gone, perhaps scared off by the lights.

'Are you sure?' he asked.

'Yeah. Dead sure. Two guys, in black like spooks.'

'You mean they had covered faces?'

She realized they had had masks, black ski-masks or terror hoods.

'I mean it. I'm not kidding.'

It was two-eighteen in the morning, and he saw she was barely covered. Her skin felt chilled.

'Laurel, you'll catch cold.'

'Honey, I'm scared. Dead scared. There were two guys. What the hell were they after in a place like this? How did they know I was here?'

How did they know Laurel was there? Why should she ask that? He tried to reassure her. 'They wouldn't be after you. Don't let it worry you.'

They sat together in the kitchen-diner, drinking tea, but her fears would not go away.

'I don't like it,' she said. 'They're after one of us, or both.'

He fetched her white coat which she put over the nightdress and bedroom wrap. 'What do you mean?'

'Listen, Peter. We ought to do something about it. Like phoning the cops.'

His head was full of doubts. 'You know my opinion of the ones round here. Owens and co.'

But Laurel had been shaken. 'Well, maybe. But physical threats are a different thing. They may try something else. It's only fair to tell the police.'

There was a phone in the cottage: it was one of the selling points so far as she was concerned. It was only when Fellowes tried to dial he discovered the line was dead; when he looked outside he saw that the wire had been cut.

They stared at each other.

'We're safe enough inside,' he said. 'Nobody got in; and in any case they won't come back. Why don't you go back to bed?'

But Laurel was clinging to him like a small girl. The whole romantic idea, this thing about taking a cottage and sharing it with him, had turned to ashes.

'I couldn't sleep. Not after that.'

He wondered if it was an excuse, a perfect excuse to invite him into her bed; but he saw that she was petrified. At the top of the stairs he put his arm round her, protective rather than passionate, and opened the door to his room.

She took off the coat and slipped under the covers, still shivering. As if something had been torn from her past, just as Sandie had been wrenched from his.

He put out the lights and she lay awake by his side piecing together what she had seen, comforted by his presence then thinking back to the warnings that she had had before coming over on this goose chase in Wales. Warnings that had been as definite as any given to Peter. Christ, it was ridiculous of little Laurel Ericson to be lying there beside him, as if they were brother and sister.

When she awoke in the morning, the other side of the bed was empty and she put out a hand, feeling a sense of loss. He was avoiding her. Hell. But then, hearing a sound, he called out from below.

'That you, Laurel?'

'Yeah. Peter, honey, I'm sorry.' Who the hell did he expect? There was a smell of coffee, and toast.

'Nothing to be sorry about.'

She dressed quickly, came downstairs and into the living room, a space only big enough for the two of them with Peter at the stove in the corner. A cubby-hole. She sensed that something else had happened, and thought it was the exchanges between them which had upset him, on top of the events of the night.

'Are you OK . . . ?'

'Just fine,' she said.

He poured her coffee.

'No sign of a break-in, but you were right about our friends in the night . . .'

The chill ran through her again. 'How come?'

'Look at the cars.'

She opened the door. The two cars were parked outside and for a moment she could see nothing wrong; then she noticed the Ford, which was nearest the door, had two flat tyres.

Fellowes was standing behind her.

'I was lucky: I can't even open yours.'

She walked outside to investigate. The air was sharp and misty, the first hint of coming frosts. All four tyres on the Audi had been carefully slashed and it rested on the shredded rubber. When she tried the doors she thought they were frozen solid.

'Superglue,' he said. 'On the locks. We must have frightened them before they could finish the job. Mine haven't been touched.'

A fine line of white gum had oozed from each of the locks and dribbled down the red paintwork. There was nothing she could do.

'Come and have breakfast,' he said. 'Then we'll let the garage know.'

A curious sense of relief, almost of satisfaction, seemed to come over her. She knew now that they faced the same devils: that she was right, and she could begin to make plans with a new self-assurance. She was locked into her own quest with the same kind of obsession that he felt for Tan-y-graig. And now she was being hounded, just as she had been warned. Hounded for associating with him, or for what she wanted to do?

'They still scare me,' she whispered.

'Who? Things that go bump in the night?'

'No. This whole goddam business,' she said. 'It's as if we are stirring up ghosts.'

29

It took him most of the day before he reached Maesteg – first finding a telephone at the farm from which Laurel was renting, then waiting for a garage truck. Laurel's car had to be towed and would be out of action until they drilled and fitted new locks, but the Ford was soon on the road.

Inspector Owens was unavailable, but Sergeant Parry, hatchet-faced as ever, took him through to the interview room at the rear of the station, and listened as if Fellowes had at last gone mad.

'Sabotage?'

'That's right . . . a deliberate attempt to wreck two cars.'

'Oh, no. Possibly kids making trouble.'

'With superglue, and a knife through six tyres, at two o'clock in the morning?'

'Well . . . I have to say . . .' the carved features stared unblinkingly '. . . you must expect some hostile reactions, with all these stories about your daughter.'

'Are you suggesting I'm being victimized?'

'I'm not suggesting anything.' That closed-off face again, not wanting to know. Sergeant Parry shrugged. 'Could be Welsh Nationalists.'

'Are they active round here?'

The policeman shrugged again. Fellowes walked back to Laurel, who was waiting at the little patisserie, and had already reached her own decision.

Later that afternoon she told him she was going to France. It was a personal watershed, transformed by the events of the night, but coming to him as a bombshell. Worse, she refused to explain what had caused her change of mood.

'Good God, Laurel. You've only just taken the cottage.' He stood under the trees, arguing.

'It doesn't matter. I want to go. And I think I should get out of your hair. Anyway the car will be out of action for two or three days. It won't take me longer than that. You can stay on there,' she said.

'But that's crazy, Laurel. I thought we had a mutual-help deal . . .'

She smiled. 'This could be part of the deal. It's something I've got to do. Something I have to check on. And I shall feel . . . safer away, after last night.'

'Laurel, don't go. I need you.'

'I've got to. It's important.'

'Important?' he persisted. 'What for?'

But she would not or could not tell him. 'Something I want to be sure about. Put it down to curiosity. And nerves.'

'Laurel, come on,' he said. 'Don't be scared of those guys last night. They won't come back again. The police will be watching the place.'

She saw it differently. 'There are certain people around here – Inspector Owens for one, and maybe the media crowd – would like to make some mud stick, and while we're together it's easier. "Schoolmaster shacks up with blonde after loss of his daughter".' She laughed unconvincingly.

'I don't care.'

'But you should. In the end it may be safer for both of us.'

But beyond that she was unwilling to confide.

He understood in a sense. In one way he wanted her there: in another he needed time to sort out his own emotions. He didn't want a sudden affair, and she had made most of the running, the only way things could have started. If he accepted her going he would drive her to Bristol and she could catch a plane from there, while he returned to Maesteg and waited for the Audi.

'You must do what you think best. And what you really want.'

Under the trees by the lake, Laurel reached up and pulled his face down towards her.

'I'm sorry,' she whispered, 'but there's one more place I want to visit . . .'

She walked to the edge of the water.

'For God's sake, where?' What was this thing that unnerved her, and sent her chasing off? 'Where?'

She hesitated. 'Somewhere in Normandy. Trust me. Just for a couple of days. Then I'll come straight back and maybe we can finish with Tan-y-graig.'

He knew that she had come for something other than a holiday; people had to follow the instincts and passions that made them. He put his arm around her. 'If you want to go, I can't stop you.'

'Peter, you're very important to me . . .' The living over the dead. But to him Sandie was in limbo, neither one nor the other, and he put on no pressure.

'I'll be here,' he said, 'waiting.'

30

On the following evening, after seeing Laurel off in Bristol, Fellowes returned to the cottage and tried to switch on the lights.

Nothing.

It was already growing dark as he found a pocket torch and checked the fuses. All of them seemed in order.

He walked outside and traced the mains cable, which looped on overhead poles from the main road, one for each of the cottages. The cable to the occupied cottage hung limply from the end bracket; the other cable was untouched.

He swore softly.

The telephone had already been cut, and now he was without electricity. The mysterious forces opposed to him, whoever they were, were trying to shut him down. He felt a thrill of satisfaction: it was as if they were scared of him. No way would they frighten him off.

That night he set down for the record, in a long letter to James, what he had discovered so far, working by candle and torch light in the small downstairs room. It was surprisingly cosy, once he had lit the log fire: the flames cast a glow on the walls that reminded him of childhood.

'This is an area', he wrote, 'surrounded by enigmas. When I brought Sandie here she seemed to have a sixth sense about something being wrong. I didn't believe her then and at first the old woman's death in that strange way in Tan-y-graig house seemed a one-off event. But when Sandie disappeared, after volunteering to wait there, I knew there was some kind of devilry. She hadn't just run off. Nobody would believe me but I *knew*, and the sudden disappearance of furniture and our own things only confirmed my belief. We have inadvertently stumbled on some mystery that the powers that be – the police and the authorities, alias the MoD – are now desperate to conceal. Don't ask me what or why but I'm going to find out, James. You have been a tremendous support, and so has Laurel; I don't know what I would have done without you. Both of you. We know now who Steadman was – Major Steadman, RE – and that the old woman was his wife. And thanks to your friend Hopkins we've traced the younger Steadman to West Bromwich, where I'm going to have a little talk with him. I'm putting this in writing to you because I'm clearly being victimized and I don't trust anyone round here. That valley is a nightmare. They have sealed up the house because of something concealed there, something that Sandie discovered. I intend to establish the truth, James, if it's the last thing I do. And if anything should happen to me, carry on and publish this.'

He worked on late into the night, making several handwritten versions, addressed to the local press, some of the nationals in London and BBC News, asking for wider publicity. He sent a copy to his solicitor, smart Austen Collard in Barnes, and as an afterthought wrote a similar account to Thomas Kelvin, his MP. He suggested the latter should ask a question in the House of Commons about events at Tan-y-graig.

He kept the letters by his bed – he wasn't risking any break-in which might try to destroy his material; nor was he frightened, since the evidence was now stacking up that someone was frightened of him. In the morning he posted them.

They did not return that night, the night prowlers and wire-cutters, though he was far from sure that he had seen the last of them. Fellowes almost wished they would pounce so that he could make contact, but no further threats were made. Yet every unexplained movement bred suspicion: that car along the road going too fast or too slow, the vans that turned up from Telecom and the Electricity Board to mend the cables. He watched and tried to establish who his real enemies were.

Daily at Maesteg police office he asked about their enquiries, half-reporting, half-questioning, and met with the same cynical comments from Owens or Parry or other men drafted in, while, on the face of things, the search on the mountains continued.

'You tell us, eh?'

'Look. I've lost my only daughter. This could be a murder case – and what in God's name are you doing?'

'Murder? What makes you say that?'

He would sit there quietly, stubborn as a mule in front of them.

'What the hell is going on at Tan-y-graig?'

'Tan-y-graig? Nothing, as far as we know.'

'Barbed wire? Guards? Earth-moving equipment?' He drove up the valley every day and stood counting the trucks, until the guards waved him away. They had churned up the soil into mud and carved the rutted approach road into grotesque rivulets.

'Heavy stuff,' he said to the police. 'Toxic waste or nuclear fuel of some kind?'

Inspector Owens laughed unconvincingly. 'Oh. I don't think so. But it's MoD property. They can do as they please there. It's not for the likes of you and me.'

'They can't do what they like with me.'

He wondered what kind of life Owens lived: whether he had a wife, and children, whether they knew of his cover-ups, but Owens's peaky face did not invite that kind of confidence.

'Listen, Mr Fellowes. There's a big search on for your daughter, but as you know she hasn't turned up.' He rubbed his hands together and glanced at the second policeman who always sat in as a witness. 'She hasn't shown up anywhere that we might have expected: in London or Shrewsbury or with that fellow she's slept with –'

'That man was a liar,' Fellowes snapped. 'Sandie wouldn't sleep around like that. Somebody is paying him to lie.'

The forehead rose quizzically above the beady eyes.

'I have to say to you again: how well do you know your

daughter? How much have you seen of her development in the last few years? What was there to stop her deciding to run away? Unless you prevented her?'

He bit back the angry denials that welled up inside him. 'This is getting absurd. You're accusing me of killing her.'

'Not at this stage,' Owens said. 'But perhaps you know some of the answers.'

'All right. Then I suppose you'll deny that that earth-moving equipment could be used to search for a body?'

'Two bodies, according to you.'

'Jesus Christ, I want more action. House to house searches. Rewards.'

Owens always countered in the same disappointed voice. 'I think you'd better establish first that she's really gone missing.'

The waiting was the worst part: that and the dread of the unknown.

He missed Laurel badly now, and wanted her, waiting for her to telephone.

He talked to James in Bristol and told him there was still no news, but that he shouldn't worry.

'Worry?' James said. 'Dad, for God's sake you worry me. What's going on? Where is she?'

Fellowes had to admit again that he just didn't know. Sandie had disappeared as if she had never been. The golden autumn weather returned, and gave a last summery gleam to the grass in the meadows, the ripening hedgerow berries and stone bridges over small streams; and he felt close to despair.

31

Days and days while the law did nothing, he cursed to himself. Nothing. Nobody understood, and nobody seemed to care. A small report in the papers, 'Schoolmaster searches for daughter', meant nothing to anyone who had never known Sandie. Never held her, seen her grow, been part of a family with her, a family that would disintegrate if she were dead.

Not that it was within his power, but something bigger than one life was surely at stake: it was the whole complex relationship between him and Sandie and James. It made him sick to think of it, pestering the police to act, pestering the media for coverage; and nobody wanted to know.

Perhaps Owens had been right: the answers would have to be for him alone. If Tan-y-graig was a mountain, then he would have to climb it. He drove up the valley to the barrier and looked at the peak every day, as if it was a personal challenge, brooding there. Sealed off.

He still had his lines of enquiry, and they gave him considerable comfort: Hopkins the private detective now researching maps in Cardiff, James in Bristol, the headmistress at St Cyprian's checking on Sandie's school friends, just in case . . . but in the end he felt it rested with him, and the knowledge brought a fresh confidence. In Owens's eyes, on the other hand, his continuing presence was a mixed benefit – the nuisance of having to listen to this megalomaniac who turned up each day on the doorstep asking for news, the advantage of having the chief suspect camping out close to the crime. So he was tolerated, but kept under surveillance as he shopped in the lakeside town, watched by curious faces who warned their children.

And with every day that passed he felt that Sandie's chances were slipping.

His first thought was to telephone K. Steadman in West Bromwich, at Hopkins's contact address, but the number that had been given was permanently off the hook.

He was also waiting for Laurel, two days, three days in France now, and decided not to adventure until he heard . . . hoping every evening that a call would come through.

Trying to concentrate and rationalize what had happened.

Trying to fit facts into theories.

Trying to read.

He cooked meals of scraps on the stove in the cottage, walked up and down by the lake which stretched like ruffled grey silk under the autumnal skies, and attempted not to imagine Sandie's death. But it was beyond his perception whether or not she was living; the picture simply would not form. Instead there was only the reality of the mountains enclosing the lake, the white specks of distant sheep, terns and gulls on the water, the cold greeny-grey light on the stone-walled fields.

He also knew one other reason why he was waiting. There had been many times since Stella's death when he had persuaded himself that he was self-sufficient. The children were almost off his hands, he was a free agent, and it would be a mistake, he told himself, to get too emotional about another woman. But he had been wrong. Now he was waiting for Laurel.

On the third evening after she had left the telephone finally rang, and his hand jumped to answer it. For the first time since she had gone he found himself laughing, and the cottage seemed a brighter place.

'Hi, Peter?'

'Laurel!' He wanted to say so much, but she pre-empted him.

'Peter, listen to me . . . maybe I'm going bananas, but I've got something to tell you. A real big buzz.'

For a moment his mind went blank, as if this was some roundabout proposal. There was interference on the line, and his heart was hammering.

'Laurel –'

'Listen, Pete . . .' He sensed the urgency, the secrecy in her voice. 'I'm flying straight back in the morning. Flight into Bristol from Paris, AF 124, gets in nine minutes past twelve local time. Peter, can you meet me then?'

There was no doubt in his mind. The airport was north of the city, close to the motorway. He wanted to see her so much. Laurel was on a high, and the excitement was catching.

'Laurel darling, I'll be there,' he shouted. 'And by the way, I love you.'

He heard her laugh and say, 'I love you too. Meet me, and we'll wrap it up.'

32

The arrivals hall was uncrowded, a plastic and chromium hangar with a small knot of hopefuls, well-wishers, relatives, couriers carrying cardboard name-plates. There were gaps between flights and Fellowes had come early; still waters run deep, James would have muttered, he thought to himself, but why should he care: out of the mystery of Sandie he had plucked a rose of hope, as the numerals for AF 124 clicked up on the board.

The Paris flight trickled through slowly, with the look of bemused relief common to all arrivals. Business men in creased suits, older couples on holiday and clutching duty-free bags, a pair of mothers with daughters, a sprinkling of single women, one or two elderly males, then the uniformed hostesses and finally the flight crew. The end.

He realized she had not come.

His feelings seemed to hit a wall of disappointment: Laurel had not caught the plane. Something inside him fought against the evidence and at the Air France desk he asked if they could check the passenger list. A girl in a tricolour scarf lined up names on a screen and assured him there was no Miss Ericson.

He found himself devastated, but he would not give up.

'Is there another plane?'

There was a BA flight due in later that day, the evening business shuttle. Or perhaps she had flown to London.

Fellowes phoned James and told him, counting the hours in Bristol, hoping in spite of his fears. Disconsolate. More and more anxious.

James said, 'Maybe she just missed the flight. Maybe she'll

come on later.' He noted his father's concern with more than a passing interest, and hoped he hadn't been stood up. 'Look, why don't we meet for a meal?'

'Sorry. I don't want to eat,' Fellowes said. 'I'll hang on here.'

Instead, they both went to see Hopkins, who shared an entrance at the side of a betting shop near Fishponds Road. At the top of some well-scuffed stairs they found the private eye in a small, overheated room, still wearing his corduroy suit.

'Secure Investments is a con,' he said, throwing across type-written notes. 'A pure bloody cover. Apparently they use these guys instead of regular MoD police because it makes things less obvious. You'll find them at Porton Down, and some of the nuclear waste sites.'

'Is that what we've got here?'

The crumpled little man shook his head, a quick sparrow-like gesture that was almost a peck.

'Don't think so. No reports of heavy loads moving in and out of the valley. Anyway the locals would notice, and would have kicked up a stink.' He tossed across a map. 'Here. Land Registry info shows that the Tan-y-graig mountain was taken into direct ownership of the then War Office under the Emergency Powers Act, 1939. That nice little earner, which has never been repealed, gave HMG the right to do bloody well anything as far as I can see.'

They were looking at a hand-coloured plan, six inches to the mile, which showed Tan-y-graig farm in a niche at the end of the valley, and the whole of the mountain behind it, as well as the farm itself, encircled by a firm red line.

'The circumference is nearly five miles,' Hopkins said. 'Fact one, the MoD own the whole bloody hill. Fact two, they have wanted it kept quiet – that's par for the course, isn't it? Fact three, the Steadmans were some kind of caretakers until the old boy died and the old girl was packed off to a nursing home. Fact four, somebody in the official hierarchy up in Whitehall must have forgotten about it once the Steadmans had gone, and was only alerted when young Keith Steadman in Birmingham played his own kind of card trick and tried to make a fast buck by conning you – 'grinning at Peter Fellowes. 'Fact five, something must have happened then to give them the shits, so they moved in these Secure Investment guys pretty damn quick.'

'And then the bulldozers,' Fellowes reminded him.

'Right.' Hopkins was thoughtful. 'You want to know my theory? Well, two things happened in a very short time: Mrs Steadman turned up her toes, most unfortunately for everyone, after walking right back to the house; and Sandie found out something when someone came to collect the old girl.'

'I know. But what?'

Hopkins scratched himself. 'I haven't got that far yet.'

Fellowes said, 'Why did they want it – the mountain, I mean? Is there any evidence of a mine?'

The little detective shook his head, and pulled open a drawer on which to rest a leg.

'No. Nothing marked on the maps, but anyway these are pre-War. Fact is, however, somebody made a tunnel, a bloody big tunnel under the hill, at some stage early in the proceedings – about 1940 or 1941.' He chortled triumphantly. 'I paid a visit to London and checked out the BM with a lass who is keeper of the records there. I think she thought I was trying to pick her up, but it was worth it. She tells me they moved all their good stuff to some place in the heart of Wales so as to avoid the bombing. "Where?" I says, and she shrugs. "Go on," I says, "I'm researching a PhD." They love any reference to research you know, and so she goes off and rummages around in a lot of old filing cabinets and eventually she comes back and gives me a name. "I don't know how to pronounce it," she says, but I soon put her right.' He beamed. 'It was Tan-y-graig.'

They looked at each other in silence.

'Whereabouts is the entrance?'

'Apparently there was a small slate quarry there years ago, somewhere under the hill. The farm must have been built around it. If you'd stayed on a bit longer you might have found it . . .'

But Sandie had found it, he thought, as soon as they had arrived, when she heard or thought she heard the noises under the earth.

'The railway,' Fellowes added. 'That railway half-way up the valley. That's when it must have been built, during the War.'

'It could be,' Hopkins said apologetically. 'Afraid that's as far as I've got.'

'Keep trying,' Fellowes said.

James went back with him to the airport, waiting for the five-fifteen plane. The same long anti-climactic pauses between the dribble of passengers through the arrival doors, the same sense of anticipation draining away.

James looked at his father.

'There could be a dozen reasons. Maybe she's decided to stay over one more day, or gone after more information, or perhaps she's not well. I'm sure she'll let you know.'

It was a long time since he had seen that stare on his father's face, a look which he labelled despair. He might have been right, of course, but Peter Fellowes knew that it wasn't: it was determination.

'Come back and drink, Dad,' the son said.

When he returned to Maesteg he drove straight to the police office to try to connect the facts, only to find that Wishart, the sardonic, dark-haired CID man, had re-appeared with Owens. It was soon evident that Owens was shifting the enquiry on to a different level. The modest attempts at cosiness, the tea and toast that previously had passed as softness in Owens's hands, were replaced by a more ruthless questioning.

'Don't tell me, Mr Fellowes – have I got this right – you're reporting the disappearance of yet another woman? The American. Miss Ericson?'

The plain table in the interview room suddenly seemed more sinister for the way that Owens sat there, straight-backed against the wall.

'She told me that she had some important news connected with Sandie. Then she failed to make the plane in Paris.'

A deepening suspicion edged onto Owens's face. Too many women were missing.

'You surprise me.'

'I'd like a check on all airline tickets sold for flights to Bristol, and hotels in Normandy where she might have been staying.'

Owens said, 'You would like . . .' A paper-clip bent in his fingers until it became a spear. 'You would like . . . let me tell you something, trying to goad the police is not the best way of defending yourself.' The back of his chair hit the wall, where the indentations grew larger with every session. He had on his hands someone who either wouldn't face the fact that none of those women wanted him, or else knew far more about their disappearance than he was prepared to admit. 'How long were you married?'

'What's that got to do with it?'

'Answer the question, please.'

Fellowes could see the answers going down in the WPC's little book.

'Just under twenty years.'

'And your wife died three years ago? In an accident?'

'The facts are all on the record.'

'I would like you to tell me, please.' He was turning the session into a prosecution attack.

'Yes. In a road accident in which I was not involved. Look, I came here to ask about Sandie.'

'Yes, Sandie. What were your feelings about her? Did you find her attractive?'

'I resent that question,' he said.

Owens was not deflected.

'Since coming to Wales, you have reported the disappearance of three women. Doesn't that strike you as odd?'

'Since renting Tan-y-graig,' Fellowes retorted. 'Doesn't that strike you as ominous?'

'It does. For someone.' Owens straightened his back again, until he seemed pinned to the wall. The paper clip went tap, tap, tap on the table like a tiny dentist's drill, until suddenly Wishart intervened.

'All right,' he said, looking at Owens. 'I think that's probably enough.'

'Enough?' Owens's mouth dropped in astonishment.

'For the time being, I mean. Until we have something more definite . . .'

Fellowes caught the note of unease in the senior man's voice. It was almost as if he was embarrassed, or knew more than he was prepared to admit.

33

In the fading light of the next afternoon, driving east to track down Steadman, he reached the top of the pass over the Berwyn and paused for a moment to look back. The roadsides were marked by rocks across the desolate moorland, and water was running strongly in the drainage ditches. Lower down on the hillsides sheep huddled out of the wind, the same wind that caught stray leaves and dusted them across the road; the same wind that made him shiver. He no longer wanted to call at the school in Shrewsbury where Sandie should have been. The memories were too acute. He felt that he wanted to kill someone in West Bromwich, with his bare hands.

He found Steadman's street without difficulty – Hopkins was precise in his details – and ran up exterior steps to a first floor flat over a row of shops that had post-War civic architecture stamped all over them. It was a run-down shopping centre in a run-down part of the town.

'Steadman?' he said. 'I'd like to talk to Mr Steadman.' Fellowes was sure he was there: Hopkins had tracked him down to this address, but instead he was confronted by an Indian-looking woman clutching a baby, with a child of three behind her legs.

She nodded. 'I'm Mrs Steadman.'

The children and the woman disarmed him. He was prepared to be angry, but somehow not in front of them. 'He'll be back in an hour,' she said. 'He's only gone to his club.' Not the Athenaeum, he gathered, but some drinking hole down the road. Her dark Anglo-Indian features split into a soft-hearted smile.

'Are you sure?' Perhaps this was some other turn-round, and Steadman was lurking inside.

'Oh, yes. I'm sure.'

He waited in the end two hours, spent in a flea-pit cinema somewhere between there and Wolverhampton, watching a sex-romp film whose title he could not even remember, before he called back at nine. When the woman came to the door again she was still holding the baby, but this time she invited him in. Steadman was sitting with the other child – a boy of three in dirty dungarees – on his lap watching TV. He turned his head and grinned, flicking the sound button lower.

'Don't mind if I don't get up?'

He was much as Hopkins had described, a man in his middle thirties with fading fair hair, a paunch and a ready patter, dressed in a T-shirt and blue over-tight trousers. His feet were in carpet slippers.

'I'd rather not talk in here,' Fellowes began '. . . I've got some rather personal questions.'

Keith Steadman grinned again and shrugged.

'Don't worry. You've already met the missus. You can say what you like.'

Fellowes glanced at the shabby decor, the two cheap plastic settees, a table cluttered with debris, some chipped wooden furniture and a small electronic organ, as well as the wordless TV. It was the room of a family trying and not quite succeeding.

'You advertised a farmhouse,' he said, 'I replied, and sent a cheque for a hundred pounds.'

'Oh, yes.' Steadman now shifted the child, who balanced precariously on his other knee, and peered again at his own letter of directions as if not quite sure he had sent it. 'That's right. Tan-y-graig.'

Fellowes tried to hold his eyes, but Steadman's glance shifted sideways. 'Nothing but trouble,' he added. 'Nothing but trouble, that place.'

'What do you mean?'

'Well, first the cops, then that little private detective, and now you.'

Lydia Steadman busied herself in the kitchen producing cups of weak tea which she offered with ginger biscuits and small round samosas.

'Listen,' Fellowes said. 'Who came here from the police?'

Steadman scratched the top of his head with his free hand, still clasping the child with the other. The little boy's nose was running.

'Frankly, I wouldn't know the name. Some creepy inspector. A short-arsed Welsh guy.'

Owens. 'And he told you about the body?'

Steadman frowned. 'Well, actually he told me you had reported the disappearance of your daughter, who went there with you.'

'And what about the death . . . of old Mrs Steadman?' Fellowes took the black and white photograph from his pocket and handed it across.

Steadman noticed the child and wiped his nose with a tissue, while he studied the picture that he had given to Hopkins.

'Aunt Maud? Yes, but that was more the other bloke who came here, the private eye. Asked me if I wanted the photo' – paid for it, Fellowes thought – 'so I says not particularly. He spun me some story about Aunt Maud having died there, but I says no way, because she was still in the nursing home.'

'What nursing home?'

'Padgate Lodge in Llangollen,' Steadman said.

'How do you know?'

'How do I know? Had a letter from the matron telling me she'd died in her sleep.'

Fellowes sat up. 'Have you still got it?'

'Here? What is this?' Steadman shifted uneasily. 'Course I have. Lydia – you got that letter?'

She found it in a drawer and passed it to Fellowes. A typewritten note of regret, on headed paper, enclosing a form for suggested funeral arrangements. Padgate Lodge had it all worked out.

'Did you see the body?'

Steadman shook his head. 'They said she'd had a stroke, and wasn't a very pretty sight, poor old Maud, so I just fixed up the last rites, as you might say. We went to a service for her in Llangollen, Lydia and me, a few days back.'

Fellowes felt outsmarted. While he had been trailing round Maesteg, pestering Owens, beginning to get to know Laurel, whoever had spirited away old Mrs Steadman's body had fixed it all up with the home that she must have come from. A quiet family funeral, no questions.

'What about the death certificate?'

Steadman looked puzzled.

'No problem. There was a regular doctor came to the home.'

'Was she interred?'

'Cremated.'

Fellowes paused. At least there was some kind of proof that the old woman had died, albeit in the wrong place.

'She was at Tan-y-graig, the first night that I was there, with my daughter.'

'So I've heard.' The bland face seemed unconcerned. 'That's what the other bloke told me. I don't believe it.'

'Hopkins?'

Steadman nodded.

'Look. I was there, and I know. I saw her dead on the floor, when we came down to breakfast. Then my daughter, who would have been the other witness, disappeared too. I swear to God. Now, can you believe me?'

'It's not what the coppers said. This Welsh inspector bloke. He said they suspected that you'd invented a story to cover the loss of your daughter.'

'But the police must surely have known about the house being cleared, and then sealed? Didn't they ask you about your aunt's effects?'

'The coppers came to tell me my aunt had died in Llangollen.'

'When was this?'

'Look. I'm fed up with all these questions.' But he put down the child, who was sucking his thumb, and consulted a calendar pinned up on the wall. Twelve days ago, when Fellowes was beginning his acquaintanceship with Laurel, twelve days ago Owens had been to see Steadman and told him about his aunt, and five days later there had been a quiet and unobserved cremation. The ashes, Steadman said, had now been scattered over the grave at Llangogarth, and he would amend the tombstone.

And yet Owens was close to accusing Fellowes of being responsible for two bodies, old Mrs Steadman and Sandie: Owens, who knew all along that Mrs Steadman was dead and due to be cremated, and who therefore must also have known that her body had been moved back to the nursing home. Owens, who had sat on the press and kept the story out of the media. In Fellowes's mind the little inspector assumed the guise of a cunning, duplicitous villain, but to what end?

'All right. Now, look. Since my daughter disappeared the MoD have wired off the house. I wasn't able to stay there.'

The child climbed back on Steadman's knee. 'I know. The coppers told me.' He grinned again. 'Gave me the money, and all.'

'What do you mean?'

'Gave me a hundred quid,' he replied. 'Said if I had any problems I was to pay you back. Otherwise I could keep it.' He wiped the kid's nose again. 'I suppose you want your money back?'

Fellowes looked at Lydia Steadman, poorly dressed, holding the second child, and the state of the furnishings. They had three rooms and a kitchen, hardly a palace, and he had passed far beyond the question of recovering his cash.

'Keep it,' he said. 'Just tell me why you advertised the wretched place.'

There were murmurs of thanks from both sides. Starting by admitting that he was struggling to make a living, Keith Steadman set out his problems. Maud Steadman, he explained, was the widow of an army major who had moved into the hill farm on a disability pension at the end of the War. They had lived there so long, according to the nephew, that the major had gone a little strange in the head, and designed the stained glass window to victims of the War; he always said that his pension would be withdrawn if he left the place.

His aunt had been persuaded to move into the nursing home just over two years before, when the major had died. Keith Steadman hadn't known them well, but he was their only close relation, and – according to him – she had said he should have the property after she died. But, he grinned, you know what old people are, a bit funny at the end, he knew she would never go back, and asked her to give him a key, so he could keep an eye. In fact he had been surprised to find that his aunt was strong enough, in the better weather, from time to time to return, and the home had encouraged it by sending and collecting her by taxi. All she had to do was telephone.

'When was the last time?' Fellowes asked.

'Oh, three – four months ago now, during the summer.'

When PC Thomas had noticed the lights, he recalled.

'And what about the advertisement?'

'Well, when the old girl wasn't there I used it from time to time, me and Lydia, for the weekends, but we didn't like it much. Bit dark and gloomy if you ask me. The old pair had hung on too long.'

'I see,' Fellowes said slowly. 'So you decided to let it out for somebody else to use, even though it wasn't yours?'

Steadman shifted uncomfortably.

'Well, not quite. I was goaded, as you might say.'

'Goaded?'

'Yes. Last time I saw the old girl she was very uptight – she still had her marbles, you know – because she'd had this letter from the landlords –'

'Secure Investments?'

Steadman nodded. 'Correct. Saying as how they were giving three months' notice and intended to repossess the place. Apparently that was in the terms of the old boy's original contract, though I didn't know anything about it. She was bloody upset, and I was a bit choked too, to tell the truth, because I thought from what she had said that I would somehow inherit.'

'Have you got the letter?'

Steadman shook his head. 'It must be with the old girl's bits and pieces, still down there at Llangollen. Anyway, I thought, bugger that, and when I went back there last month it suddenly occurred to me that it would help with the readies to rent it out for a bit. And then, blimey, no sooner in the paper – I had a temp in Bristol for a few weeks so I put it in there – than you were ringing up.'

He was also one of those people, Fellowes realized, who never liked things too straight, almost as if life required a certain amount of subterfuge as the means of survival.

'So why did you put the contact address as a newspaper shop in Birmingham, rather than here?'

Steadman gave that don't-blame-me-I'm-only-a-big-overgrown-schoolboy grin.

'It's Lydia's home,' he said. 'I thought it might be safer just in case things were . . . well, you know, dodgy.'

'Dodgy? On a straightforward let?'

Steadman put down the kid again. 'There now, run along and find your mum.' He switched off the background flickering of the TV and the images faded to darkness. His chair creaked.

'Well, they weren't too keen when I tried to arrange it through some agency in Maesteg. And the fact is I'd also had a visit, couple of weeks before, from these Secure Investment guys. Man and a girl, in a Rover, said they'd got my name through talking to Aunt Maud, and knew that I used the house.' He paused. 'This ties in a bit with what you say about the place being cleaned out. They says they wanted to clear it at the first opportunity, as soon as the old girl could be persuaded to sell up. I wasn't to go back there, and nobody else was to use it. Well, sod that, I thought, it wasn't their bloody property, or not yet, and buggered if they were going to stop me making a quid or two while I saw the chance, and needed it. So I puts in the ad and thumbs my nose, and didn't tell anyone like; but I used the missus's address, just in case.' He hesitated. 'I'm sorry you got caught.'

'Yes,' Fellowes said slowly. 'So am I,' but he could no longer be angry. He found he knew the reason why Mrs Steadman had gone back.

He was also thinking hard. Something had stirred them to action, the authorities, after all those years, and set in motion a chain of events that had got out of control. He still had to find what it was.

34

Padgate Lodge was a large Victorian house on the fringes of Llangollen, black-roofed and white-fronted with witches' hats on the turrets. It looked what it was, the castle of some nineteenth-century businessman which had fallen on hard times and ended up as a nursing home. Fellowes parked by the bushes and entered the mahogany hall. It smelled of indifferent cooking, disinfectant and incontinence.

The matron was small and formidable, an SRN from the West Midlands who escorted him to an office and offered condolences. He felt she might thrust a pot-plant on him in token memory.

'Where did she die?' he asked.

The pale hands rested nervelessly in her lap.

'Poor Mrs Steadman.' Her head hung just for a moment in a gesture of mute sympathy. 'She had this habit of wandering. Some of them do, you know. They can't stay still, as if they want to go back somehow into the life they knew . . .'

He nodded.

'What happened?'

The matron hesitated. Her white hair made her look motherly but her chin was aggressive. 'She was found by the police . . . somewhere on the other side of town. They believed she was trying to return to her old home.'

Thirty-odd miles away, he thought. People were disappearing when they came in to contact with Tan-y-graig. Abducted by the authorities? The very concept was absurd . . . and yet . . . and yet.

'Did they say where?'

The matron shook her head. 'No ... no. Not very far away – they can't get very far you know' – she bent her head forward and whispered conspiratorily – 'but she was already dead. Dead when they found her, poor lady. It obviously had been too much for her, and she had collapsed and died in the street. We don't like that kind of publicity, of course, so we didn't tell the relatives. It would have been too upsetting.'

'So the police brought her back?'

The matron nodded. 'On a stretcher. It was terrible. We had to bring her round the back way, so that the other residents . . .'

'What time in the day was this?' he asked.

'Time? Oh. I can't remember. Quite late, I suppose. Late in the morning.'

'And then you called in the doctor?'

'Of course. For the certificate.'

'What kind of police?' he said.

'What kind? I don't understand.'

'Were they in uniform?'

She thrust out that chin suspiciously. 'Well, no. They were in plain clothes. But they said who they were.'

'Driving a police van?'

She began to look embarrassed. 'I didn't see the vehicle. I didn't notice. I was too busy arranging things.'

Thirty-odd miles, he reckoned, from Tan-y-graig. Say one hour's driving, and Mrs Steadman could have been back there before midday.

'But was she here overnight? The night before?'

Fellowes saw the flush of embarrassment rise in her cheeks.

'Of course she was. We check all our patients at night.'

And then he knew she was covering up for the fact that they had lost her that previous day, and only been told in the morning; or telling him what the police had rehearsed with her. Yet it still did not explain why so many of those concerned were involved in some secret conspiracy.

He thanked the matron, asked if he could see the room. Again she looked embarrassed.

'I'm afraid that it's been reoccupied. We have such pressures,

163

as you will appreciate, on accommodation in establishments like this.' She smiled warily, rising to her feet to escort him.

'What about her personal effects?' He explained that he had seen Steadman, who had told him that some things were still held there, including the letter from Secure Investments about the future of Tan-y-graig.

She shook her head. 'The police said they'd take them away, and deliver them to Mr Steadman. So as to save us the trouble.'

And me, he thought. He had been one of those people who never did himself justice, baulked at the high fences, let others push in front of him, but not now. Not even if the whole damned apparatus of the State was lining up against him. The matron was walking back with him down the long linoleum corridor, scorch-marked by wheelchairs and trolleys, when he asked, 'Did she have any friends here? People from the same valley? Near Tan-y-graig?'

The matron pursed her lips. 'You know what it is when people get to that stage . . .'

He saw the sad cases sitting in the day-rooms as they passed the open doors. Slippered feet and dressing-gowns.

'No-one at all?'

'Only old Mr Connor, I suppose.'

'Connor?'

'Well, he used to farm near Crickhowell, but I believe that at one time he lived much nearer to Maesteg. I heard them talking about it once.'

Fellowes stopped. 'Do you think I could see him?'

The matron shrugged. Somebody was calling for help. 'You won't find him very . . . well, you know.'

'I understand.'

She led him back to the first day-room and pointed to the figures in the corner, a group of four elderly people, two men, two women, eyes fixed on the television which was turned up full blast.

'Mr Connor,' she said. 'This gentleman would like to meet you.'

Connor was a man who had shrunk, the loose flesh hanging

from his face and frame, with clothes that were now too big, as if they'd been bought in sales though at one time they must have been expensive: a tweed jacket and stained trousers. His eyes had a watery look, boiled eyes that were swimming in milk.

Fellowes crouched down beside him, directing the questions into his good ear. The others looked on in open-mouthed astonishment before switching back to their programme.

'I believe you knew Mrs Steadman?'

'What?' The head was swivelled from Fellowes to the television and back again as if Connor was watching some very slow tennis match.

'I believe . . . you knew . . . Maud Steadman.'

A glimmer of recognition. The old head accepted the fact.

'Do you know Tan-y-graig?'

It brought no flicker of response.

'Tan-y-graig . . . ?' Fellowes shouted.

'Oh. Don't tell me.' The words creaked out as if from a very old gramophone.

'Don't tell you what?' Fellowes found himself shouting, oblivious of the puzzled faces impatiently fingering buttons and pieces of cloth, who vaguely resented this intrusion.

Connor had relapsed into silence.

It was worse than a whole classload of difficult and insecure kids. Fellowes had dealt with them, as well as his own children, by giving them confidence, drawing them out.

'You've been a great help,' he said, 'about Maud Steadman.'

'Who?'

'Maud Steadman.'

'Oh, yes.'

'She was there many years?'

'Who?'

'Mrs Steadman.'

'Oh, yes.'

Fellowes counted them up. 'Forty-five years at least. Was she there during the War?'

The last word seemed to punch a button inside Connor's slow recall, for he roused himself and for the first time looked at his visitor. The matron had returned and hovered in the doorway, making signals.

'No. Not during the War. I was there during the War.' A tremor passed over the surface of his ancient, dried face. Fellowes bent forward insistently.

'Where? Where were you during the War? What did Maud Steadman – Mrs Steadman – talk to you about? Happenings at Tan-y-graig?'

'What?'

Patiently, Fellowes repeated the question, watching it sink in almost physically, until Connor remembered.

'About the lorries.'

'What lorries?' Fellowes's nerves began to tingle.

'The lorries. During the War.' The word seemed to tumble out as if he was still shaken.

'What were they doing? Where?'

But Connor just shook his head, as if he was unwilling to dredge up more; as if some great catharsis had blotted out his memory.

'Crickhowell,' he said. 'I moved to Crickhowell.'

'When? Where from, Mr Connor?'

'From Pen-y-banc.'

Pen-y-banc. Fellowes recalled the empty farm down the valley from Tan-y-graig where he had made his first call that morning after leaving Sandie and going to telephone for help. Pen-y-banc with its broken chicken-wire fences and weed-grown, boarded-up doors. The abandoned farm two miles down the road.

'What happened, Mr Connor?' he asked urgently. 'What happened at Pen-y-banc?'

'What?'

Connor's hands began to shake. The matron came over and said, 'Please, I think you should leave him alone,' in that starchy, professional way that implied she was back on duty. But Fellowes persisted.

'What about the lorries? The lorries during the War?'

A shudder seemed to convulse the old fellow, who started shaking, then buried his head in his hands.

The other heads swivelled in baffled sympathy.

'The lorries went into the mountain . . .' And he broke down in confusion, unable to say more.

'I really think you'd better stop,' the matron said.

35

He knew now it was something big. As he turned out of Llangollen, the little black and white visitors' town, his thoughts were of convoys of trucks driving into the mountain. Affairs of State, not in the public interest, sufficient to cause Sandie's disappearance, and no reply from Laurel? A fine sweat, almost a chill, crept over his forehead. Sandie had seemed to hear noises, as if the natural and supernatural had joined in uneasy alliance. It was ridiculous, but the sweaty almost feverish fear that was gripping him would not let up. His heart banged in his chest like feet on a grating. The whole thing was bunching him up, and underneath was a secret horror that he was fighting an evil which had entered them all.

The cottage stood empty, close to the edge of the lake, cold as he came back to it but apparently undisturbed. The telephone and the electricity were back in working order, so presumably the opposing forces were too clever to repeat the same trick. He unlocked and walked inside, telling himself not to be chicken. He had alerted his MP, and questions would be thrown at the Defence Department, the wheels of government would turn . . . yet in the deep porch of the cottage the shadows seemed more like threats.

No sign. No sign of Laurel or Sandie but at least there were letters, forwarded to him from London. A couple of buff envelopes, one of them sealed and official, marked 'On Her Majesty's Service'. At first he thought it was income tax, some recoding adjustment, and thrust it aside, forced himself to make tea and heat up some beans from a can, aware that

he needed to eat. Only then, when he glanced at the back of
the official letter, he noticed that it was from the Department
of Education and Science.

'Dear Sir,' he read,
'The attention of the Department has been drawn to a series
of recent allegations and events in which your name has
featured, and we understand that police investigations are
continuing. In consequence it has been suggested that you
may no longer be a suitable person to remain as a qualified
teacher. I am therefore directed to request that you should
report in person to this office within the next two weeks
so that a full psychiatric assessment can be arranged. Until
such an assessment is satisfactorily completed the Secretary
of State is advising your school that you should be suspended
from further duties on full pay.

I am, sir, your obedient servant . . .'

He found that the chill had come back, eating into his bones. He
ought to have been angry, he knew, and seen a deliberate plot
carefully put together to discredit him . . . but what if they in
fact were right? What if he was really constructing a mountain
out of a molehill? Psychiatric tests. Suspension. A further sense
of unknown forces, winding up enemies against him. It was
growing dark outside but even darker in his mind.

It was in this mood, shaken like the confusions before some
kind of mental paralysis, that he opened the second envelope and
found a postcard inside. Someone had readdressed it from the
school, knowing very well what it meant, or what it purported
to mean. His hands shook so much that he could hardly read it,
in spite of the bold, clear writing. Dear God, he breathed, it can't
be . . . and then he thought they can't do this . . . but there it
was leaping at him . . . the brief scrawl. Signed Sandie.

Unbelievable, but fizzing there in his hand, and he wondered
if he was going insane. Stunned, he took the card over to the
window and examined it in the light. Out there the water was
the colour of ashes. In his hand was a cheap picture postcard, a
photograph of Tunis. Tunis, for God's sake, some modern street
of shops, undistinguished, it could have been anywhere hot

and dry with waving palm trees. Totally confused, he turned it over.

'Don't worry, Dad. Sorry I had to go suddenly, but someone called. It was a once-in-a-lifetime offer, and I couldn't refuse. All well, back soon. Love, Sandie.'

The strength had drained from his legs, and he felt for a chair, staring and staring, trying to make sense of the message and the location. Blood pounded round in his head. Rationalize; *think* He wasn't Alice in Wonderland, this was contemporary Britain. It simply did not seem possible that she could have flown to Africa – had she had her passport with her when she had gone to Wales? Impossible, as absurd as his fears about the powers of darkness intervening in human affairs, and yet the doubts were like tiny pinpricks.

The handwriting, big and bold, slightly childish, very like what he remembered: but he could not be sure. It was as if she had written it . . . or had it been ghosted for her? Automatic writing from the other side of darkness? As far as he remembered she formed her letters like that, but he had no examples to compare. Two letters sent from London to tell him he was insane . . . or how scared someone up there was? The signature – that signature – was that really hers? Did she write 'Sandie' that way, with the big S and the looped d? He realized yet again how little he really knew her, how little he'd seen of her writing these last couple of years. Oh yes, he wrote to her, once a week during term, but she had rarely replied and he had scarcely expected it. Teenagers didn't write, they did their business by telephone, but now the sins of omission were catching up with him once more. Why should she do this to him? It must be true, it must be . . . but . . . so long as he wasn't mad, fighting off invisible pursuers or enemies in his mind . . . he could not believe it was genuine. Not after all this time . . . unless it was under duress. In the end he could not convince himself.

Alarmed, he began to drink whisky, but the alcohol stayed like a black cloud dulling the edge of his brain. James, then, he would tell James, and get a second opinion, and if he went back to London, as the DES hoped, or even to her school in

Shrewsbury, he would be able to find specimens of her own hand. But with a growing sense of despair he concluded it was all trickery.

The message next, reading between the lines, but that told him little enough. There was a hint of reality in saying someone had called, suddenly out of the blue, but no hint of who or why. More significantly, she had not been in a position to refuse. Tunisia must surely be a red herring, some kind of sick joke; perhaps the most hopeful thing was that she claimed she was well, and would be back soon. And yet there were damaging fears that people with sick minds were prepared to play hideous deceptions. Nine inches away from his hand was a card that tried to say something, and in a haze of exhaustion he threw it down on the floor.

That night he had a kind of nightmare. A yellow, wax-like torso was sitting somewhere accusing him, but the face in the skull was Sandie's, lined and white, grinning then drawn in anguish and then merging into Laurel's, softer, unfocused, dissolving. He struggled to reach a teapot and the teapot became a cat in a witch's hat which spilled something dark on the floor. Dark and warm as used motor oil, but he knew it was blood.

He woke up sweating and groped his way to the window of the upstairs bedroom. The moon shone gently but the night seemed full of invisible cat-calls twitching and howling at him. Was this the way madness developed, and was that what they wanted? He swung his fist at the mountains.

Downstairs in the small hours he made coffee in the kitchen, warming up against the cold. With the fire out the old stone building was damp, reminding him of a prison, each of the rooms like a cell. That brought him back to the nightmare of Sandie, dead or imprisoned somewhere, and the shadowy powers who were trying to fool him. The postcard from Sandie was faked, he was now sure of it, but why had they gone to the trouble of post-marking it from Tunis? And why didn't those same forces lined up against him and lurking out there in the dark when he and Laurel were together come in now and get him as well? He stood outlined by the window, staring over the lake, almost

171

daring them. If they didn't move directly it must be because they feared him, or perhaps feared what would happen if he disappeared too: James alerted in Bristol, Hopkins the private eye, Austen Collard in Barnes, some of the media probably, Tom Kelvin his MP poised to raise awkward questions. It gave him a good deal of comfort.

In the morning he drove back to Maesteg. A faint late October sun washed over the surface of the road, and the mountains behind. In the distance he caught a glimpse of the high brown sugar-loaf of Tan-y-graig, where Sandie had felt from the start that there were dragons. He bought some equipment in a small hardware store, secateurs, a flashlight, a pocket-knife, and put them in a new anorak. He then went to see Owens, and showed him the postcard.

Owens shrugged and rubbed his moustache.

'On the one hand,' he said slowly, 'it's not impossible, is it, that she met up with a boyfriend, somebody other than Blackburn, it wouldn't be the first time, would it, and decided to go off to Tunisia with him?'

'Nobody knew where we were, apart from James and me.'

The policeman drummed his nails and looked at the haggard face in front of him.

'Well, that's your story. On the other hand you could have set it up. Got someone to post you the card.'

Fellowes placed his hands squarely on the edge of the desk. 'Listen to me for a moment. I've been to see Steadman, Keith Steadman in West Bromwich, and what do I find? I find that you were there in person, telling him that his aunt, the old lady we found dead, had pegged out in a nursing home. Then when I visit the home, Padgate Lodge in Llangollen, the matron informs me that some of your plain-clothes officers arrived back there with the body on a stretcher and a rather different story. This time the version is that she'd collapsed nearby and been found dead in the street. The next thing that anyone knows, the old girl has been quietly cremated, out of harm's way. Yet I've been in here to see you nearly every day for two weeks and not a word of this, not one word, has been communicated to me. Isn't that rather strange?'

Owens stood up, nodding to the second policeman to make sure that he stopped noting. 'I don't know what you're talking about. What body on a stretcher? I didn't send men there. You can come here with what stories you like, but you can't prove them.'

'I can get Steadman to swear to what you told him. And the matron of the nursing home.'

Owens put his hands in the pockets of his jacket. 'Can you now? I wonder.'

Owens's lack of interest was an almost physical pressure to beat him back, but Fellowes persisted.

'I'm raising matters with my solicitor . . .' The words hardly seemed to matter.

The police inspector nodded. 'You must do what you think best. And so must I.'

'Does that mean you're under instructions from some higher authority?'

'Look. Will you have a cup of tea?'

Fellowes rose in disgust.

'No. I don't think we've that much in common, let alone the pursuit of the truth.'

It stung the policeman to snap at him, 'I think you'd better go.'

Fellowes stormed out of the building determined never to return, and only when he was outside did he pause to reflect that Owens had left his questions unanswered.

36

When he returned to the cottage, a further letter lay on the mat. Picking it up he saw the portcullis and stamp of the Houses of Parliament.

'Dear Mr Fellowes,' he read,
'Thank you for your letter of the 15th instant, suggesting I should make enquiries and raise questions in the House about the farmhouse called Tan-y-craig' – he did not even spell it correctly – 'and the registered firm known as Security Investments. I appreciate of course that you feel a deep concern about the unexpected disappearance of your daughter and connect this in some way with the events which you allege. I have to say, however, that I have discussed all these matters with the Home Office' – Home Office for God's sake – 'and consulted the Secretary of State for Defence, and both have advised me that for the present it would be inappropriate to pursue further enquiries, in the public interest. I have accordingly decided not to raise the matter in the House of Commons for the time being. I do however retain a strong interest in the issues which you have mentioned and assure you that I shall continue to keep the needs of my constituents, including of course yourself, very much in mind. Assuring you of my best wishes at all times,

Yours etc., Thomas Kelvin.'

Etc., etc., etc., Fellowes thought, looking at the unreadable scrawl of the signature. Perhaps this too was a concocted letter, like the Tunisian postcard and the DES summons. When the authorities ran scared they would close ranks in self-preservation, and he could almost hear the gratings clanging into place. He was being frozen out just as surely as some kind of D-notice had been imposed on the media, and the question in his mind was still, why?

He could ring his MP, of course, who was in a marginal seat, but Kelvin had clearly been got at by the same forces that were bugging him. But they were not supernatural, they were the police and the security boys, the whole damned process of government. Sandie and Laurel had come to mean more to him than the lot of them rolled in a ball and splattered downhill together.

'James?' He sat with his elbows on the table, later that day, briefing his son by phone about his visit to Steadman, and three letters of discouragement.

'Jesus, Dad. What have you got involved in?'

'I don't know. I can't imagine.' Those black secrets were still hovering outside his understanding. 'Some terrible cover-up.'

'Come away. It's dangerous.'

'What makes you say that?' Fellowes's voice sounded twisted. 'How do we really know Sandie hasn't just gone off with some mysterious new boyfriend?'

'Dad. I know Sandie. We've had to get alongside each other since Mum died. Sort of filling the gap.'

He was thankful for the reassurance. James must be right, of course, and yet the nagging doubts remained.

'How do we know that she isn't dead? Killed because of something she saw or heard?'

'For God's sake give it a rest, Dad. You've had that postcard.'

'I know. It troubles me – that degree of deceit.' He paused. 'Listen, James, whatever happens, don't worry about me.'

His son picked up the nuance at once.

'Dad. What are you going to do?'

'Nothing much,' he said doggedly. He would not disclose plans over the phone, in case they were listening. Something like that had happened to Laurel.

'Look, Dad, whatever this is you can't fight it on your own.'

But Fellowes had the faces of Sandie and Laurel clearly in his mind's eye, and beat back the sense of ghosts. The people manipulating him were purely flesh and blood.

'Just don't worry,' he said. 'I'll phone you in a couple of days. If you haven't heard by then you know what to do.'

'But Dad, you can't trust anyone. For Christ's sake, wait. What the hell are you planning?'

'I'm not sure yet,' he said. 'But it's best that I do it alone.'

37

The steely sliver of moon was largely hidden in cloud, thick greasy cotton wool cloud, when he went back to Tan-y-graig that night.

As soon as he passed Pen-y-banc he parked the car and walked on foot with just enough light to reflect from the slick surface of the road and the pale stone of the walls. It was further than he expected up to the first barrier and he wondered if he'd been too cautious. Surely they wouldn't be patrolling at night now that the house was empty? But then he saw the lighted cabin on the other side of the gates: they must have rigged electricity from the line that had gone to the farm. They. There were lights on the gates as well. Red warning lights.

He started to make a detour from the road, climbing over the wall on his right-hand side and landing up to his knees in nettles. There were several fences to negotiate before he reached the farm's main boundary, more or less in line, as far as he could judge, with the gates on the road. The occasional squeak of some animal, the long sighs of the wind, were the only things breaking the silence.

To his left the little cabin with its two lighted windows was out of sight behind the trees. To his right and further forward perhaps half a mile distant, he should have seen the white bulk of the house, at the end of the track up which he and Sandie had driven, past the dew-ponds of the old pastures. None of it was visible now, as the clouds closed on the moon, but just beyond the boundary wall stood the eight-strand barbed-wire fence. He had known it was more than a cattle fence — even if there had been cattle – when he saw it before: it was an anti-personnel barrier out of a prisoner-of-war film, firmly fixed to concrete poles. He shone the torch to make sure, before climbing over the last wall. If they came for him now he did not give much for his chances.

The cutters were in his anorak, zipped across the front of his chest: garden secateurs really, which he hoped to God would be strong enough to cut through the wire mesh.

Snip. Snip. In the darkness he was ruining the blades, but at least he was making a hole.

He scrambled through and paused; everything inside him went cool. *Don't go back now.*

Tan-y-graig house was somewhere over there on the right. When he was away from the hole he risked the flat bicycle torch again, moving quickly up the track towards where the house should be.

It was not there. Where there should have been a building he groped in the dark, first towards a black void, a pit that should not have been there, and then made out a mound of rubble, jagged and irregular like the aftermath of an explosion. An obscure lump in the darkness. The two big yellow bulldozers glimmered phosphorescently to one side.

It was increasingly cold and a sharp wind stirred up the dust.

Slowly, as his eyes adjusted, the outlines became more defined into half-recognized landmarks: an old zinc bath, scum-ridden and full of timber, the concrete washing-line posts still standing in the forecourt, the old dog kennel left intact, but the house itself had gone. Disappeared. And not in any structured way: knocked down to walls no more than knee high, it stood like the ruins of an abandoned fort, little more than foundations, pushed here and there into bigger piles of debris. He picked his way cautiously forward, then stood listening. Somewhere back there in the darkness guards were manning the gate; he wondered again about night patrols. What if there was some virus locked up here in a forbidden hideaway known only to the authorities? Recollected tales of anthrax and germ warfare. *Don't be stupid.* The fence and the lights on the gates were territorial warnings, nothing more.

All was quiet, and he moved across the site like a blind man, intending to negotiate the yard and cautiously explore the barns, which as far as he could tell were still standing. But the old house had been so flattened by the two big machines that he found himself blundering into a no-man's land, eventually discovering that he was inside what had once been the ground-floor rooms. Here was the smashed front door, and that edge of half-buried metal was formerly the kitchen Aga, too big and solid to move. He stumbled across the brickwork that once must have been the division between the kitchen and scullery. In God's name what were they playing at?

Something was very familiar about the end of that external wall. Among the collapsed stones he traced the outline of an arch, the arch of the little blue window that Sandie had first noticed. The supports had been broken and it stood half-buried in the rubble. Pieces of smashed glass, blue and white, reminded him of the memorial that they had never identified: nothing had been spared. He chanced shining the torch to see if he could make sense of the fragments, but it was hopeless, they were shattered beyond repair. Whatever was commemorated there seemed to have gone for ever.

It was in brushing away the broken glass he saw again the markings, scratched into one of the stones, that Sandie had first noticed. He risked the light and pulled away some of the debris to see the marked stone more clearly: the same military cross and War Office arrow that had been on Steadman's headstone in the churchyard at Llangogarth. His mouth went dry; he wasn't imagining things, he wasn't living a fantasy, standing there in the dark, searching for a lost daughter. The forces might be lined up against him, beating their wings, but he was in Tan-y-graig, or what remained of it, where he and Sandie had come, and it was telling him something.

The marker sat in the wall some two feet above the ground, directly below the smashed window, but the demolishers in their high cabs must have been unable to see it. Moreover, the stone was loose: either it was poorly cemented or the bulldozers had shaken it.

Scrambling, sweating, cursing, he tried in vain to prise it

free, broke his nails on the surface, cursed again, and finally remembered the pocket-knife. He fumbled with the blade in the dark, dropped it, retrieved it and pushed it into the mortar; nothing seemed to matter now except to scrape the thing free. Then suddenly it was moving, it was yielding – he had worked it out to see a hollow in the wall. A safe; a hiding-place.

He shone the torch inside and put his hand in a cavity where it touched something hard and cold. A metal box, a small metal deed-box, covered in dirt and rust; the outside wall must have been damp. No more than nine inches long, oblong, locked solid with rust. He felt again to find a key but there was nothing more.

The box sat in his hands, a black tin the size of a building brick but much lighter: when he shook it he heard nothing inside. Papers perhaps, but it would need to be forced. He switched off the torch quickly. No sounds except the wind. The moon shone fitfully on the shoulder of the mountain.

He had the same impression as Sandie, that there were voices whispering. It chilled him.

He pushed the box under his arm and headed out of the ruins, jumping the broken walls. Was it only two weeks since Sandie had explored the same room, climbing across the junk pile of chairs and tables and tea-chests to find the window? Sandie . . . Sandie. *Don't let me fail you*. The thought of her could reduce him to tears, but the box was a token of something, a message from the past: it had to be, he told himself, unless Steadman had also been mad. The secret of Tan-y-graig.

Get out. Self-preservation took over. Get away while you can, the small voice inside him repeated. He listened once more. Nothing. Nothing but his own heartbeats. On the other side of the yard he could see the outlines of the old farm sheds in a black line. The bulldozers had not yet finished their unknown task. This had been Sandie's view, the scene from her rear bedroom looking up at the hill: the sheds were built on to it, using it as a backdrop. Three long sheds with sloping corrugated roofs, lined up against the rock face, disused, abandoned with the farm.

Or at least so he had thought. He saw now in the faint moonlight that a tracked vehicle had been across there, and the path to the right-hand shed had been beaten flat. His heart began to race again as he stumbled across to investigate, clawing his way over the debris. The earth there was churned and broken; he felt the woodwork of the shed door, and shone the torch again, through a crack, but inside was nothing but a hollow darkness. The door was secured by heavy-duty double padlocks that glistened silver. He realized that they were new.

He was becoming less cautious. There was a mystery still but it no longer unnerved him: he held the key in his hands.

Before he could move he heard noises – the sound of a car – and saw headlights sweeping up from the gates. A Secure Investments car, its white paintwork reflecting in the wash from the moon. He ducked but for one fleeting second its beams must have nailed him against the entrance to the sheds.

He heard it screech to a halt, then the car doors slamming, and shouting, and at least two men walking towards him.

'Stop! Halt!'

Shit. Don't let them catch you. Fellowes was up and running, legs pounding into the blackness of the surrounding fields. A wire fence which tore at his clothing; the lights were behind him somewhere, bobbing and weaving, unsure where he had gone. He waited for the shouting to die, and wondered where he was heading, what he was doing: security men were guarding this site, and he no longer trusted them.

He heard them restarting the car, its headlights shining on the wreckage of Tan-y-graig. It stayed there for several minutes, probably sending a message for reinforcements. He reckoned he hadn't much time.

He ran back as far as he could along the line of his entry, still carrying the deed-box. It was hopeless to find the same hole and he settled for a second exist. This time it seemed much harder, showing how tired he was, hands clumsy with nerves, scarcely able to handle the cutters . . .

He sawed away with the blunt blades.

The soft plip of broken wires, then he was through, up and over the boundary wall, down to the road and running. The car was at Pen-y-banc. His heart was hitting his ribs. Escaping, still carrying the box.

He stopped. He could see the outline of the abandoned farmhouse, his car, and the car beside it. Secure Investments had already arrived.

He turned away uncertainly, out of sight from the road. So easy to walk towards them and explain that he had wanted to see what was going on at Tan-y-graig ... but that was what Sandie had done. He had the box under his arm and they were not going to get it before he had a chance to examine it. Legs shaking, breath rasping, the enemy a hundred yards away inspecting the Ford Capri, he crouched down to try and think. Cold, and scared. All the other anomalies were flashing through his mind: Steadman himself, the way that the police had prevaricated, the muzzling of the press, his MP's refusal to probe, the letters from the Education Department and the card from Sandie. Laurel's failure to return. No ghosts there, yet he couldn't get them out of his head. What sort of authority, what kind of society, he wondered, wanted to take such trouble over its secrets? What kind of ghosts at Tan-y-graig were 'not in the public interest'? Ghosts that had stolen Sandie. Like habeas corpus, the freedom of the individual was not all that it seemed in the textbooks.

He was down to a walking pace now. *Whatever it is I want to know. I want to find out. I want to expose the truth.* It was too dark to see them but somewhere down in the valley the bastards would be staking out the road. There was no way he could claim the Capri without disclosing himself, so he shook his head and ploughed on, very tired now by the terrain and the tension. *Help. Go get some help.* It was another seven or eight miles down to the end of the valley and two more on to the cottage; he knew he wouldn't make it across country. And anyway they would be waiting, once they worked out who he was. Owens would see to that.

A belt of trees, and then he found some kind of path, running down through the middle. He was stumbling on railway sleepers rotten with age: the remains of the narrow-gauge line that ran parallel with the road. Saplings were growing through the track bed, and the rails had long been removed. His toe caught in a points switch where the line had been doubled to create a passing bay. It would serve as a landmark: the lever could fix the spot. He kicked away the earth under one of the sleepers close to the handle and tucked the box underneath. Even if they picked him up no-one would get it now, unless he told them.

He waited. No-one was moving.

The end of the line must also mean that he was close to the only other house in the valley which knew about Tan-y-graig. The big house where he'd met Davies. The path he had reached through the trees must have been the road that curved upwards when he had driven there.

He did not trust Davies either – he had lied about Tan-y-graig – but the truth could be flushed out from him. If anyone knew about Sandie it was going to be Davies. Fellowes no longer felt scared. Just tired. Too tired to go on, he began to plod slowly towards the house.

Go and have it out with him. These were the gate-posts, at last, that he remembered, with the notice still hanging in its plastic sleeve. 'Maesteg Railway Extension'. In spite of himself he smiled. What the hell would they think when he turned up, a scratched and limping scarecrow? Well, he was too weary to care. Beyond the gate-posts was the lawn, an ellipse of uncut grass over which he now trudged, too exhausted to walk round the path. Three steps – he could hardly climb them. His hand was shaking as he rang the bell.

The crop-haired man stood in the doorway but he saw with some relief that the girl in the grey suit was behind him. He stumbled through a token story about having lost his way.

'You'd better come in,' she said, almost as if expecting him.

38

He was shown into the well-lit hall with the wooden staircase leading upstairs. The girl said her name was Jane Morrisey, and that she looked after the house, but she did not introduce the man. A slightly different story, he noted, from the one she had relayed before when she claimed not to know of the existence of Tan-y-graig, implying she was merely a visitor. Dressed now in a blue woollen sweater she was polite but distant, as if not wanting to hear the account he gave of losing his way on the hills. Davies was away, she explained. He had gone back to business in London.

'You look all in,' she said.

'Did you know Tan-y-graig house has been demolished?'

She shook her head. 'You can't see it from here. I suppose it was unsafe.'

She led him through to the kitchen, a big Edwardian room with modern appliances, and he found his legs still trembling as he sipped hot, sweet tea. He tried to assess that calm, methodical face, mid-twenties probably, with its neatly cropped hair. That kind of woman, controlled and meticulous, carefully made-up, too business-like to be rural, reminded him of something . . . he realized he could well be looking at an under-cover officer. The stocky young man behind her with the suspicious gaze left him in little doubt: these were some kind of team. Fellowes began to sweat again.

'It's not very advisable,' the girl said, 'to go walking on hills you don't know, at night on your own.'

Fellowes had to agree.

'Would you like something to eat?'

He shook his head. 'I'm fine. Just tired.' The kitchen was massive, as if to cater for a small army, well fitted out in pine. Two large freezers stood against one of the walls, enough for a winter siege.

He determined to persuade them that he was an innocent walker until he could get hold of Davies, until he could sort all this out, but it was late, he was weary, and Maesteg seemed miles away.

'Look,' she said. 'We can't let you go tonight' – he wondered about the implications of that phrase – 'but you're welcome to a spare bed.'

He tried to say it was all right, all he needed was to ring for a taxi, but they were both insistent.

'Oh, please. You must. You need a bath and a rest.' His hand had been cut, and she put a plaster on it. 'It would be stupid to go.'

'Be our guest,' the man said.

Fellowes allowed them to convince him, half-hoping, half-fearing, wondering if he should also ask them to let him ring James, then decided against it. He did not want to raise suspicions.

The man led him upstairs.

'How long have you lived here?' Fellowes asked him.

'On and off,' the man said, opening doors. 'Bathroom here, bedroom next door.' He laid out some towels and pyjamas. It all seemed so bloody civilized he thought it could not be true. When he went to the bathroom the man was standing in the corridor apparently studying a picture, but he did not look the type. He saw Fellowes and smiled.

'Nice to have some new faces,' he said. 'Gets a bit lonely here.' But he would not enlarge on it.

The water soaked into his body, relieving the aches and tensions. It was a big old bathroom with mahogany fittings and brass taps, unmodernized. A draught blew under the door and when he turned the taps off he could hear noises below. Car doors, people talking, but he could not be sure. When he emerged the passage was empty. He thought about prowling along it but decided not to chance his luck until he knew more about them; after all what had he found, as distinct from these suppositions and impressions in his mind? Benefit of the doubt, wasn't that what he told his kids? It had been a long day, beginning with his talk with Owens and ending here.

He put on the pyjamas and walked back to the bedroom, a room of cream-painted panelling hung with innocuous pictures: two lovers walking on sands, birds circling over a cliff, indifferent Victorian art. It was that kind of house, and that kind of brass-bound bed, with a hand-embroidered coverlet. There was a small radio, a bookshelf of paperbacks, a clock showing half-past midnight. Civilization of sorts.

Then footsteps along the passage, light but firm, whether the man or the girl he could not be sure. And the key turned in the lock. He lay in the bed listening to the treads fading, then slipped out and tried the handle. Locked. They had made him a prisoner.

'Take it slowly,' he thought. *'Don't let them get you.'* Time would be on his side; time plus a curious awareness that this was what had happened to Sandie. She had been taken hostage for something, possibly even brought here. He began to explore the room, testing the locked door and the single window which opened on to a drop of twenty feet to the ground. Difficult but not impossible, but he wasn't going that way, at least not yet. Perhaps they expected him to, and would be waiting downstairs with some kind of welcoming party. No way, tired as he was, would he rush into that: instead he examined the bedroom. There was an empty wardrobe, a big, heavy, carved oak monster that looked made for the house, a chest of drawers full of blankets that told him nothing, the few books, a pile of old papers. There were times when you had to give in. The waves of exhaustion broke over him.

When he awoke, the door was still locked and the room was still there. He was hungry and they must have heard him rattling the handle for in a few minutes the man from the night before appeared carrying a breakfast tray, accompanied by a second heavy.

186

'I want to go to the bathroom,' Fellowes said.

'That's O.K., provided that you behave yourself.'

'Look, what the hell is all this?'

The number one man shook his head, and said politely, 'Afraid I'm not allowed to discuss it.'

'Discuss what, for God's sake?'

'Nothing. We're not allowed to talk.'

He was up against that same wall of indifference that he had seen in the girl. They didn't seem to want to harm him, they were not threatening him, it was just that he had to stay there.

'How long?' he asked.

The lead man shrugged. 'A couple of days, that's all.'

'That's all? What the hell for? What is this place?'

'Not allowed to discuss it,' the lead man said.

Fellowes sat on the bed and tried to stare them out, but they simply avoided his eyes.

When he got to the bathroom he stood on the seat and looked out from the louvre at the top of the frosted-glass window. At the rear of the house a long, untended garden, a lawn between straggling rose-bushes, stretched away to a summer-house and beyond that to a wilderness. If he could get there unnoticed he reckoned he could give them the slip, but again that twenty-feet drop would have to be negotiated. This time, however, the drainpipe ran close to the sill and he judged it could hold his weight. The window was on a latch and shivered gently when he pushed it. Whoever they were, these jailers, they had given him an open prison.

He went back and ate the breakfast of two boiled eggs, toast and coffee, feeling a good deal better. When the two young men came back for the tray, Fellowes said, 'Look. I want a telephone. To tell them I'm safe.' Anyone, James or Collard, even the school.

'You stay right where you are.'

'Who is in charge of this place? Let me speak to Miss Morrisey.'

But they simply ignored him, locking the door.

Nothing was worse than inaction. He contemplated the window, the long run down to the trees and whatever lay beyond them and knew it was hopeless in daylight. As if to remind him to stay where he was the crop-headed man appeared on the gravel below, taking the air, with his hands in his pockets. The only thing that was clear was that they weren't sadists, were not in the business of hurting him. He was effectively a prisoner because of something he knew, or that they thought he'd seen or might discover. He began to prowl round the room.

It gutted him to feel so helpless, trying to imagine what kind of lunatics had set this thing up, controlling the valley, concealing what was in the mountain. The possibilities could be checked off and rationalized into an essay: examine the main reasons why the valley at Tan-y-graig has become a State secret. Well, there was a tunnel, somewhere under the hill, used according to Hopkins for hiding the BM's treasures during the War. The little railway had been built to help transport them. Perhaps some of them were still there, but then why demolish the farmhouse? Had there been some terrible accident that would account for the trucks, or a more recent leak of something lethal, chemical weapons or radio-active waste? But even so the precautions, and the secrecy, were excessive; and they must know that when they released him he would want an enquiry.

It blew his mind to be held against his will like this, his only crime a mild trespass. People were disappearing when they came into contact with Tan-y-graig. The place was haunted in his own memory by the old woman's face: Maud Steadman who had been drawn there by some last urge. Laurel had understood that. Laurel, who'd implied she'd discovered some big secret, and then had never returned.

Under the banked-down surface, throughout the day as they came with silent meals he swore that he would get even, and began to go through the room looking for any signs.

It was one of those square box places used for the second-best bed, dusty, a dead pot plant on the window-sill, a howling draught down the chimney, two church-hall-type easy chairs faded with age, a crucifix on the wall, a pile of papers in the corner, two rows of books gathering dust: a survivor of a room. Perhaps they had put him there simply because it was solid, with that heavy locked door and the sheer drop down to the drive. *All right, he would wait until dark.*

The bookcase, then, searching for something to read. He ran his fingers along the two rows of books, bound volumes on the bottom, *Hymns Ancient and Modern*, and deeds that won the Empire stuff, paperbacks on the top, mostly dog-eared and recent, Jack Higgins, Desmond Bagley, Mary Higgins Clark, Scott Fitzgerald's *Tender is the Night*. It pulled him up short. Where had he seen that last volume before, in that edition? Sandie of course. Sandie had been reading it and asked him what he had thought of it in the car coming down.

He blinked back tears of frustration as he picked out the book. Did it mean she had had it with her, did it mean that this was her book? He simply could not bear it, it might be a pure coincidence, conjuring hope from the air. The book gave him no message, only a helpless ache, and yet . . . and yet . . .

It was no good pretending. He could never be sure, and he slipped the book away again, but as he did so he saw something behind it, at the back of the bookcase.

He retrieved it and turned it over. An oval of blue quartz, on a cheap copper backing. For a moment he could not remember where he had seen it before. And then he knew. Sandie had come across it on the floor of the old woman's bedroom, and placed it on the bedside table when he went in to say goodnight.

A huge surge of relief swept over him. Thank God. Thank God. She'd been here and now he had proof. A key piece to the jigsaw. Whatever else Davies and the rest of them were, security or MI5 or whatever, he was conspiring in an abduction, and like lesser men would stand accused through the due process of law.

Fellowes put the brooch in his pocket. When they brought him an evening meal of soup, eggs and bacon and tinned peaches they found him surprisingly cooperative, even relaxed. He seemed resigned to his fate and had finally stopped asking them questions.

39

When it was thoroughly dark he told them he wanted a bath and left by the bathroom window with the taps still running. The drainpipe tore at his hands and seemed to judder on the wall, but the cast iron pipes held firm. In the process he had skinned his palms, but otherwise he was intact as he made a run for the summer-house.

Trees loomed up, the moon was momentarily clearer with diamond-hard, frosty stars, a blessing and a disadvantage, and he was through the wilderness and running. Needed to run to keep warm, having left his anorak behind. He made ground and came to a wall, low blocks at the end of the garden. There were only the three people in the house and they would have problems finding him once he was into the fields.

Toe-holds and footholds and then he was over and downhill, outside the grounds, running wildly, in the direction of the road. No time to pick up the deed-box but that should be safe enough.

Running like a madman, with his mind in a turmoil. Davies. Owens. Sandie. What had they done with Sandie? Laurel, for God's sake, too? Needed to get away. Needed to telephone. *Don't trust. Don't trust anyone.*

Stopped, clutching his ribs. *Think, in spite of the agony.* No sounds of pursuit. He wondered if by now they realized the bath water was still running in the upstairs room.

Jesus Christ, it was cold, a settled, numbing, frosty cold as soon as he paused. His clothes were too thin for this weather, the sweater no protection against the icy air. He was beginning to shiver, and started to run again, legs pounding, chest raw. No expertise, no sense of direction after the moon was lost behind fresh banks of cloud. A refugee, flitting through a freezing landscape.

Hitting the road at last it was easier there and he slowed to an exhausted walk, ready to scramble again at the sound of a vehicle. But it was eerily silent. He loped by the row of cottages next to the sheep farm and even the dogs did not bark, close-lipped in the dark. The telephone box was still useless.

Paralysed with cold, but somehow he had to continue. He hated it now, hated this lonely valley and the background, sinister echoes that he at first had thought were only in Sandie's mind. Noises from under the mountain. A white blanket of frost was on the tops of the walls, plates of frost covered the road, and it took him another hour before he came across a phone box, on the road by the lake, that was still working.

Don't give up. Don't give in. He must get a message through somehow. He found some coins in his pocket and dialled James with clumsy fingers.

The phone rang forever in the flat off Whiteladies Road, and he remembered how solidly James had slept on the put-u-up after offering him the bedroom; but he kept on and on. James must be there. He must. They understood each other now, in the depths of adversity.

'What?'

When his son replied he was so cold he could hardly articulate, and stumbled over his account.

James tried to calm him down. This was someone driven over the edge, phoning him up in the small hours, trying to explain some story about a man called Davies who had a safe-house in Wales where he had been taken prisoner. And Tan-y-graig smashed down, and a deed-box he had buried somewhere.

'Take it easy, Dad. Are you all right?'

'Yes.' But Fellowes's teeth were chattering, his speech slurred with fatigue. James wondered if he was drunk.

'They are looking for me,' he said. 'They are looking for me.'

'Who, Dad, who?'

'I don't know . . . I don't know . . . but they've had Sandie in that house.'

'Go to the police,' James said. 'Go to the police.'

Inside the box Fellowes argued.

'I can't. Owens. Road blocks. These people have got the car. *Don't trust anyone.*'

'What?'

As his senses revived, James tried to puzzle things out. His father was either going slowly mad, or there were indeed secrets around, secrets for which Sandie had been silenced, in which case the world must be told. Not the Tan-y-graig people who were in some way involved but Scotland Yard and the other powers-that-be. Peter Fellowes sounded desperate. He needed support, perhaps even medical help.

'Try the emergency services, for God's sake. You've got to. Listen, dial 999. Cut out the local people. There'll be a central control room. Tell them where you are, get them to send an ambulance. I'll come straight up to Wales. You hear me, Dad? You hear me?'

Fellowes was too exhausted to care.

'I hear you,' he said, and swayed as he put down the phone.

He stayed in the box, half-frozen, unable to move, unable to think clearly, the yellow light beaming down. Better than the darkness outside. A single car on the road did not give him a second glance.

He dialled again. 999.

'Which service do you require?'

'Ambulance,' he said, and mumbled out some story, when the calm voice asked what had happened, about illegal imprisonment in a strange country house, and his missing daughter, and something in a tin box. He sounded drunk. She'd heard them all before; and when she asked where he was he said he didn't know. Eventually she got the call-box number and traced it on the map.

'Wait there,' she said. 'We'll be along.'

40

He held on for what seemed an hour, blowing on his hands, stamping his feet to keep the circulation going. Wanted to run, find a house and rouse them, but now he was committed, waiting for medical help. Wondered why the hell they took so long, as if they were phoning around.

Outside the box the frost settled like snow on the grass, the road, and the opaque glass of the kiosk.

He watched the water on the lake, thinking once more about Sandie. Knew she would never have survived nights in the open like this. He thought then about Laurel and wondered why she had failed him. *Trust no-one*, the inner voice said.

He tried to count off the minutes, but still no sign of a vehicle. He flapped his arms to keep warm, and groped back inside the box. The deserted road ran into darkness, hemmed in by bushes, hoar-frosted and silent.

Eventually he heard a car engine, long before he saw the lights cruising the distance, as if it was looking for something. He had a sudden urge to run again but by then it was too late. The police car was looking for him, picked him up in its headlights and stopped, a blue light winking on top.

'I'm w-waiting f-for an ambulance,' he gasped.

The young policeman took his arm. He was buttoned up in a heavy car-coat, and felt the other man tremble with cold.

'Don't worry, we'll get you home.'

Fellowes shuffled on numb feet towards the open rear

door, and the dark overcoat inside. A high-cheeked, familiar face.

'Get in, please,' Chief Inspector Wishart said.

The young policeman unscrewed a flask of hot coffee.

'Here. Drink this. Do you good.'

Fellowes felt it warming his throat, then his hands and his whole body. The drink seemed to run through his muscles, bringing on violent shivering, and Wishart said, 'Take it easy. Just tell us what happened.' He pulled a blanket off the back window ledge and settled it round Fellowes's shoulders: the kind of rug they draped over heads.

Fellowes drained the coffee gratefully, remembering how Wishart had appeared when he became the prime suspect, taking over from Owens as if on higher authority. The interior light came on and for a few minutes they sat together in the car, cat and mouse watching each other, as he slowly thawed out while the driver phoned something through. Then the car reversed, pointing back towards Maesteg.

'Tell us about it . . .' Wishart said gently.

Fellowes pulled the quartz brooch from his pocket.

'See this? The Davies house is more than a regional office, in spite of the story he gave me. And Tan-y-graig is owned by an MoD cover company called Secure Investments, the ones that have wired it off. I suspect they own the place next door. The only other house nearby.'

Wishart examined the brooch carefully, then returned it.

'We'd better go back there,' he said, bending forward to instruct the driver. 'I'm sorry? What does that prove?'

'Prove?' Fellowes stared out at the night. The heavy frost had turned the landscape into a sinister fairy-land. 'Prove? I can't yet prove anything, but the people in the Davies house have held me there for twenty-four hours.'

He noted the car was turning off the lake road again.

'Hey. Where are we going? This isn't the road to Maesteg.' The darkness, the cold, the white hedges confused him, like looking at a film negative.

Wishart smiled. 'Please don't worry. We picked up the distress call and said we would collect you.' He held on to the inside strap as the car swayed round a corner.

'This is the road back to Tan-y-graig.'

'I know. I just want to show you something. Something that will help to explain things.'

The warmth had returned to his body, and as it did so his suspicions grew. Why had they been on duty, available to pick him up?

'Explain?' The ghosts moved back into his mind. Some horror had overtaken Sandie.

'Who are you? What sort of game is this?'

Wishart produced a photo-identity card, and turned his face towards him.

'You'll feel a lot better soon.'

Fellowes's voice was calm but murderous.

'Why are we going back?'

'To show you.'

'To show me what?' Fellowes pointed up in the darkness, towards the Davies house, invisible but menacing as they climbed past the silent sheep farm and towards Pen-y-banc. 'What the hell is going on up there? Listen to me. I swear that's where my daughter was taken.'

'Taken, Mr Fellowes? Have you got any evidence that would convince a court? I've only your word on that brooch.'

'It was there in Tan-y-graig. I saw it. I swear to it.' The words faltered in his mouth. *Don't trust them, any of them.*

Wishart heard the engine note slow and said, 'carry on,' to the driver. 'Don't worry. If there's anything in what you say we'll do a thorough check. We may need a search warrant, but that will be easy enough.'

He decided they were acting like ghouls, automatons directed by forces outside his understanding.

'I want the place searched now,' he raged. The blanket was huddled round his shoulders as if he was a suspect. 'Let me go.'

Pen-y-banc flashed past in the cold, abandoned and empty.

'I'll radio back,' the CID man promised. 'Look.'

As they rounded the bend he pointed ahead through the windscreen and Fellowes saw there were bright lights at the top of the valley. Floodlights. The wire gates that had sealed off Tan-y-graig were open and swarming with men. Half-a-dozen army trucks, Landrovers and Bedford three-tonners, were parked nose to tail inside, along the verge, and the two big yellow bulldozers had been drawn up beyond them, across the start of the track up to Tan-y-graig house. In the glare of the floodlights he could see soldiers waiting, inside the three-ton trucks or sheltering by their sides, soldiers in battle kit, steel helmets, camouflage jackets. Twenty or thirty he reckoned, and a handful of police. They stamped on the freezing grass and their breath was rising like smoke.

Fellowes was silent.

'Feeling any better?' Wishart asked.

'Worse.'

The police car stopped, waved down by one of the soldiers.

'Sorry, sir. That's it. Nobody allowed above here . . .'

The policemen sat in the car, its engine running.

'I should switch off, if I were you, sir.'

'OK,' Wishart said.

The soldier was painted in zombie colours, his face streaked with black and green dye, the colours on his jacket making him a walking tree. Wishart consulted his watch.

'How long?'

'Just in time. Only ten minutes to go.'

'Ten minutes to what?' Fellowes screamed, consumed by a terrible fear that she was inside the hill. Sandie. Dead and soon buried. Dear God, he would never see her, never again have the chance . . .

'Don't worry,' Wishart urged. 'Wait.'

It seemed like an eternity to be sitting there, the minutes ticking away, the soldiers running and shouting in the freezing night air, a couple of the trucks reversing further down outside the gates. Engineers, Fellowes saw from the painted insignia, the heraldry decorating the tail-gates. Engineers like Major Steadman.

'Eight. Seven. Six.' Minutes when he felt his past was ticking away. Like the last moments of drowning. His past with Stella, holding Sandie in his arms, christening her, then the long childhood that was in retrospect no more than brief summers, moments of happiness before she seemed to grow up into a frizzy-haired schoolgirl and next minute a young woman.

'Five. Four. Three,' Wishart said. 'Put your hands over your ears.'

Three years since Stella had died, and it had all gone wrong. Sandie kicking over the traces, wanting to run away from the kind of empty home that was all he could offer. A massive, aching void. And James, dear James. *Forgive us our trespasses* . . .

A vast light flickered on the hills, a sudden brief lightning, replaced by a thunderous sound, a confined, awe-inspiring boom, a sound barrier explosion which shook out some of the lights. Inside the car they felt the hillside tremble, as if the whole mountain of rock that was Tan-y-graig was tearing itself apart. Even when the big bang ceased he heard – as he raised his head and took his hands from his ears – the residual rumbling of boulders loosened by the blast and shaking in the earth. Inside and outside the mountain layers of rock were reforming.

The soldiers who had been crouching beside their vehicles emerged and began to relax, talking and joking.

Some of the lights returned. An officer walked over, cradling an automatic rifle.

'That's all,' he grinned. 'No smoke. No flames. Just one hell of a bang. I wouldn't like to have been inside there.'

They got out and stood looking up, craning to see the mountain in the dark, as a curtain of dust, rubble and tiny chippings, pattered over them all.

41

For a moment they were stunned. The explosion had been so violent, so trapped between the hillsides that it seemed to echo for ever in rivulets and growls of sound deep underneath them, and even when it had ceased, and the secondary tremors were still, no-one seemed anxious to speak, as if they had witnessed something defying description. Then Wishart said slowly, 'That's it. That's the reason for the secrecy.' He exhaled a sigh of relief. 'I'm sorry . . .'

Fellowes was shaking his head, his ears still ringing. 'What do you mean?' He saw other policemen now, walking across, and one of them was Owens, dressed in a khaki parka like a small, hooded bird.

'A huge ammunition dump, volatile and unstable, under the mountain,' Wishart said. 'Wartime, deteriorating. Dangerous. The farm had been sitting on it.' He paused. 'I thought you ought to know.'

Fellowes was hoarse with confusion, his voice a kind of dry whisper.

'It doesn't bring Sandie back . . .'

'I'm aware of that –'

'And it doesn't explain what has been going on in the Davies house, or why people tried to frighten me.' The doubts were returning fast.

Owens came up and saluted. His beady eyes stared at Fellowes standing there clutching his blanket.

'Oh. You've decided to arrest him then?'

'No,' Wishart said. 'Not quite.' He moved to jog Fellowes's

elbow. 'Come on. We'll take you home now. I thought you would like to see the reason for all the security, and the barbed wire.'

They climbed back inside the car. The demolition troop was beginning to move forward, down the track to the site.

'Get moving. Back to Maesteg,' Wishart ordered.

Fellowes said, 'In God's name what happened to Sandie?' A black despair in his voice.

Wishart was leaning across, his face like a totem pole.

'What happened to that box?'

'Box?' For a moment he did not react.

'The deed-box. You said you found a box.'

He knew then he should not trust them. Knew. They had heard the 999 call. They were trading the box for Sandie . . . for information . . . or – he began to hope against hope – Sandie herself.

'Tell me what's happened to her,' he screamed.

'The box. First. Please.'

He fought against revealing it. 'It's nothing,' he said. 'Just an old tin box. What do you want that for anyway? I want an immediate search of the Davies house. You said you would get a warrant. It's my daughter that's important.'

The car slipped past Pen-y-banc, where he saw more police vehicles, armed police, sealing the road again. His suspicions were mounting, as the shock of the explosion died.

'Get on with finding my daughter.'

Wishart's carved face began to seem less patient, even threatening.

'Look. You've already confessed to breaking and entering. Stealing property. You've had a postcard from your daughter in Tunis. If she wants to run away with a boyfriend she's old enough to know her own business.'

'I believe she's up there!' he raged.

'Shut up, and listen.' Wishart's tone was bleak. 'Your own conduct doesn't stand up. Why did you come here with her in the first place? *Why?* What have you done with her? That's an equally legitimate question. And why break in to Tan-y-graig?'

'I've been held against my will,' he shouted back. 'A prisoner in that place up there.' He clutched the blanket round him and shivered again from helplessness and a blind anger. 'So was my daughter. Her copy of a book is there, for Christ's sake. *Tender is the Night*.' The irony was not lost on him. 'You're all in this together.'

'Don't be ridiculous. Any fool can come to us with a story of some book that he's found, and a cheap brooch.'

'Liar,' he said.

Wishart grew increasingly annoyed.

'That's a very serious accusation.'

'You bastards. All of you.' He was going out of his mind. The car slid past the shuttered houses, the sheep farm, the wrecked telephone box that he had come to use as a landmark. He wished they would all disappear as if the whole thing was a nightmare.

Wishart's voice switched to reason again.

'You're making things very difficult for yourself.' His hand rubbed condensation from the offside window. 'Very difficult. We could book you for trespass and theft, on your own admission: you realize that –'

'Try it.'

'Listen. I want to help you. We want you to cooperate. Why do you think I took you up there?' He shook his head. 'For heaven's sake don't be a fool. You've over-reached yourself out there on the mountain. Ill-prepared. All you have to do is tell us where that box is while I take you back for a check-up. We'll book you into a private room. Get a good sleep and a bath. Man, you look knackered. Simply go back to Maesteg, please, and leave the rest to me.'

For the second time he had the sensation that he was in custody, a prisoner on remand in the car. And knew he had to get away.

'I must have a leak,' he said. 'That coffee. I drank too much when I was cold.'

'Wait a bit.'

'No. I can't. I'll wet my pants.' He put his hands between his legs.

'All right. Pull over,' Wishart ordered.

The car stopped close to a wall. Dark. Overhanging bushes, frosted with crystals. If he could only jump over and run . . .

'Get out,' Wishart said; but when Fellowes did so Wishart stood with him, watching him urinate in a little cloud of steam against the wall.

'Get back,' Wishart said. 'We're going on.'

He was determined now, fearing if they took him to Maesteg they would have him under lock and key, out of harm's way. That would be the end of it all. He climbed back slowly. The door was re-locked.

'Drive on.'

The car began to move again, gathering speed but as it did so he made a lunge for the wheel over the back of the driver, between the seats.

'Christ's sake, be careful . . . What the hell are you doing?'

He tugged at the steering wheel viciously, pulling it to the right, and the car swerved across the road in a shriek of brakes, Wishart and Fellowes flying forward but Fellowes cushioned by the impact of the policemen in front. Wishart's skull collided with the driver's in a dull crack, but Fellowes didn't waste time enquiring. As the car hit the opposite wall he opened the nearside door and threw himself sideways and out, rolling into a ditch. There was a shout from someone, and screams of pain, but he didn't wait to see – for the second time that night he found himself winded and bruised but up and still running.

42

The lights of the car had gone out under the impact, and once he was over the wall he could see nothing. He knew he was going to be cold again, bitterly cold, and found he was still clutching the blanket which had been wrapped around him, something he was going to need as he made his way into the night, climbing this time, walking and stumbling, not running . . .

Hills and valleys and more hills. He climbed across gates and fences, a limping, haphazard progress, anxious only to get away. The distance was impossible to estimate; every mile seemed like a hundred in the freezing darkness. He knew he needed some shelter but feared if he stopped they would find him. They would all have it in for him now: he had caused the police to crash, might well have caused death or injury. The nightmare had become reality.

Get away. Put distance between them as fast and far as he could, before they came searching, before he dropped from exhaustion.

It was nearly five o'clock when Fellowes saw the first glimmers of a reservoir through a break in the cloud. He did not know where he was, only that it lay there below him like a long stain of ink.

When the sun rose and the mist cleared he saw traffic on the road, a tiny black ribbon of asphalt winding down towards the water. He had gone very high, higher than he had thought, a speck on the landscape to anyone looking from below, and whenever he saw movement – a car, a solitary motor cyclist – he froze. Hunkered down under the blanket he could become a boulder.

Rain swept in from the west, turning the tops of the mountains into soggy cardboard. Hail stung his face and hands and he was soaked to the skin, the blanket heavy and useless. He holed up again in a crude shelter high on the hills, a tin-roofed box smelling of sheep shit and wool, and watched a car on the road one thousand feet below. A Landrover by the look of it, with police markings. So they were out to get him, but without enough men for a drag-net. It sat in a passing bay, as if they were waiting instructions, and then moved on over the pass. Fellowes reckoned that they had lost him.

In Maesteg the police had reached a very similar conclusion, as Wishart dried out with Owens in the little police office. Wishart, although nursing a broken finger and a cut on his head, was determined to see things through.

'You've got to find him. Otherwise there'll be hell to pay.'

'Don't try and tell me that,' the little Welshman said angrily. 'I suggested you should run him in before we got to this stage.'

'He's not a fool. An educated man. In contact with his solicitor. He could have taken us to the cleaners.'

'You'd better tell that to Davies.'

'I've told Davies. His people had him there, would you believe it, and then they let him *go*.' Wishart digested the unhappy fact that they had failed to keep him. 'I want a search of the area. Complete. Every fucking mountain.'

'Give me the men then.'

'I'll give you more than that.' Wishart's voice was heavy with anger. 'I'll give you the Defence Secretary to say what he thinks about the way this has been handled. Foreign Secretary too. What do you think about that?' Pacing restlessly about the little office where Owens sat with his back to the electric fire, he studied the map with the red line round Tan-y-graig, and swore softly.

'If this business gets out . . .'

'Look,' Owens said. 'What, for God's sake? If what gets out? My orders were difficult enough without you trying to interpret them. I was told you had this damn-fool secret, an ammunition tunnel in the mountain an' that, but I didn't know who had taken the bloody girl.' His suspicious little face turned on the chief inspector. 'All you tell me is that there is a security blanket. Jesus Christ, who is running this operation?'

Wishart, who knew more, was brutal. 'Not you, when the chips are down. All you have to do is to find this lunatic. If he gets out of control more heads than yours will roll. Mine and Davies's too, most like.'

Owens realized that he'd been used, fed half-truths and half-excuses which he had swallowed like a fish on a line. He began to prevaricate. 'I don't understand what the problem is. It was ammunition, wasn't it? A bloody big bang, heard all the way down here . . .'

'The problem,' Wishart snapped, 'is something for Davies.'

'Abduction's a criminal offence –'

'Leave that to Davies.' Inside himself Wishart was scared. A professional had to live by the rules, and he had climbed fast, not by licking people's boots but by offering to clean them and do the dirty work. It had meant rapid preferment, but that had its flip side too and in his case it meant liaising with Davies's Defence crowd in Whitehall, no questions asked. He had had to use Owens, and Owens had always been weak.

'Our job is to nail Fellowes.'

'I don't see –'

'You don't have to. We'll just silence him, one way or another. Damage to property, burglary, assault, trespass, creating disturbance.'

Owens was jumpy. He gestured at the map. 'It's a big haystack. Long way to look for a needle.'

'I'll get some more police sent in. Standby team from Hereford, and tell them to skin the bastard,' Wishart said furiously. He stared out through the window to the green fields behind the house, awash now with the rain. 'This weather won't help the poor bugger.'

Close to five in the evening, when the cloudburst had stopped, retreated and given way to a pale wash of grey, Fellowes came down to the settlement, it could hardly be called a village, in the crook of the pass that he had monitored for hours. It lay at a fork in the road, one branch going off to the reservoir, the other branch heading south, a short cut over the mountains. The police had already been there, he'd seen them earlier that day, but by now he was hungry, weary and drenched. He wrung out the surplus moisture from the blanket as best he could and slithered down towards the road.

There were five occupied houses, quarry or road-worker places, two sheds, a derelict chapel and the Post Office store. He had watched from the hillside and seen only a handful of people throughout the afternoon. What interested him more were the left-over papers hanging up outside the shop, and the new notice there.

A police car had come back down the road, a neat white toy under the crags and the driver had gone inside as if making a delivery. Then the two uniformed occupants had stood looking for a while at the poster before they drove on.

Haggard, torn and shivering, the subject of their attention was six hundred feet above them.

Fellowes moved nearer, waiting for the dusk, ravenously hungry. The road was deserted, lights came on in the slate-roofed houses, the woman must be coming out soon to remove the unsold papers. He folded the blanket carefully and made a run for it, quickly in front of the houses, snatching one of the papers and disappearing up into the fields again. The paper was the *Clwyd News* and banner headlines said 'Dangerous Man Escapes. Suspected of Daughter's Murder.' The poster, in English, read 'Police Warning: Have You Seen This Man?'

Don't let them fool you.

The thought of murder sent a chill through his body and he began to run and run again, until he was away from that place and collapsed under a wall. Numbed and horrified he read the story slowly, as if it represented someone he had never heard of, this demented homicidal maniac thought to have been responsible for the disappearance of his own daughter and an American woman with whom he'd been seen in Maesteg. He was wanted by the police for questioning in respect of these matters, an assault on an officer, and breaking into the security zone at Tan-y-graig. Tan-y-graig mountain itself had been used to store wartime munitions which had been found to be dangerously unstable and therefore detonated. The resultant explosion, it said, had shaken windows as far away as Llangollen, and while being moved for his own safety away from the danger area Fellowes had attacked the police. He was said to be violent and should not be approached by the public.

For his own safety, he thought savagely, blowing on his fingers to induce some degree of warmth. To shut him up, in fact, if only he could read their motives, or even understand how much they knew themselves, Wishart and Owens and the rest of them. Those soldiers guarding the barriers at Tan-y-graig, they had been under orders, so no doubt the police were too: but why, and from whom?

It began to rain again, drizzling, cheerless rain, and he crawled away looking for shelter. Then, on an inside page, he found an explanation of the explosion. He crouched to read it in the dusk, before the light failed. It said that at the back of Tan-y-graig farm, concealed among the barns – the newly padlocked doors that he'd seen – wartime tunnels had been driven through the fissurate granite. Constant temperature tunnels at fifty degrees Fahrenheit, six to eight feet high, sealed tunnels inside the hill. And there had been stored, during the height of the War, first of all treasures from London and later high explosives for D Day. The lorries, he thought, the lorries. Some explosives had apparently been left in the custody of a Ministry of Defence firm, until such time as they were discovered to be unstable and steps were taken to detonate . . .

He finished as the light faded, and still he did not believe them. If that was all, why the excessive precautions, and in God's name what had happened to Sandie? It was another embroidery, another ominous distortion of some horrible truth. God damn them, God help them. The paper had come to pieces in his hands; he crumpled it up and threw it away.

43

In the morning, Owens had driven back to the Tan-y-graig site. Just inside the wire gates he stopped to chat with some of the men still on duty: two from the North Wales force, two from Secure Investments standing around in the dawn that was creeping pink and cold over the side of the mountain.

'No sign?'

'No sign, sir.'

Owens put his hands deeper in the pockets of his reefer jacket. 'As they say in the books, sometimes the murderer likes to revisit the scene of the crime . . .'

'Is that what he is?'

Owens shrugged. 'Somebody took the girl.'

The policemen had heard the stories recounted from the inspector's office. 'She's in Tunisia apparently.'

Owens laughed importantly, as if he knew more than them. Wishart himself had said the postcard was no more than a bluff: get some fool to fly out there, or give it to someone to send back. 'He had the time like to fix that up.'

The older of the two policeman, married with a couple of children, concerned about roofs over heads, said, 'What do you think he'll do now?'

Owens shrugged. 'Go back to the cottage maybe. He persuaded the other woman to rent it for him. The American. His son is waiting there now.' They had been through the place with a tooth-comb.

The policeman looked at Owens's boots. Why should an

inspector wear boots? Perhaps to make him look bigger, he decided.

'What does the son do?'

'Oh. I don't know. Some kind of student. He thinks the father is living in a fantasy world.'

'Do you think so too, sir?'

Owens considered the ground, studying his boots, then rising to stare at the ruin, opaque in the half light, that had once been Tan-y-graig farmhouse. They had been playing games with him, Davies and Wishart, he knew that now.

'I think the whole lot of us have gone flaming mad. Fellowes and everyone else. You know, a kind of madness sets in.'

'Is that so?'

Owens nodded, and a sudden anger irradiated his small features, normally so secretive and cautious. He glared up at the mountain as if it was something personal and then stumped back to the car to ask about the reinforcements.

Everything was very green. Fellowes found the world moving. He was lying on the grass, a damp, soggy mat of grass where he must have collapsed in the night. Five or six feet away the blanket lay discarded, too wet to be of use. He trembled with cold but the rays of the rising sun were too feeble for warmth. The pit of his mouth was dry and he was starving but it cheered him that he'd somehow survived.

Exposed. Collapsed in a hollow high up on a hillside looking across the valley somewhere below Tan-y-graig. Without knowing it, in the night he'd come almost full circle, as if drawn by a magnet, over the mountains and back again. Anybody might have seen him; sprawled in the field, except that from a distance the blanket would have looked like a rock. In the wide, desolate landscape nothing was moving, but he traced the lines of the fields, down to the valley bottom and the road, then up to the white house on the other side, half-hidden in its belt of conifers. The Davies house: and there, directly below it, straight as a parting through hair, the track of the old railway.

He came down the side of the hill and crossed the fields to the road. It was empty and he ran across and climbed the opposite wall. Excitement stripped away tiredness as he ran the last few yards up the broken ground towards the embankment, now covered by self-sown woods; then he was hidden inside them.

The urge to retrieve and unravel the secrets of the box he had hidden there was overwhelming – if only they hadn't found it. He froze again, cautious, fearing an ambush, some further kind of trap: but why should they know he had been there? The old metal lever, rusted and immobile, marked the switch points that had long ago vanished together with the rails themselves. Only the rotting sleepers tracked a line which had ceased to exist. He reached the handle – still no sound nor any sign of movement – and began to dig with his bare hands.

Nothing. Then he realized that he had gone wrong; his memory must have been confused by the nights of exposure. Cursing and swearing, he tried to keep a grip on reason. Don't let them fool you. Don't. It was the wrong spot. The sleeper he had selected was the one further back, not so close to the lever, but in his haste he had forgotten.

He kicked away at the dark earth, thinking, 'Please God, this time; now;' and reached in with his hand. He hadn't thought he had been so thorough when he concealed the tin, but there was something hard inside there, under the wood.

At last. The box, he thought, the box. There it was in his hands, the small rusted deed-box that Wishart had been so keen to retrieve. My God, this is what it's all about. It must be, it must. Some terrible, decaying secret that Steadman had locked up for posterity. Squatting down, almost caressing it, he brushed off the remaining dirt, and then began to panic. If he had this they might kill him, just as they might have killed Sandie. He began to run sweatily, darting like a hunted animal back into the cover of the trees.

Later, when his spirits recovered, he put ground behind him again, moving higher up on the hills, empty, bleak country with its own windswept grandeur, until he could see Lake Maesteg and the pub and the shop where he had originally called on that first traumatic morning. The morning Sandie had died on him.

When the sun had warmed him a little, and he was certain there was no pursuit, he stopped to examine the deed-box more closely. So light that it might even be empty, and the cheap lock had rusted solid. Another wild goose chase perhaps, had it not been for the other mysteries at Tan-y-graig, but without a hammer and chisel he had no way of finding out. He battered the box with a stone, kicked it and punched it and cursed it, but nothing gave. It sat there and seemed to mock him.

Suddenly, in despair, an overwhelming revulsion made him loathe it as if it was a living thing, and somehow responsible for sowing a black confusion in his mind. He hated this rusty tin casket, and hated everything surrounding it, Tan-y-graig and all its secrets . . . and wanted to throw them away just as he could throw away the box. Almost before he knew it, he had hurled it against the rocks, watching it scraping and falling down the hillside below him, faster and faster, until it hit a crevice and disappeared from sight.

44

Madman at large. A tractor was ploughing a field, forcing him to keep out of sight, and every car on the road below seemed full of menace. Fellowes feared that a line of men would come sweeping over the hills, but nothing happened, as if he had ceased to exist.

I'm not mad. I'm not mad. I'm sane.

Ghosts of Sandie and Laurel, but the only ghosts were in his mind. Once when Sandie was five he had taken her into a cavern and she had screamed and screamed, as if she was living a nightmare; when he had brought her out she had said how she hated it, hated those 'dark underneaths'. He was seized by a terror that those fears had become realities.

Panic gripped him. He felt abandoned by logic and in the presence of hell: the dread of discovery and the fear that he might never know what had happened there at Tan-y-graig. He stopped, his stomach like an iron fist clenched up inside him, and listened to his own heartbeats.

You fool. You fool. Give up and you're beaten, reduced to suicidal depression, a shambling on-the-run figure tortured by guilt. *Don't let them. Don't let them beat you.*

Those unknown forces were somehow locked up in the box, and he had thrown it away. He was running and scrambling back after it, searching and clawing at the sides of the gulley into which he had thrown it, praying, 'Please, please,' as if the act of recovery was also an act of contrition.

Cut his hands. Tore his clothes.

Nothing. Gone. Vanished.

Oh God, help me.

Then he saw it. A small, black deed-box, slipped, wedged between rocks, and he was sweating, cursing, in the effort to retrieve it. Hugged it to himself in triumph. A rusty, steel container which he shook against his ear: definitely something there, a faint – oh so faint – sound like a murmur inside it.

He hammered it again in fury, with rocks and stones and stakes, but it was rusted solid, then picked it up and carried it. His oyster. His cross.

James would be somewhere waiting. What they wanted was proof of what had happened to Sandie, and the infamy of Tan-y-graig, and he fought against devils of tiredness and cold and black fear, in the knowledge that he held the thing that Wishart needed.

That evening he came out of the valley of Tan-y-graig under the cover of darkness, still clutching the box. One last, long, tired scramble along the lake towards the cottage.

About half a mile away he waited and watched for movements for a long time, then crossed the little railway and worked his way through the trees until he was looking down on the two small stone buildings facing the lake. There was no sign of life, except for a spiral of smoke from the central chimney stack.

It might of course be a trap. He had to make sure that it wasn't, even though he saw no police. James might be waiting inside, but equally it might be those other forces that seemed to want to destroy him, to silence him as surely as they had silenced Sandie.

Late in the evening, James came, driving up in the battered Saab which he had bought in Bristol. He seemed to have been buying provisions, and started unloading boxes of groceries. Just as his father had with Sandie, a lifetime ago. The watcher in the trees kept silent. Tiredness wrapped round him again and he found himself drifting to sleep.

The noise of another car jerked him awake, and he watched it bumping up the lane, its headlights blazing. A white Rover, with a fluorescent red stripe.

Two uniformed men went inside and then he saw James at the door, talking to them. Fifteen, twenty minutes, he reckoned.

James could be in their pocket, set up there as a decoy. *Trust him.* *Trust him.* Out of their previous coolness had grown a mutual respect, and he believed it still held.

He waited until they drove away. Waited until the lights went out in the cottage. Silence broken only by seagulls blown inland and riding the water as if a storm was coming.

He ran across and tapped on the door.

'Jesus, Dad,' James said, then equally quickly, 'Come in,' shutting the door behind them. He was in the familiar, tiny granite-flagged kitchen where he had first kissed Laurel, a time which now seemed a dream, so long ago. The floor was pockmarked by generations of farming boots, the stone sink grey with old scars, the dim light over the table scarcely enough to read by, and yet it was like coming home as James hugged him.

Arms-length, he looked at his son. James was tall, goodlooking, three inches taller than him with a head of fair hair that fell sheepdog-like over his eyes. He flicked it back and cried in relief.

'Dad. Dad. What's happened?'

Fellowes slumped in a chair.

'Bolt the door. Make sure there's no-one there.'

His son quickly closed off the house.

'Dad. You look terrible. What have they done?'

It was too soon to tell him, and in any case the words would not come. He blurted out that he was fine, but how was he sure they were safe?

'It's OK,' James said. 'The police have asked me to tell them if you try to get in touch. That's all . . .'

For a moment Fellowes scarcely believed him, but the look in his son's eyes pleaded with him for explanation.

The box lay on the table between them.

'What in hell is that?'

'Open it,' he muttered, 'Carefully . . .'

Without a word James went outside, partly to reassure his father, partly to search for tools, a hammer and an old blunt screwdriver which he found in the shed. He stared at his father's face.

'What is this, Dad?' As if it might explode.

'Open it,' Fellowes ordered in a voice that shook with emotion. 'Open it, carefully.'

Slowly, James ran the screwdriver round the rusted edges of the lid and inserted it, hitting the handle gently, then harder. Conscious of his father watching him, slumped in the big chair, seemingly drained of effort.

'Dad, it can wait. You need a hot drink. Food . . . Sleep . . .' But Fellowes shook his head.

'I want to see what is inside.'

So James began the slow task of inserting the chisel on all four sides of the box, prising it open. It took a good ten minutes before he was able to say, 'OK. That's it.'

The box lid was loose on top, its hinges broken, the lock itself twisted free. As if it was his father's responsibility, James held the thing out towards him.

'All yours,' he said.

45

They were interrupted by the hammering outside.

'Police. We know that you're there . . .'

They looked at each other without speaking, in the pained silence of guarding a terrible secret. Then Fellowes put down the box and said quietly, as if he was praying, '*Sandie*. They know about Sandie.'

James thought at first that he had sterilized his own anger, but it came flooding back. He gripped his father's arm.

'Don't let them get it. *Open the box.*'

Fellowes felt the pressure of fingers, responded to the look in his eyes, but shook his head slowly.

'I want Sandie first.'

The hammering increased.

'Open up, or we'll smash down the door.' A fierce light beamed through the curtains.

'Let 'em in,' Fellowes said.

The words fell away into silence.

Then a loudhailer called, 'We are warning you . . .'

'Don't give up now, Dad.'

'I'm not giving up. Dead or alive. *Let them in!*'

'Dad. You're ill. You need a doctor . . .'

The look in the older man's face disabused him. Peter Fellowes did not need anyone; he was ready for them on his own. James realized too late what he ought to have done: concealed that box, telephoned Collard about his legal rights, contacted the media . . . but his father's eyes said, No. He gave in, and opened the door.

A semi-circle of men stood there, black-coated and armed police, centring on Wishart and Davies.

It was Davies who took command.

'May we come in?' His eyes searched through the room and saw the box on the table. Then they were crowded together, Davies and Wishart, Peter and James, elbowing for space in the cottage.

'Peter Fellowes,' Davies snapped. 'I've reason to believe you are in illegal possession of unauthorized documents prejudicial to the national interest.' Someone switched on the remaining light, over the kitchen sink. Davies's face had the mottled colour of pressed meats. Then he smiled, put his hands in his pockets and rocked on his solid legs while the armed police were shooed outside.

'Well . . . you've given us . . . you've given me . . . one hell of a dance.'

'I wouldn't call it a dance. I would call it either kidnap or murder.' The once-rounded face was staring at Davies, hollow and gaunt.

Wishart picked up the box, and a long slow sigh exuded from Davies.

'Where the hell is she?' Fellowes shouted.

They stared at each other.

'She's going to be all right, don't worry. Just sign the papers first.' Davies nodded across to Wishart, who produced a folder from a briefcase.

'Just sign these first, please.'

Fellowes refused, pushing the folder away,

'*Where is she?*'

'Dad, don't . . .'

'There's no need to panic,' Davies said smoothly. 'No-one intends any harm –'

'Just tell me what's happened.' It was a blur in his mind . . . the secret of Tan-y-graig and the utter desolation that was beginning to lift as he realized she was not entombed there. Yesterday in his despair he would have settled for less, simply some kind of assurance that she was still alive, but now he wanted the truth and in some way an act of vengeance. The black box had disappeared.

216

Davies leaned against the table. The door opened again and another policeman came in. Fellowes saw that it was Owens.

'Sign the papers first,' Davies said.

He heard James shouting, 'I'm going to telephone your solicitor . . .'

Davies said, 'You'll want more than a solicitor, old boy, by the time that I've finished,' in that controlling voice.

'You've been holding my daughter illegally. Lying . . . deceiving –'

'I'll say what's the law,' Davies said, indicating the documents now laid out on the table. As he motioned to Wishart to open the folder, his voice became suddenly reasonable. 'So far as the others are concerned, they've had the position explained to them, and they've both signed.'

'Both?'

He nodded. 'Your daughter and Miss Ericson. Sandie and Laurel.' He extracted a bunch of papers. 'Here. I've brought a set for you. Chasing you around North Wales. Sign here and we can all forget. We can let bygones be bygones.' He saw Fellowes start to protest. 'I suggest that you read it first.'

There was an ominous quiet while Fellowes stood by the table and took the documents handed him.

'Extract from the Official Secrets Acts 1911 and 1920,' he read. 'Section 2 of the Official Secrets Act 1911, as amended by the Official Secrets Act 1920, provides as follows . . .

If any person having in his possession or control any secret official code word, or pass word, or any sketch, plan, model, article, note, document or information which relates to or is used in a prohibited place . . . communicates . . . uses . . . retains . . . fails to take reasonable care of the sketch, plan, model, article, note, document or information: that person shall be guilty of a misdemeanour.'

'Read on,' Davies urged.

'Section 1(2) of the Official Secrets Act 1920, provides as follows:

If any person retains for any purpose prejudicial to the safety or interest of the State any official document, whether or not completed or issued for use, when he had no right to retain it . . . or fails to comply with any directions issued by a Government Department or any person authorized by such department with regard to the return or disposal thereof . . . he shall be guilty of a misdemeanour.'

Davies nodded. 'Turn over. Sign on the other side. That about wraps it up, provided you're sensible, and keep your mouth shut.'

'Get lost,' Fellowes said.

'I'm sorry?' The big man kept his temper. 'I think you've misunderstood. Sign here. That's all I'm asking of you, and I promise to take no further action. Otherwise, I have to warn you,' he said quietly, 'that a series of charges will be made: multiple charges for breaking and entering, theft, damage to Government property and actions prejudicial to national interest under the aforesaid legislation –'

'*Where is Sandie?*' Fellowes shouted.

'I assure you, she's safe . . .'

'Prove it.'

Davies said, 'Sign first.'

'No deal.' Fellowes heard James gasp, and tried to signal, 'Don't worry.'

'What is more,' Davies said, 'if you stand out it will all be for nothing. We've got the documents.'

Fellowes stood there tight-lipped, defiant.

'You can't force me to sign.'

'Do you believe in ghosts?'

Fellowes shook his head.

Davies shrugged. 'You look as if you've seen some. That is what troubles me. You'd better think it over . . .' and pointed again to the papers. He turned to Wishart. 'I want him under guard overnight.'

*   *   *

Davies went outside to the car, preferring the radio link, and spoke directly to London.

'I've got him but he won't sign.'

The voice at the other end was firm.

'You were told to remove the evidence at all costs.'

'I can't remove Fellowes,' he said.

'The Americans won't like it.'

Davies frowned and sucked his teeth. 'They may have to lump it, sir.'

'No revelations on any account. I gave Washington my personal assurance.'

'But it started with that American woman. If she hadn't pestered the Pentagon . . .'

'I'm less concerned about her than this man Fellowes. He's got to be muzzled.'

Davies considered the options.

'We've already got the stuff from Tan-y-graig.'

'I don't care about that. Make sure he doesn't talk. You've got plenty of time. Do you want some more help?'

He looked back at the cottage, with armed police standing outside.

'I'll get further with him alone.'

'What are you telling the police?'

'Virtually nothing. Just enough to keep them onside.'

The voice at the other end paused.

'Screw him,' it said.

Davies got out of the car and stood for a moment bare-headed. Give him a good night's rest: the man looked as if he could do with it. Wishart was watching him, his angular face unreadable.

'I'll take the box now, Bob,' he said.

He suddenly felt stimulated by the prospect of action, even – he joked to himself – of another accident. He sat in the car again and opened the glove compartment. The gun was safely inside there: standard Browning nine-millimetre high power pistol.

He made sure it was loaded, and checked it over.

'OK,' he said. 'Let's get to bed.'

The driver knew by his face that this would be an interesting assignment.

From the upstairs window Fellowes commanded a view of the lane, and could see the police below, ringing the house. The cottage was oppressively silent. He pulled the curtains, washed and shaved, took whatever food James offered. Tiredness rolled over him. He jumped when his son touched his shoulder. Sandie had been left alone in a place not unlike this, eight or nine miles away, on the morning she had disappeared. He had worked over so much in his mind, words and imagination, that it exhausted him now to think of the ordeal that she must have endured, but he tried to put such thoughts aside. Get Davies, he said to himself, and don't let Davies get you.

From the second bedroom – the room which had been Laurel's – he faced over the water, which had a gunmetal dullness. The bedroom had been prettied up with a pale blue carpet and chairs, and the casement windows were fitted out as window seats. When he opened them he saw the police watching, from a patrol car below.

'Get some sleep,' James said.

It was no good. Like a man in a padded cell he beat round and round for answers, asking why the small tragedies of his own life, and Sandie's, had somehow become caught up in this overall deception. The ghosts were still in his mind.

'Listen,' he said to James. 'Tomorrow you go to London. Get hold of Collard. Talk to him about what's happened . . .'

'But Dad, I'm staying with you.'

He shook his head. This thing was now one to one, and a fresh confidence swept through him, as if all his life he had grown to meet this challenge.

'Leave Davies to me,' he said, and sat on the bed. Something had kept Steadman there year after year on a kind of special pension, knowing and not knowing the secret of Tan-y-graig. A secret he had taken to the grave, but something so disturbing that he had been forced to create his own private memorial. Something that after his death had driven Maud Steadman back there . . . Outside it began to rain.

46

Davies came back at ten-fifteen next morning, in the same car with Wishart. From the window Fellowes watched them bumping over the crossing, then up the lane. The seaweed-green Rover, Series 820.

He walked out to greet them, ignoring the police. Davies was sitting in the back, leaned over the driver to say something in his ear, and then emerged. The same heavy figure and high-blood-pressure face, fierce eyes looking for trouble.

'It's a brisk morning,' Davies said.

Fellowes said, 'Yes. What happened to my daughter?'

Davies held out his hand, containing the buff folder.

'I think we have other business first. I hope you have slept on it.' Having his orders confirmed made compromise that much more difficult; it wasn't a question of personal rights, much larger issues of State had been placed squarely in his care.

'Come on. Please sign. Then we can forget about things.'

But he had misjudged the man.

'I want the truth,' Fellowes said. 'What has happened to Sandie? What went on at Tan-y-graig?'

'Sandie's all right. Look. Can we go inside?' It was as if he felt exposed in the open, preferring the dark, almost furtive interior of the old cottage. Reluctantly Fellowes agreed.

They stood facing each other, Fellowes with his back to the fireplace, Davies blocking the door while Wishart talked to James outside.

'What have you done with her?' Fellowes's voice was deep with bitterness.

'Please calm down. She's quite safe.' The superior, self-confident tone induced an irrational loathing. 'Just sign here, and undertake to say nothing . . .'

Fellowes laughed in his face. 'No way. I want this whole damned business out in the open. *Where is she?*'

He watched Davies's face darken as the other man understood he still could not force him to sign.

'Your daughter has signed.'

'Why?'

'A case of necessity.'

'Where?'

Davies sighed. 'Bird watching.'

'Bird watching?'

'All right. Listen. Shut up. The time for games is over.' Suddenly there was a gun in Davies's hand, a snub-nosed automatic pistol. 'Shut up and listen to me. They had to be removed for their own safety, your two women . . . but there could still be an accident.'

'What the hell do you mean?'

'Your daughter and that interfering American. For God's sake, man, don't try and be difficult.' His thick-set body radiated a determination to overcome this temporary obstacle. 'If you do what I tell you, you're safe. They will be safe. Otherwise I can't guarantee –'

'For God's sake, stop fooling.' A cold, hard fury built up inside him.

'I think you'll understand when you see them,' Davies said.

They drove there in Davies's car with a police vehicle behind. Fellowes with the driver in front, Davies and Wishart in the back seat.

'There's no need to be alarmed,' Davies said smoothly. 'No-one need come to any harm . . .'

They headed west, skirting the lake, and climbed through the high passes on the other side, then down again towards the sea. At midday they reached Ffestiniog, a valley stacked with broken slates, then Porthmadoc, small and busy, Criccieth with its ancient fortress and the long curving road of the Lleyn peninsula.

'Cardigan Bay,' Davies said. As they reached the end of the peninsula the car turned off the road and bumped across rutted tracks towards a wired-off enclosure.

'We get out and walk here,' Davies explained.

At the edge of the wire Wishart unlatched a gate and Fellowes made a sudden move.

'Don't do anything stupid now,' Davies muttered; the gun was lodged in his pocket.

They were inside a compound marked 'Private. Keep Out.'

Davies said, 'We need a boat.'

A large, prefabricated shed stood at the edge of the water, where grass and pebbles ran down to a rocky shore-line; out in the bay, perhaps a mile away across a stretch of glass-green water, Fellowes saw a collection of islands. A Secure Investments guard was unlocking the galvanized doors of the boat shed.

'Look,' Davies said. 'It's about time we were sensible. You play ball with me and I'll –'

'I don't want sense,' Fellowes shouted. 'This thing is beyond reason.'

Davies shrugged.

'You mean you don't want to see them?'

Fellowes stood still, trying not to hope for too much. Sandie. Laurel. Davies handed him binoculars and he looked across and saw a small collection of huts on the main island. An island that seemed to crouch there under a watery sun and the blustery wind.

'A bird watcher's paradise,' Davies said.

'A prison,' he replied.

'All right,' Davies said. 'We'll go across, and then perhaps you will see sense.'

Two of the guards were carrying down a rubber dinghy, big enough to take three people, with the outboard attached. He watched while they struggled across the rocks of the foreshore. The little cove was hemmed in by trees and marked off by wire boundaries, the same kind of fence as the one at Tan-y-graig.

Davies told him to get in. Wishart would stay on the shore. Sandie was over there, separated by a mile of cold water. They clambered in. Davies, holding the gun in his left hand, adjusted the choke with his right, pulled at the starter and the motor burst into life. The dinghy bucked across the water, straight as an arrow.

'Look, for God's sake.' Davies made one last try, shouting over the noise. 'Let's be civilized about this.'

'Civilized?' Fellowes turned his face to the island now coming up fast. He did not bother to reply, for he could see them now, coming out at the sound of the engine. Unmistakably Sandie, hair blown about in the wind, in the same jeans and sweater in which he'd left her, and the smaller figure of Laurel. Then they were jumping and waving, together with the woman in grey from the Davies house.

Davies ran the boat towards a tiny jetty. Sandie was running and shouting and in her father's arms at last. Sandie alive . . . and Laurel more enigmatic, standing beside him. Ghosts who had come back.

Davies watched them, then walked across.

'Now will you trust me?'

'Sandie? Sandie? What have they done? Are you all right?' How could he ever know?

One look, and the tone of her voice, gave him that reassurance. 'Daddy, don't worry, I'm fine. They took me away almost as soon as you'd gone. As soon as he saw the old woman,' she said, pointing at Davies. 'He took me to that other house.'

'And held you there against your will?'

'Not held . . .' Davies said. 'Protected for her own good. In a safe-house.'

'A safe-house, next to the property at Tan-y-graig? You kept her there as a prisoner.' In a voice swollen with anger Fellowes added, 'If you've harmed a hair of her head . . .'

Davies only smiled. 'Of course not. Why don't you trust me . . .'

The longest days of Fellowes's life ran before him now in a series of flashbacks: that first weekend with Sandie, Maud Steadman's body, the empty, echoing loss inside him when

Sandie and then Laurel vanished, followed by his own nightmare wanderings. He clenched his fists as if he would throttle Davies, but Davies held the gun.

'. . . or stay here with them until you sign.'

Fellowes stood on the shore with his daughter, and the woman he had come to appreciate for the hope she had given him. Laurel, who had started enquiries on the other side of the Atlantic, which had led to Davies being ordered to seal up the rumours, once and for all, and nearly split a mountain in two.

'Peter,' she said. 'I had an uncle. Leo. Officially killed in action in Normandy, summer of 1944, but I know he died in a tragedy. When I worried the Pentagon about a letter written two weeks after his alleged death in action, written from Llangogarth camp, nobody wanted to know.'

'There are certain things best concealed,' Davies said. 'For reasons of security.' He pointed the gun at Fellowes, then at his briefcase. 'Either you sign or you stay.'

Fellowes thought of the trucks moving into the mountain, and Steadman's private memorial, and finally put it together. There had been some huge cock-up, some secret hidden in the mountain and concealed by the military historians.

'OK,' he said. 'Give me a pen.'

With a sense of relief, Davies offered him the folder, as Fellowes lunged for the gun. It spun out of Davies's hand and fell harmlessly between the two men.

'You bloody fool,' Davies was screaming; but now Fellowes had the weapon, and stood twenty feet away, pointing it at him.

'Who are you? Who do you represent?'

But Davies shook his head. He saw Fellowes tell the women to get back aboard the boat. The wardress in grey had appeared, and Fellowes waved her back.

'What are you going to do?'

'Leave you here,' Fellowes said.

As Fellowes, Sandie and Laurel set off, leaving Davies and the girl on the island, the air seemed to break up in noise. A speedboat was cresting the water with blue lights flashing and a helicopter

225

came in low from somewhere over the hills, hovered then circled the dinghy, beating the water beneath them like an egg whisk. It hung up there defeating thought, and the waters of the bay reverberated with the racket of engines, as the chopper dipped lower until it almost clipped their heads. The dinghy bobbed like a cork.

A winch-man was dangling down, waving against the roar, impossible to hear but they understood well enough. He was pointing to the mainland where they could now see the cars, a white and blue paddy waggon, a squad of blue uniformed men.

Fellowes waved in acknowledgment, the winch-man was hauled inside and the helicopter lifted away, keeping a watching distance. The maelstrom it had made of the water slowly subsided but the speedboat was buzzing them now, while a big launch circled behind as if to cut off any thought of escape towards the open sea. Where the hell did they think he was running to, Fellowes wondered; he was running right back to London and Parliament and the media and the Old Bailey. To expose the ghosts of Tan-y-graig.

He smiled at Sandie, and Laurel held his free hand.

'I went to France,' she shouted, 'to look up Leo's grave, in the war cemetery at St Valéry-en-Caen. But the dates they gave me, and the dates of the GIs buried with him, were all wrong. Then some guys kind of collected me. Brought me to Cardiff, then here.'

'Dad, what do they all want? It's terrifying,' Sandie said.

'Don't worry. It's all over bar the shouting.' He thought of Laurel's evidence, the false dates that she had uncovered, and knew they could not keep him muzzled. He tried to gesture to the chopper to go away but it maintained its position, almost stationary, a hundred feet in the air while the speedboat closed up. A loudhailer boomed at them.

'Drop the gun and head straight for the shore.'

He laughed and flourished it at them, holding it by the barrel, then threw it in a long, lazy arc across the water. The light glinted as it fell. He did not care. Nothing mattered now he had found them, and truth must out.

The chopper peeled off, and headed for the island. Fellowes was closing with the shore rapidly, and a line of police advanced to meet him, carrying guns, some of them in body armour, looking like Samurai warriors.

'Must think we're tough,' he grinned. Let them put it to the test.

'How did they react so quickly?' Sandie asked.

'Davies would have had a radio link.'

Then the chopper was back over them, just as they came to the beach, with Davies waving to them from inside the open door. But there was no time to speculate for Wishart was there, as they stumbled ashore.

'You're under arrest,' he said.

Fellowes stood at the edge of the water with the two women as they were ringed by police. He looked back at the island where they had kept his daughter and across to the helicopter from which Davies was emerging, a heavy, ruffled figure, brushing his hair and talking, a hundred yards away outside the perimeter fence.

'What for?' He was confident in his civil rights; James would brief Collard in London.

'Holding a senior MoD officer at gunpoint is an offence.'

'So is pointing a gun at me. So is abducting my daughter.'

'Dad –' He saw Sandie trying to warn him.

'So is obstructing officers in the course of their duty. And stealing papers from secret premises . . .'

Fellowes laughed at them. The rain which had threatened all day began to set in firmly and the police made a cordon round him.

Davies was walking across, in a borrowed raincoat, belted and buckled.

'Let's go inside,' he said. He did not seem to like the daylight.

The interior of the boat shed was empty apart from some oil drums and a pair of trestle tables. Wishart switched on the overhead lights.

Davies strode across.

'Look, old chap. You're in enough trouble. I don't want to make matters worse. You've got your women back' – Fellowes hated that patronizing, chattel-like attitude, but for the moment swallowed it – 'listen to me. You've been meddling with things that don't concern the individual. Matters of State. You could face a whole series of criminal charges, but I'll waive the lot if you reconsider, sign on the dotted, and swear to keep your mouth shut.'

'About what?' Fellowes said stubbornly.

Laurel had pushed through beside him. 'I'll tell you. There was a major rehearsal for a secondary invasion attack on the Pas de Calais, a couple of weeks after D Day. Unfortunately it went wrong. Inaccurate weather forecast, a sudden storm swamped the barges, others were rammed in the dark, and fired on by our own side . . . It was a terrible tragedy – the loss of a raiding force – and it would have jeopardized cooperation if it had come out then. Acrimony, propaganda for the Germans, imagine it. A major assault-craft disaster in the Irish Sea . . . that's how my uncle died.'

'Shut up,' Davies snapped.

But Laurel could not be silenced.

'A top level decision was taken to hush the whole matter up. I started to investigate and got the brush-off. I was warned to be careful. It wasn't deaths at sea, it was deaths in action in France. So I found I was hassled; I couldn't trust anyone, perhaps not even you.'

'The lorries,' Fellowes said. 'The lorries that went into the mountain?'

She nodded. 'That was where the dead were interred, after they were washed ashore in Cardigan Bay. People were moved from the valley and the farmhouse made into a mortuary. Steadman was put in there as a kind of caretaker, but eventually it preyed on his mind. I thought so as soon as you told me . . . but I could not be sure.'

Fellowes said, 'How many?'

She said, 'I don't know. The authorities never disclosed it. Eight or nine hundred, at least. No-one will ever know.'

The figures chilled him. This appalling catalogue made him want to shout and curse at the unfairness of so many, many wasted lives. He trembled with outraged horror. Someone had

228

delivered to Davies an almost god-like authority to cover up an inter-services disaster. He thought of the hundreds of bodies washed up on the sands and taken into the mountain and finally he understood the ghosts and the murmurings of Tan-y-graig. Ghosts that had cried out for recognition for nearly fifty years; and Davies had conspired against them all – the original nine hundred, Sandie and Laurel and Maud Steadman, Wishart and Owens, the media and Parliament.

'Now sign, please. It must not come out. Not after all this time. Think of the distress it would cause. Unnecessary distress.'

'No. Go ahead. Prosecute me,' Fellowes steamed. 'We'll see what happens when the media get hold of things.'

Davies turned on his heel and walked away into the shadows, talking to Wishart. When they returned, the policeman was holding the black box.

'Look,' Davies said. 'The only remaining evidence is inside here.' He snapped open the top and took out four crumpled and stained typewritten lists. Long scrolls of names which curled around on his fingers. Steadman's own record.

There was an echoing silence in the high drum of the building where light bulbs swung on bare wires.

'Clear the shed,' Davies ordered. He did not want unnecessary witnesses. Fellowes heard Sandie calling out, 'Daddy', as if from a long way away and then she was breaking through the police, running towards him.

He held her tightly and hugged her. They could never take her away now, whatever she had signed.

'It's going to be all right.' Inside himself he felt a contemptuous anger for these men who obeyed instructions irrespective of conscience.

They could hear the rain beating on the roof overhead.

'Not a day for a barbecue,' Davies muttered. And then to Wishart: 'Here. Fetch me an empty drum.'

At first Wishart did not understand.

'For Christ's sake, don't just stand there. Fetch me an empty oil drum.'

Wishart and one of the police began to roll one across. It had been used for waste, and the top had been removed.

Davies took the sheets of Steadman's names and held them over the drum. Then with a pocket lighter set fire to them one by one.

They watched in silence as if he was conducting a ceremony. All souls. The charred remnants fluttered into the bin and were lost in the thick black residue, but a chance draught swayed one small fragment which hovered in the air. Fellowes caught it and glimpsed just for a moment six lives from the past:

Dean J. Alport Pvt 17th Infantry
Alun B. Annerley S/Sgt   "
Jason P. Arnkamp Pvt 4th   "
Norman L. Baldwin Pfc 17th Infantry
Richard Baumann T/5 14th Armoured
Lee J. Beckenbauer Pvt 83rd Infantry

'Give it back,' Davies said. All that remained of one long, terrible roll of honour. Buried in Tan-y-graig. They watched it consumed by flames.

Davies's eyes showed no compassion. To him it was just an assignment.

'Come over here,' he said, and drew Fellowes out of earshot of everyone, Sandie and Laurel and Wishart, down to the end of the boat shed. Their footsteps rang on the concrete floor and Fellowes saw the skid marks where the boats had been dragged up, the boats which had ferried to the islands. The whole place had been out of bounds, a security area. Davies held his arm and began to speak urgently.

'Listen to me. All the actions I have taken have been on the highest authority. You follow me? Over nine hundred bodies were interred there at the height of the Normandy battles. It had to be hushed up. It would have played into German hands to admit that we killed them ourselves. After the war nobody wanted to re-open a chapter like that, until your wretched Laurel started asking tom-fool questions. Questions that upset the Pentagon and Number Ten.'

'So you just salute and take orders, no questions needed —'

'Listen to me, I say. I have been under instructions to remove the evidence at all costs. You understand? No muck-raking. Not another Slapton Sands.'

'You exceeded your duty . . . any conceivable duty.'

'Not at all. I simply sealed the mountain. Unfortunately, just as I started, Maud Steadman returned and died, and you turned up with your daughter.'

'You bastard.'

Davies laughed softly. 'What was I expected to do? Kill her off, or let you into the secret? Precious little time to decide, but obviously if I could get her out of the way we could sew the whole thing up, empty the farmhouse and dynamite the hillside.'

'You kidnapped her. That is a criminal offence.'

'No. Not at all. I took her to a place of safety, for reasons of security. And she's committed to silence under the Official Secrets Acts. Try making anything stick.'

Fellowes felt he wanted to be sick. 'I'll see that you don't get away with it. By Christ, you won't silence me. You falsified Mrs Steadman's death, and sent me phoney papers. And put a gag on Owens.'

Davies looked at him calmly. 'Challenge me, and you challenge the powers of Government. I have sufficient statutory authority to muzzle the press. As for that fool Owens, he didn't know what he was looking for.' His heavy face turned away, staring towards the sea. 'In short, I had to bury the evidence, once and for all. Nine hundred GIs killed by friendly fire, sealed in a mine, ignored, is not something any of us are proud of. You won't find it in the official records.'

'I call it the biggest mass murder in British history.'

Davies drew in his breath. 'You can say that and still not understand the orders to keep it under wraps, and the lengths we would go to?'

'Get off my back,' Fellowes said. 'It won't stop the truth coming out.'

'Don't give me that line, please. You've got no proof . . . even if you knew the names.'

Blindly, angrily, Fellowes could only say, 'You are the complete bastard, aren't you?'

231

'Don't rile me,' Davies countered. 'Attempting to disclose highly sensitive information and retaining it without rights will get you ten years. We'll see to that.'

Fellowes drew a line with his foot, a scorch mark on the concrete as if to say thus far and no farther. 'I don't care.'

'Think about it first,' Davies said. 'Before anyone gets hurt . . . and I mean that. It would be a pointless exercise.'

Fellowes recognized the threat, undefined but real, that could cloud his whole life. Out there, through the boat shed doors, he could see chinks of light and a grey slant of sea and sky. Behind him, Sandie waited with Laurel.

He walked slowly away from Davies, back towards the two women who meant everything.

'What do you want me to do?' he asked Sandie. Sandie, who left alone had begun to explore, and perhaps in her way had guessed, the secret of the hill.

She shivered and clung to him. 'Nothing, Daddy,' she said. 'I just want you.'

And Laurel . . . ? He found himself gazing at her eyes, which sparkled with tears. 'Peter,' she whispered, 'perhaps in the end it is better not to disturb the dead, if only for the sake of the living.'

Standing there, in the cold light of the boat shed, he understood that people could know the truth and be able to do nothing about it, when confronted by fanatics like Davies and the powers behind him. But he also knew, deep down inside, that he and Sandie and Laurel had found a deeper truth that was hidden before.

He put an arm round his daughter's shoulder and then the other round Laurel, and kissed them both.